Evernight Teen ®

www.evernightteen.com

ISBN: 978-0-3695-1446-2

Cover Artist: Jay Aheer

Editor: Melissa Hosack

This is a work of fiction. All names, characters, and places are fictitious. Any resemblance to actual events, locales, organizations, or persons, living or dead, is entirely coincidental.

C. LEE MCKENZIE

DEDICATION

When you play tennis and want to improve, always get onto the court with someone who plays better than you. The same strategy applies to writing for publication. Over the years, I've been lucky to exchange manuscripts with some excellent writers who have helped me improve each of my stories. I'm grateful for you all.

L.K. Madigan, Yvonne Ventresca, Heather Couthard, Mel Higgins, Gabi Coatsworth, Sonia Antaki, Gillian Foster

C. LEE MCKENZIE

THAT MOONWATER WITCH

C. Lee McKenzie

Preface

How did it happen that the Storm Haven villagers whispered suspicion into each other's ears whenever Calista or her mother, Miriam Moonwater, passed by? How did it happen that for most of her father's life, Samuel D'White had no friends near their home and had to journey to his childhood village to ask for favors or companionship?

And when did this mistreatment start?

If someone had kept a written history, instead of passing fireside stories from parent to child, it could be read, and everyone would know the answers to these questions. But no one wrote down the facts, so the causes for the persecution of the Moonwater D'Whites are a mystery.

Today, the villagers are certain of only one thing. The family must be avoided. It is the "why" that has faded from memory.

So it is still a common occurrence when shopkeepers, housewives, and field workers narrow their eyes to slits and lean close so their words won't escape into the air and—most importantly—won't mist their way up to the top of Vengeance Mountain.

Here's what they cup into their palms.

"Take care. Here comes Miriam Moonwater's girl."

"Calista? I hear her father came from the reputable D'White family."

"He did—poor man. Not welcomed here for certain. Must have been hard."

"Who but people with something to hide, would choose to live in the last cottage at the very edge of Storm Haven?"

"Exactly. And next to the cemetery."

"Only a Moonwater would do that, of course."

"But why did they choose such a place?"

"The old stories are—"

"Hush, best not bring up the old stories."

Fear is the main source of superstition, and one of the main sources of cruelty. To conquer fear is the beginning of wisdom.

—Bertrand Russell

Chapter One

Calista sensed a threat and slowed her pace. Pulling her shawl closed at the neck, she scanned the bushes that lined the dirt road. The rustling of leaves brought her to a halt just before Micah Kennewick stepped out and blocked her path.

"Hey, ugly. Where you going in such a hurry?" Micah pointed a finger at her the way he might if he held a sharp object.

She gripped the handle of her straw basket and set her jaw. She would not let this bully see any fear. She was about to push past and ignore him, but two others ducked out from hiding and stood behind him. Now, there was no escape unless she high-tailed it back the way she'd come. If only her mule hadn't stumbled and wrenched a knee, Calista would already be down the road on Flower's sturdy back and out of reach.

Of course, she could outrun all of them. That she was very sure of because she'd done it since she was eight. Heat rose in her cheeks at the memories of all those other humiliations, all those times when she had to fight back tears of fear mingled with frustration. More than anything, she'd longed to throttle Micah and his minions, but she had always been one against three boys—sometimes armed with stones. Now at eighteen, she wasn't about to let them see her flee like a scared little girl.

She willed her heart to settle into a steady rhythm and drew herself to her full height. Intimidation her goal. "Let me pass. I'm off to the village."

Kip Delany, another Storm Haven male who'd come into the world mean and full of hate, shouldered past Micah and snatched the covered basket from Calista's hands. "Something smells downright good. Let me see what you got."

She grabbed at the handle. The basket upended and freshly baked muffins tumbled onto the ground.

"Oops!" Kip snickered.

Bailey Phelps, the shortest of the three, laughed and kicked one of the muffins off the road and into a ditch. "They make good kickballs."

Calista stifled a gasp. Bailey had just ruined her morning's work and cost her a day's income. Eyes smarting, she snatched up the basket and backed out of their reach. Keeping her voice as steady as possible, she said, "So now you must be more than proud of yourselves."

She had other things she held back. *You are pathetic excuses for men. There's nothing so weak as a strength used to harm others.* But, as always, she was outnumbered, and while she'd like to hurl more than words at them, years of growing up in Storm Haven had taught her better. Telling them what she thought of them would merely stir up more of their wicked natures, then she'd surely have to outrun them or risk harm at their hands. Alone, they were only bullies, but in a pack, they'd blackened the eyes of younger village boys. They would not be above hurting a lone girl who challenged them.

They laughed, and Micah stooped to pick up a muffin. He tossed it in the air and then threw it at her, striking her on the shoulder. “Go home, Calista Moonwater D’White, and stay there.”

She was out of their sight quickly. Long and lean, Calista was always taller than average, but by the end of her schooling, she’d looked down on all of the village boys and most of the men.

She kicked a small pebble out of her path.

*I hate every single one of them. They have no right to...*With each step, she stomped down as if she could grind them to dust.

A sudden wind gusted at her back, and then a sound like stealthy footsteps came from behind her, but when she whipped around, the road was empty.

Chapter Two

Calista waited and scanned the road behind, her heart tapping faster than she'd like to admit. It was upsetting that Michah and the others might be following her. Once she was sure no one was, she turned toward home again and safety.

When she reached the cottage, she unlatched the gate and shoved it open. As she stepped onto the path, her mother opened the front door and hurried to meet her.

Miriam wasn't as tall as her daughter, but like Calista, she had hair the blue-black color of the raven, and she bound it with a ribbon at her neckline. "You're back so soon. Did you…" Her mother touched the empty basket and, frowning, looked at Calista.

Calista was about to explain what had happened when a black horse, trudging ahead of an open wagon, came down the road toward them.

"Thomas Tidwell," her mother said with a sad shake of her head. "Died on the fifteenth day of this harvest month, he did."

Calista and Miriam stood by the road, heads bowed in respect, as the wagon passed with Thomas's casket jiggling in the back. Each time a wheel dipped into a rut, the wooden box danced sideways, then back to center. More lively in death than in life, Thomas led the remaining Tidwell family and a trail of other villagers to his place of rest, Storm Haven Cemetery, where they would pass under the arched sign, *Welcome Forever*.

The mourners who passed didn't look their way. No one who walked the road in front of the cottage ever did. And no one ventured by their cottage unless they had dead to bury, which didn't happen too often. The cemetery's silent population grew at a slow but steady pace of one or two elders each year—unless there was an accident—or worse—a killing.

Once the mourners passed, Miriam took Calista by the shoulders and looked into her eyes. "Now tell me what happened. Everything."

What happened today had happened with some variation ever since Calista could remember. Her telling was really a re-telling, so Calista described her encounter that had been like so many others. As always, she held back just how fearful she'd been. She didn't want to heighten her mother's worry.

Her mother listened, and although her face remained as still as an undisturbed pond, her back straightened and her grip tightened. "Well, then, come. We have some baking to do." Her mother led the way into the cottage. "It was good that I bought more flour this week after all."

"I'm sorry," Calista said. "I didn't—"

"None of that," Miriam said. "This is not your fault."

But Calista couldn't help but think otherwise. If only she were clever enough or strong enough to best those village bullies. She brushed away an annoying sting of tears that always came from her frustration, and then followed her mother into the cottage.

In the warmth of the kitchen, Calista set to measuring cups of sugar and the correct weight of butter. While Miriam broke fresh eggs and whipped the ingredients into a sugary froth, Calista remained silent, letting the anger brew inside her. But as she stirred the pureed pumpkin into the mixture and blended the flour laced with cardamon, that anger slowly ebbed. It was difficult to hold onto dark thoughts when what she was creating was meant to bring comfort and satisfaction to others.

Her mother slid one batch of the pumpkin muffins into the oven and then pulled Calista onto a kitchen chair. Once they were both seated, Miriam took her by the hands. "I know how you must feel, Calista." Then, with eyes veiled by something Calista had never understood, she lifted her daughter's chin. "But I've told you, you are more than just another village girl. Those boys sense that, and that's why they treat you as they do."

No one thought of her as *just* another village girl. She knew that. "But what does that mean?" She'd always asked that question whenever her mother mentioned how she was different, and she already knew how her mother would answer.

"Patience." A sigh weighted with secrets escaped before Miriam said, "You will understand when or … if the time is right."

Calista had never tried to push her mother into revealing whatever she held back. One didn't push Miriam Moonwater D'White—even her daughter. Miriam was a gentle woman, with what Calista's father used to say was a girdle made of iron. But Calista wished she knew when *the time would be right*. For as long as she could remember, she'd wanted an answer to her question. With this morning's attack so fresh in her mind, it was difficult to hold back from making stronger demands for an explanation.

"Patience," she repeated with a nod. She'd try for patience this time, but she wasn't sure she could do that much longer, not when she saw no end to the mistreatment.

Before two hours had passed, a fresh batch of pumpkin muffins was done, and the basket was full again, the kitchen rich with the scent of spice.

"I'm taking these to Mr. Bennet's bakery," her mother said.

"No. This time I will be ready for them if they come at me." Calista was not about to let Micah, Bailey, or Kip keep her from carrying on business as usual.

Her mother started to object, but Calista held up her hand. "I can do this. I want to do this." In truth, she *had* to do this or give up venturing into Storm Haven altogether and stay always isolated in the cottage. And that was out of the question.

Miriam took a moment before handing Calista the basket of muffins bundled inside a clean cloth. "Then here you are, but please be careful. If there's any trouble, come back. Don't—"

"I'll be fine." But Calista wasn't that sure. The only thing she was sure about was that they had a long-standing agreement with Mr. Bennet to honor. He'd pay them two scolas for each muffin and sell them at his bakery for five. While his selling price was a bargain, what he paid her was far too little. Not even Mr. Bennet baked a tastier muffin. On that, the entire village agreed. They didn't say so in words, but they did so by all of the scolas they left in Mr. Bennet's till and by the quickly emptied shelves where her muffins once sat on display.

"After old Thomas's service, everyone will want one of these." Her mother touched Calista's hand, leaving a floury print. "Death makes people hungry and in need of sweet comfort."

Whether it was grief or joy that spread through the village this time of year, the pumpkin muffins comforted the mourning or enhanced the high spirited. In the winter, the villagers flocked to the bakery for the hot cinnamon ones. In the spring, lavender. In the summer, peach.

Calista took down her woolen shawl from the peg by the door. On her journey home, the sun would dip behind the peak, and once it became dusk, a chill wind would sweep down from Vengeance Mountain.

Some said that a vengeful giant lived in a high mountain cave, and he brought certain death to anyone from the village who dared climb into his domain. But Storm Haven was full of old stories that nobody quite remembered the same way. And no one could tell you where the stories came from. They'd always been a part of their lives, something as familiar, yet clouded and scary, as the mountain itself.

Calista refused to believe any of those tales. Always shrouded at the summit by dark clouds, the mountain was forever threatening, but it was just a mountain, she told herself. And there were no giants in this world. That was sheer poppycock. Besides, Micah and his gang were the real threat, the danger she had to watch out for.

This time, they would not catch her unaware.

She hoped.

Chapter Three

Calista stepped out into the chilled air and stared up at the craggy face of Vengeance Mountain. "Stuff and nonsense. There is no giant," she said as if that would make it so, and for a moment, her huffed words formed a tiny patch of fog.

It was well past midday, and the late fall days had grown short. Already the shadows were lengthening. She'd have to hurry to be home before dusk. Snug in her heavy shawl, she set off down the rutted dirt road, her stride long and the sound of her booted footsteps determined.

When she came to the Kennewick farm, she walked faster, keeping her eyes on the bushes and checking for any signs of Micah and his friends. This time, the road was empty, and soon she was across from the Wakefields. From farther ahead came the banging of shutters at Storm Haven Inn. The innkeeper was already closing his windows to keep out the night cold soon to come. With this reminder that she was later than usual for reaching the bakery, she walked faster.

At the boulder where the road curled back around like a lazy serpent, she halted. In a few steps, she'd enter the village.

Tensing her shoulders, she drew in a deep breath. She never felt welcome here no matter how often she came. When she'd been a child, she'd followed her mother's advice and ignored the sour faces turned her way. She wasn't a child anymore, and she'd stopped shrinking from confronting the villagers. Now she looked into their eyes when she passed, and when she did, they always glanced away first. She wasn't ashamed of being a Moonwater or a D'White, and she wanted them to know it. She had every right to visit the shops on the square, and if some surly villager gave her so much as a glare, she'd send them off with a few sharp words. She'd found that everyone she challenged verbally melted away, giving her free passage.

If only that would work with Micah and those others. She shook her head. "Stop thinking about them. Deliver the muffins, collect the scolas, and return home," she muttered to herself before taking the last steps that brought her into sight of the familiar square.

She'd always admired the magistrate's house with its steeply pitched slate roof. This solid stone building was the first to greet people when they entered the village. Here was a place able to withstand great trials, even fires that three times had engulfed the wooden structures adjacent to it.

Its weathered wooden fence protected the leggy hollyhocks in summer and sprawling pumpkin vines in fall. In winter, it banked a thick layer of snow.

In front of that fence stood the village pillory where anyone breaking Storm Haven laws spent miserable hours, their heads thrust through the top hole and their arms and legs fastened securely through four others. She'd always hated seeing someone suffer in that way, and when an unfortunate soul was locked in it and miserable, she made certain they at least had water and, when possible, something to eat. She didn't care that her kindness only served to make the villagers even more hateful toward her. Wait until one of them is pilloried, she thought. Today the torturous device was empty. One less torment for her to endure.

A few feet farther along and next to the General Store, the blacksmith's shop doors stood wide open, and its forge belched fire. Inside, the blacksmith brought down his hammer with a loud clank, shooting sparks into the air. On the opposite side of the square, the tailor's shop butted up against the greengrocer.

Her destination, Mr. Bennet's bakery, was the last building on the left. Storm Haven church, a prim whitewashed structure with a bell tower, perched at the end of the square. At precisely seven AM every Sunday morning, Parson Garrison rang the church bell and broke the peace of Storm Haven to summon the villagers. The only other times the bell pealed were for trials, weddings, or funerals, and on Christmas morning. Calista had never entered its doors. No Moonwater ever had. A familiar shadow of sadness darkened her heart. The church was another place closed to her.

She made her way to the first shop, glancing in the window in time to see the tailor turning his sign from open to closed. He hesitated when he spied her through the glass, then he snapped the shade down into place before she had time to raise her hand in greeting. She moved ahead quickly.

The greengrocer had already rolled his cart inside, and the click of his lock sounded loudly across the late afternoon.

A cluster of village women, satchels filled with produce, spotted her and drew into a tighter knot. They didn't bother to conceal their heavy-lidded suspicion and could have been the ones from last week or last month or years ago. One leaned into the other, and Calista once again thought she heard words like wicked, unnaturally tall, and Moonwater all murmured together. The conversations were never clear so that she could understand them—just snorts and hisses and clicks of disapproving tongues.

"Mean-spirited-ninnies," she said under her breath. So what if she was taller than most people in Stone Haven? So what if she lived next to the cemetery?

She was different, so did that make her bad? The villagers were worse than mean-spirited-ninnies, they were closed-minded, intolerant fools. She pulled her shawl closed at the neck and pushed past the women who clutched their cloaks to their bosoms and stepped back to avoid her touch.

Mr. Bennet's bakery was next, and the aroma of sweet tarts and yeasty breads filtered outside. She peered inside at the crowded room of mourners. Her mother was right. Death stirred the appetites of those left behind, and what better way to comfort the living than hot-from-the-oven pumpkin muffins?

Calista opened the bakery door and stepped inside at the same moment Mrs. Pinehurst was on her way out. There was no avoiding each other, and Calista found herself pressed against the older woman's broad belly.

Tiny zaps of energy discharged inside Calista's mind. She blinked rapidly, trying to make sense of what was happening to her. Even though she stood facing the inside of the bakery, she wasn't seeing it at all. Instead, she was seeing another place. A bedroom. Two women. One lying in a bed. It wasn't clear who she was. Eleanor Pinehurst stood over the woman, her face contorted, not by grief, but … glee? She held a—

"Well? Are you going to let me pass?" Mrs. Pinehurst's irritable voice shattered the vision.

Calista stepped back, relieved she couldn't see any more of these strange and disturbing images that seemed to be flowing from Mrs. Pinehurst's thoughts into hers. She gazed down into the woman's pale eyes and tried to speak, but what she'd just seen stopped her words, and only a rush of breath spilled from her lips. She had to grip the basket of muffins to steady her hands.

"What are you staring at?" The woman fumed, but her indignation was tinged with a trace of misgiving.

She dodged around Calista, clutching her string bag bulging with Mr. Bennet's breads and cakes.

"S-sorry," Calista stammered, dropping her gaze to her covered basket, but it was too late. She'd seen something, and she didn't know why or how, but for one moment she'd been inside Mrs. Pinehurst's mind, and now she shared something with her that she shouldn't.

A dreadful secret.

Chapter Four

That night while she and her mother ate, Calista held back mentioning what had happened at the bakery with Mrs. Pinehurst. The more she thought about the incident, the more she doubted that she remembered the moment correctly.

No one slipped inside the thoughts of others. That was a ridiculous notion.

After her mother tried to start several conversations that only elicited a quick yes or no or a nod from Calista, Miriam fell silent, so the kitchen pulsed with an unusual quiet throughout supper. But once the dinner plates were in the sink, Miriam sat across from Calista and grasped her hands. With a gentle squeeze, she asked, "What happened in the village today?" Then more firmly, she said, "And don't you dare tell me nothing."

Her mother had a keen sense for knowing when Calista was troubled, and long ago, Calista had given up trying to dodge these kinds of questions. She wished she had an easy way to explain the shock she'd experienced.

"I … uh…" She stopped because now with their hands clasped, Calista felt that same odd stir she had when she'd touched Mrs. Pinehurst. Nothing specific this time, but brief sensations. A flicker, like captured fireflies passed between their palms. Then glimpses of strange images. Sorrow draped her mother's heart. A large lump of something the size of a fist sat at her center. It wasn't clear, but dark and troubled. So many feelings. Calista was suddenly privy to all of what was very private. She felt her face flush with embarrassment. She had no right to explore anyone's feelings in this way, most especially her mother's.

Pulling her hands free, Calista said, "A

strangeness. That's the only way I have to explain it."

"Then tell me the details, and perhaps I can help." Miriam sat back and crossed her arms. "I'm listening."

Calista told what had happened, but she couldn't bring herself to reveal the true cruelty of Mrs. Pinehurst's secret. It seemed wrong to share it, even with her mother.

For a time, her mother remained silent, her face drawn into worried creases. Then she got to her feet. "Come. It's time you discovered who you are."

"Who I am? I don't under."

Her mother led her from the kitchen into the next room where she knelt to pull aside the carpet worn thin by years of use. Calista gasped when Miriam lifted a floorboard and retrieved a small wooden chest, its rounded top sprinkled with dust. It was secured by a heavy iron lock. What did it hold that required it to be hidden and locked? After all, they had little of value to keep safe.

Placing a hand on the lid, her mother remained still without saying more. It was as if she was considering whether or not to open it after all.

"Are you all right?" Calista knelt next to her.

"Yes, but this is an important moment. I'm finally answering the question you've asked for years, and I want to tell you in the right way." Her mother took another deep breath before going on. "But perhaps just the simple truth is best." She sighed, considering her choice of words carefully the way Calista had seen her mother do her whole life. "This belonged to a very powerful witch, your great-grandmother."

Startled, Calista looked up into her mother's face. "My great-grandmother? She was a—"

"Yes. And my mother as well. I told you long ago that you were no ordinary village girl, and after today, you know I told the truth."

In school, there'd always been supernatural tales the older students scared the younger ones with. These stories were about witches that walked the paths of Storm Haven, about their evil curses that could render unsuspecting villagers mute or turn them into large rats. Calista's common sense had counseled her to ignore such nonsense. But after what her mother had just told her, she recognized a core of truth in these schoolhouse yarns. It was possible that they weren't only made up, but that they'd been aimed at her and her family.

Gently cupping Calista's face between her hands, Miriam said, "Since you were a child, I've feared this day would come, and it has ... as much as I've wished otherwise. I'd hoped the village would be different, that it would be enlightened and ready to accept you by the time you became aware of your gift. At the very least, I wanted the old stories completely out of memory." The look that Calista remembered but never understood was in mother's face again. *Worry? Or something worse?*

"Gift?"

"The Moonwater magic."

"What if I don't want this … gift?"

Her mother gazed at her the way she always did a newly hatched chick. Delight and wistfulness played over her face. "Once a woman with Moonwater blood comes into their magic, they have no choice but to accept it. I had to, and after what you experienced today, I'm sure your gift is much stronger than mine. It was in your amber-flecked eyes from the beginning. They're the same as your great-grandmother's. And, like her, you've always enchanted animals. Any plant under your care thrives. The muffins you stir rise lighter and are more flavorful than any I've ever tasted. You have such goodness within you, a Moonwater's sense of right and wrong, all of the strengths that mark you as a powerful witch."

Calista sat stunned. Witch. She was a… Impossible. A tart taste crept into the back of her throat and she swallowed, blinking back the sting of tears. When she spoke, her voice came in uneven, cracked tones. "But… You never said … you…Why didn't—"

"Oh, Calista. I'm so sorry, but I—" Her mother pressed her lips together, then straightened, clearly resolved to deliver her message without faltering. "As I told you, we were waiting for all to be different in the village, and your father and I thought it best to keep this from you until you were old enough to understand. I suppose we both secretly hoped that if we didn't tell you, this gift might skip a generation, even cease to manifest itself in our family." Miriam's voice grew breathy as if she had grown suddenly tired and needed to set down a heavy load. "But, in truth, we both knew that was wishful thinking."

Calista heard the logical explanation, but she was still having trouble making sense of all that her mother was telling her. "I don't think I'll ever be old enough to understand this."

"Of course you will. You've inherited Amara Moonwater's talent, so you must have inherited her capacity for managing it as well. But with caution." Her mother lightly tapped the lock. It vanished, and the top of the chest opened by itself.

Calista rocked back on her heels, not able to breathe. Shock quickly gave way to foreboding. First, the encounter with Mrs. Pinehurst. Now her mother's magic. The stories she'd heard in whispered snatches were suddenly making sense. They were about the Moonwaters. They were about her. She exhaled the breath she'd been holding. She was someone that others were suspicious of, a witch, but not just any witch. She was a Moonwater witch, and that was, according to what she'd just heard, very special.

Until today witches had been nothing more than a myth from long ago and without one pinch of fact. She'd lumped it together with the one about the giant who lived atop Vengeance Mountain. Now her beliefs were in utter disorder and confusion.

"Making that lock disappear is the extent of my witchcraft, Calista. A parlor trick for our ancestors."

Calista blinked, trying to stop the persistent sting at the corner of her eyes. She wished her heart didn't continue to buck. Oh, how she wanted her father to be here, to hold her and tell her stories about goddesses, how she was one of them, how nothing could ever hurt her because she was so strong. She needed him to make her bold against the world the way he always did when she felt threatened.

"Come." Her mother pulled her nearer. "This is your destiny. You have no choice but to embrace it."

Calista pushed down the foreboding that threatened to overpower her and peered inside the chest.

Chapter Five

Ordinary.

That's how Calista would describe the single item in the trunk—a plain white book about the size of a diary. In one way, it was a relief to find nothing shocking or witch-like. In another, it was disappointing. Perhaps she was overreacting to this unexpected news. It might take a while, but it was quite possible she'd get used to the idea of her family history and her destiny.

Her mother withdrew the book from the bottom of the chest and held it out to her. Its cover bore no title, but when Calista took it from her mother's hand, it glittered like a captured star. Surprised, Calista almost let it fall to the floor.

This wasn't an ordinary book at all. Staring at it as if it were something about to spring to life, she had the distinct feeling of standing on the edge of a precipice. The floor seemed to tilt underfoot, and when she tried focusing on what she clasped in her hands, she grew dizzy.

As soon as she slid her fingers over the cover, bold scarlet letters appeared. She caught her breath and then read what they spelled. "Amara Moonwater." When she said the name, a sensation surged through her body. Exciting. Frightening. A sense of something vast, without limits.

She peeled back the cover, somehow knowing that once she looked inside, the strange events of today would become commonplace, and her world would be forever altered. She hoped that whatever changes came they'd be good, not bad. But good or bad didn't matter because, from what her mother said, Calista had no choice but to go forward.

The lettering on the first page was a jumble of marks.

ᛟ ZZ ᚹ

The first looked like an X with an upside-down V on top. Two zigzagging shapes close together followed. The third one resembled a P, but not exactly. The rest of the writing was equally obscure.

She looked up, questioning.

"Runes. To protect the words from eyes that should not see them. This is your great-grandmother's book of magic, the record of her thoughts and experiences. It holds her spells and potions, too. She passed this on to my mother, and then it came to me. Now I am passing it on to you as you must one day. Mother to daughter forever."

Must? It seemed this book came with an obligation, one Calista didn't know she could fulfill. She might not have a daughter. Any child.

She set that thought aside and asked, "But I can't read this writing."

"Look again."

The unreadable shapes had reassembled themselves, or her eyes had adjusted. She could now easily make out the writing.

On this first day of my power, I begin my Book. I will set down a record of all things magyk I discover. May these words continue through time, and may they not be lost as were those of my notable predecessors.

"What does she mean, 'lost' and 'notable predecessors'?"

"Much of our family was destroyed by superstitious villagers long ago," her mother said. "The books that our ancestors created were burned along with..." She shot to her feet and slammed the lid on the chest with some force. "The earliest book we have is that one."

Calista looked up at her mother and tried to read her expression. She was upset, to be sure, but there was something secretive in her face as well and traces of anxiety. "And you? Do you have such a book?"

Her mother shook her head. "No. It was unwise. My mother stopped the practice after "—she cleared her throat— "and she bade me do the same."

"I don't understand. Why was it unwise if—"

Her mother turned away. "The power didn't come to my mother or to me. We could work magic, but not the kind the Moonwaters had been famous for. My mother felt it better to set it aside. Your father liked that I did, too. He worried about the danger it might bring to our family." The longing in her voice reminded Calista of how lonely her mother was without him. Briefly, the loss of her father pushed aside the uneasiness she felt about all that was happening at the moment. Then she returned to the business at hand.

"And what of me? Should I make a book of my own?" Calista didn't think through the question or why she asked it. The day had muddled her mind. She shouldn't even consider creating a book of magic when she didn't understand one thing about such matters.

"I must leave that to you." Her mother leaned down to her and held up a cautionary finger. "But know this. If you set down in writing any experience some might think unnatural—any potion, any incantation, you must guard it as if your life is in jeopardy." She gripped Calista by the shoulders and stared into her eyes. "Because it will be."

For the first time in her young life, Calista heard the knife-edge of fear in her mother's voice. There had been great sadness when her father died. There had been concern in years of poor harvests and anger when neighbors shunned any of her family, but never fear. And now she recognized what she'd sensed earlier while clasping her mother's hands. Fear was what crouched at her center, a large fistful of it.

"The people in the village? They would do us real harm instead of only ostracizing us?"

"Their memory of the old days is dim and grows dimmer with each generation. All that's left is unreasoned suspicion without knowledge of the truth. We want to keep it that way because it is safer for you and for me."

"I don't understand," Calista said.

"We must avoid calling attention to ourselves. That way they will ignore us, and only occasionally resort to taunts the way Micah and those boys did this morning. Do you understand?"

Calista nodded, but she didn't understand at all. Surely, unreasoned suspicion was more dangerous than the truth. This was something she'd have to consider.

"You will want a family and a home one day, and I want you to have it in safety."

Calista could point out that as long as she remained in Storm Haven, she might be in danger of many things, but finding anyone to marry was not one of them. She'd never had a boy look at her the way she'd seen them look at other village girls—their eyes soft with longing, lips parted in timid smiles. Even her father had come from a village to the south. And her grandfather and great-grandfather, if she remembered clearly. Her mother didn't need to hear any of that. Her grief had ebbed, but at times it filled her eyes, and the loss of her one love returned as sharply as the memory of his last breath.

Although Calista never mentioned it, she'd decided her life was full enough without venturing into a relationship. And after learning what she had today, she had no intention of going in search of a man as strong as those who had married a Moonwater in the past and lived in Storm Haven.

So Calista decided to remain quiet whenever her mother mentioned having a family or a home of her own one day in the future.

She stood up and kissed her mother's cheek. Then taking the book, she climbed the stairs to her room and opened it again.

In the flickering light of the candle, she waited until the runes had fallen into a graceful script across the first page.

To the Moonwater witch of the future who reads this book. You are endowed with a majestic power that you must use with care.

Know this. You will face danger. You will face death. But no matter the obstacles, you must seek out the goodness in all life, protect and cherish it, for there is where true magyk resides.

Calista ran her finger over the oddly spelled word, *magyk*. She was curious about why Amara had written it in this way here. She read on.

Harm no one.

Listen to the earth and her creatures. The earth will guide you onto the right path. Her creatures will counsel you into right action.

The ghosts that cling to it will have needs. Prepare for your part in setting them free from longing and old regrets.

Be true to yourself and honest in your dealings with others.

Be alert to any signs of The Vengeance. It will not be what is foretold.

Calista stopped at that last line. The Vengeance?

Surely this didn't have anything to do with that ridiculous myth about the giant perched atop the mountain ready to swoop down if any dared enter his domain. She wished she understood what this so-called Vengeance was really about.

She stretched up from her desk and paced. Perhaps if she took long enough, she could figure out what she should do with this information. There was so much she wished she understood. How creatures were going to give her guidance was one. And what Amara meant by ghostly needs. That was more than disquieting.

In spite of the din of unanswered questions, she was too tired to think more about today's events or the mysterious messages in Amara's book.

She would read more the next night when she could think clearly. Surely, tomorrow wouldn't be as chock-full of unusual occurrences.

After Calista dressed in her nightgown, she blew out her bedside candle and slipped under the covers, staring into the darkness. This day marked the end of her life as a village girl and the beginning of her life as a witch. That was going to take some getting used to.

"It won't be that difficult, dear." The woman's voice was sweet. It came to her like a flickering of tiny lights in her chest, not the sound of words in her ears.

Calista bolted upright, her skin needled by the shock of hearing it. With a shaking hand, she lit the candle again and held it overhead, but the room was as it had been, empty except for her wardrobe, writing table, and chair. "Who—"

"I'm Mrs. Wilhelm, the third from the left, near the main gate."

That made no sense at all.

"You're a sweet girl. Now I have a chance to tell you so."

"I have no idea what you're talking about." Calista set down her candle and stooped to look under the bed.

"You won't find me there." The voice was sprinkled with laughter.

"Then where?"

"I told you already, but where I am isn't important anymore." The woman's sigh brushed along Calista's mind. "What is, is that I now have someone to chat with other than the bitter Pinehurst woman—"

"Pinehurst woman?" Was the name Pinehurst going to pop up everywhere in her life this day? Calista tried to shut out the moment she'd stood belly-to-belly with Mrs. Pinehurst at the bakery door. That vision disturbed her more each time she recalled it.

"Yes, and young Squire Nielson. He's another one that goes on and on."

At the mention of that name, Calista shivered. His death had been so terrible. Why would this … this whoever they were bring up the poor squire?

"Besides, you're someone who must hear what I have to say."

Calista pointed at her chest—an unspoken "Me?". For the third time today, she was speechless. She hoped this wasn't going to be a constantly reoccurring condition. She needed to be able to speak out in her defense. All of the villagers shied away from a verbal contest with her and slunk off with useless threats when she unleashed her tongue and keen mind. She needed her voice.

"Come to visit me anytime," Mrs. Wilhelm said. "Tomorrow is perfect. There's great excitement next door now that you've come into your own. I just hope you're up to the task ahead."

And in the next moment, the pinpoints of light

she'd sensed vanished from inside Calista, and there was a sudden space in her chest as if a bit of her had fled.

Sitting on the edge of her bed, she covered her face with her hands. She had no idea what all of this meant or who was talking to her. Very unnerving.

In the next moment, her eyes went wide. "Young Squire Nielson. Next door. The third from the left, near the main gate. Oh no!"

Chapter Six

The next morning, Calista dressed quickly and stepped out into the crisp air. Chores had to be done first, so she took care of Greta, who never failed to give them a good amount of fresh goat milk. The hens were generous, and she gathered six eggs. After checking Flower's sore leg, she put their mule out to pasture to fill her ample belly with sweet grass. Flower did everything slowly, including healing from injuries, but she wasn't limping as badly as yesterday. For some reason, neither her mother's nor her poultices hurried Flower back to full health. Miriam often attributed this to Flower's stubborn nature.

Last night could not be as Calista remembered. But she had to make sure, so once she closed the barn door, she was off to see for herself.

On her way to the small gate that separated her farm from the cemetery, she passed the thicket where a few hares nested. Her heavy boots must have signaled her arrival because, by the time she reached the gate, her favorite gray hare loped at her heels.

"Where are you off to so early this fine day?" the large gray hare asked.

Her hand froze on the gate latch, and she looked down into the intense stare, numb with disbelief. It was not possible, but she could swear she'd heard that voice coming from the furry creature at her feet.

"No." She shook her head.

"That's not a proper answer," the gray hare said. "I asked you a question requiring information, not one that can be answered with a yes or a no."

"I'm … sorry?" She pressed her fingers against her temples, then sank to her knees beside him. "I'm not used to hearing you. It was a"—she searched for the right word— "surprise."

"Oh, yes. Of course. But you see, I thought you'd always heard me in the past." His whiskers twitched. "You seemed to."

Perhaps she had, but not in this way. She always spoke to animals but never expected them to reply.

"You called me Harold. Of course, that's not my name, but I thought it a good one."

Made curious even more by this statement, Calista cocked her head. "Sorry. What is your name, then?"

"Wallace."

"I see." She cleared her throat. "Well, Wallace, I'm off to find a Mrs. Wilhelm." She looked into the cemetery, hoping she was wrong and her conversation last night was nothing more than a vivid dream brought on by all of the strangeness yesterday. "Have you heard of her?"

"The third from the left, near the main gate," Wallace said.

"Oh." The small sound escaped her lips, a wispy ghost in the cold morning air. So it was true. Mrs. Wilhelm was one of the permanent residents of the Storm Haven Cemetery.

"Come. I like chatting with that one. She has stories from a very long time ago and knows so much about my ancestors' former thicket before the cemetery displaced it." He hopped ahead, leaving Calista to follow, confused and wary.

The part of the cemetery that bordered the Moonwater D'White farm was older than the village. Its higgledy-piggledy headstones bore indistinct traces of those first people to travel through the mountain pass before it was called Vengeance Mountain. No one alive today knew where these people came from or who they were. No one alive today cared much about their ancestors, it seemed. But her mother had implied it was a good thing for the past to remain shrouded in mystery, so perhaps it was just as well the history of those early settlers lay buried with them.

Always darker than the rest of the cemetery, this section smelled sour, and it felt soggy underfoot, even in the high heat of summer. She used to wonder why a low wall of stone enclosed this group of graves, but then she'd decided it might be a way to honor—perhaps distinguish—these early people from more recent ones.

She followed the hare, and once past the low rock wall divider, a flimsy ribbon of fog wound around her skirt in a cool, caressing hand of welcome. She paused at Old Thomas Tidwell's mound of freshly churned dirt to nod in respect before catching up with Wallace.

He hopped this way and that until he came to a stone carved into a kneeling angel. "Mrs. Wilhelm." He dipped his ear toward the small monument. The dates carved into the granite spanned a lifetime of seventy years, and the final date marked more than fifty years before Calista's birth.

Calista stared at the grave. "The third from the left, near the gate." Talking to animals was one thing, but talking to the dead was another matter. She wasn't ready to hear them, and she didn't understand why she suddenly could after seventeen years of blessed silence. She must be going mad. Perhaps that was another reason her mother seemed so worried last night. She'd never heard that madness ran in the Moonwater blood, but there was much she'd never heard, or so it seemed. It would be just like her mother to hold back such disturbing news. She was never one to cause upset in others. Calista still didn't believe any of this could be happening to her.

"You didn't believe me?" As ghostly female form filtered up from below, Calista took a long step back with a gasp, but Mrs. Wilhelm didn't seem to notice and set to arranging her dress. "This was not my last request," she said, pointing to the dress. "One of my daughter's mistakes." She put her semi-transparent hands on her hips and looked to the sky. "One of many, but that is water under the bridge."

The conversation with a dead woman had indeed happened last night, and it was happening again, this time in the clear light of morning. Calista needed to come to terms with this new way of things. She couldn't ignore how unusual everything had become anymore. It must be dealt with. She'd have to find a way. Quickly, it seemed.

"To begin with," Mrs. Wilhelm said, "do a few favors for those who are troubled. They have needs, and now you have the power to help them."

Realizing that the woman could hear everything she was thinking, Calista asked, "Do you read all of my thoughts?"

"Only the ones I want to. I'm the representative of this section. It's important that I set these residents' concerns before you." She settled lightly onto the head of her kneeling angel. "Are you prepared to listen?"

Calista wasn't prepared to hear anything Mrs. Wilhelm's spirit had to say, but she nodded. It might be prudent to show that she was *willing* to listen to this long-departed Storm Haven woman, if not *ready* to do so.

She wasn't sure what an upset ghost might do to her.

Chapter Seven

Mrs. Wilhelm seemed to like Calista's response and, from her perch atop her kneeling angel, said, "Wonderful. Then we shall start in the order of the received requests. That is how I've decided it should be done. Fairness, you know."

The cold increased and numbed Calista's fingertips. She regretted rushing from the cottage without her heavy shawl, but before the cemetery, the morning hadn't been as nippy. She wrapped her arms around her middle.

Mrs. Wilhelm called the name, Josiah, and when the spirit of a man curled up from the grave just in front of where Calista huddled, she fell back trembling. She no longer felt the chill, only panic. She considered running, but Mrs. Wilhelm shook her head. "You have nothing to fear from the dead, my dear, but mind those who still draw breath."

Calista looked toward the gate and the path to her cottage. It would only take a quick sprint to be through the side gate, across the thicket, and inside her kitchen.

"Trust me," Mrs. Wilhelm said, leaning close as if to impart secrets. "You are quite safe here."

Calista felt a soft *There. There.* in the way the woman spoke to her, but she couldn't stop the unease from roaming throughout her. "Safe? That's impossible. With my thoughts open for exploration, how can I feel anything but defenseless?"

"Not to worry, my dear. I have the privilege of reading your thoughts. The others do not. It comes with the position." Mrs. Wilhelm smiled. "Be assured that your thoughts are safe with me."

Calista wasn't sure about that, but it didn't seem she had a choice.

"Right. So let's make the best of it," Mrs. Wilhelm said.

The spirit named Josiah, who'd startled Calista, stood with his hands clasped, his head bowed. When she calmed enough to look at the figure before her, she knew this person. Farmer Kennewick. Before the man died, her father had worked for him to earn scolas during lean times. For years, the farmer's son, Micah, had treated her terribly—the way he and his friends had just yesterday, and Micah's father had done nothing to stop him. The farmer's beard lay full across his chest the way she remembered, but he'd shrunk in height. Then she thought, *No, it is I who have grown since the man passed.*

At first, Farmer Kennewick didn't look directly at Calista, then slowly, his face sheepish, he leveled his gaze at her. "I would ask a favor of you," he said. "But first I must tell you I regret my actions toward you when you was a child."

She didn't reply because she didn't have experience with accepting apologies. No one had ever offered her one before.

At her feet, the hare cocked his head to stare up at her. "You might try saying, apology accepted. You know, take the higher road."

It seemed that Wallace had a philosophy, as well as words to express it.

"Yes. Of course," she managed, nodding at Farmer Kennewick. "I … accept your apology."

"Thank you. I liked your father. He and I worked good together, but in all honesty, I feared your mother. The old tales, you know. They might go quiet, but they won't never be gone. Your father understood why I kept my distance from his family."

Calista noted what he said about old tales never being gone. Then she remembered what her mother had told her last night. *All that's left is unreasoned suspicion without knowledge of the truth. We want to keep it that way*. She nodded at the farmer. "My father was always understanding, so I will follow his example."

"I was a harsh father, and when my daughter married a man I did not approve of, I took away her mother's locket, hid it in the cellar, and shut Grace from my heart. So I would ask you to return that locket to her for me. I want my daughter to know how I still suffer for what I done."

How was she supposed to manage that? If she remembered correctly, Grace left Storm Haven and moved to Scrawly Springs. The only time Calista had ever had anything to do with the girl was when Calista was dodging the barbs of some of Grace's friends. They'd follow and taunt her on her way to the schoolhouse.

"Your head's more into the clouds today, Calista. Did you grow taller overnight?"

"How cold is it up there?"

They'd taunt her and then run off together, laughing.

She shuddered again, this time at those scraps of painful memories. And she didn't like the idea of going into Farmer Kennewick's cellar in the least. Besides, Micah lived in the house now as far as she knew. She had every reason to dislike that boy, and she surely didn't trust him to treat her kindly if he caught her on his property.

Again, the hare helped her. "Tell him you'll try. That's all he really wants."

The farmer nodded at Wallace. "You are very right about that."

Calista did as Wallace suggested, but even as she spoke those words, she doubted she'd follow through.

She didn't have an inkling of how she could.

Before the ghost of Farmer Kennewick stepped away, he said, "In the same place as the locket, I hid over a hundred scolas. Money for the bad harvest years, you know. Give half to my daughter when you give her her mother's locket, and keep the other half for yourself."

"Oh no. I couldn't."

"It will lighten my burden of regret for how bad I let Micah treat you, and I will have repaid you in a small way for this favor. Please."

Calista didn't have time to protest more before his ghost wafted away like gauze on a breeze.

"Ida, your turn," Mrs. Wilhelm called.

Ida Lakeshire, a frail bird-like woman, materialized in front of Calista, wringing her tiny hands together. Calista remembered those hands and how they'd shooed her away from the Lakeshire's door when she tried to sell a few muffins. It was after that last attempt to peddle their goods directly to neighbors that her mother had negotiated with Mr. Bennet. As she told Calista, "You will suffer many things in this world, but not humiliation because of muffins."

Calista remembered how her mother had embraced her that day and how they'd laughed together about her mother's muffin humor. That was a year before her father's painful death. A year before hearty laughter ceased in the cottage.

"I should have bought your muffins. I'm sorry." Ida slowly brought her gaze up to look directly into Calista's eyes. "If you'll forgive me, I hope you will tell my husband how sorry I am we quarreled my last day, and that I love him."

Calista didn't answer, but she did nod. She'd had two apologies in the space of a few minutes, but it still felt quite strange to hear *I'm sorry* directed at her. She stood in silence as Ida Lakeshire burst into small, nervous particles that fluttered into her grave.

"Minnie Wakefield." Mrs. Wilhelm called the names as if she were taking roll in the schoolhouse.

Minnie died last year. The woman never treated Calista unkindly, but like so many villagers, she never stopped others from doing so. Her cottage stood empty, but rumors were that Minnie's daughter might return to live there. Calista remembered Selena Wakefield as a pretty girl and not mean like so many others. She left Storm Haven soon after Squire Nielsen's tragic death. But everything was in flux after that, and Selena wasn't the only villager to pack up and leave. Murder upset the community and suspicion spread like a cancer.

Calista felt a coolness as if someone had brushed the back of her hand with a cloud. It was Minnie who'd come near and touched her. This time Calista didn't recoil, and that surprised her, then a quick stab of fear quickly followed. Her mother had warned her about the danger of anyone in the village learning of *unnatural* exchanges she might have. She'd said her father worried about the danger that might bring to the family. Calista could not risk becoming used to chats with the departed Storm Haven residents. She had to remain vigilant.

She stepped back. "What is it you need, Minnie Wakefield?"

"Please destroy the diary I left in the box on the mantel before anyone reads it. I fear Selena will not understand what I put in that book about her. I don't want her to hate me." The ghostly Minnie turned to leave, then said. "I did not wish you harm."

The last name Mrs. Wilhelm spoke was young Squire Nielson. Calista had seen him riding his fine horse and dressed in his well-tailored clothes. He'd at least acknowledged her with a nod when they met along the road and hadn't pretended she didn't exist. For that, she'd always been grateful.

Micah Kennewick found the poor squire shot in the woods, his horse grazing nearby. The village buzzed with speculation for weeks, then fell to talk of who should own the squire's horse. It was Micah who got it in the end. He'd brought the poor fellow to the Healer. Granted, it had been too late, but the deed should be rewarded. That was what the Elders concluded, but to Calista, there had never been something right about Micah doing a good deed of any kind.

The squire whorled up from the earth, eyes filled with hate. She feared he might be aiming that hate at her, but there was no reason for that. She'd never done him any harm. Standing before her, unlike the others, he had no apology to offer, and his energy didn't exude a speck of regret.

"Most foul murder," he said, his spirit vibrating with anger. "I had not lived but two and twenty years, when a disguised thief spooked my horse, and then shot me dead. He stole my purse and my life from me. I want justice. You must help me!"

Not even the hare had suggestions for her now, but she did feel some relief to know the squire wasn't directing all of that hate toward her.

Trying not to stammer, she said, "I—I will do what I can." At the same time, she realized, she'd have to track down a murderer. She didn't have a single notion of how she'd do that.

She'd been terribly wrong in thinking this day would be less confusing than the one before. It seemed that each day from now on was going to have serious shocks.

Chapter Eight

Calista paced in front of the barn, muttering to herself. “I don’t want to do any of the things the ghosts have asked of me. I mean, it would be utterly impossible.” She paused. “Well, not impossible,” she continued with one measured step after another, “but dangerous and insane. And what about my mother? She would have none of this business.”

She stopped pacing, her hands on her hips, her foot tapping. “But I can’t be cowardly now, can I? And I did say I’d try.” She glanced toward where the gray hare nested and shook her head. “Wallace, what have you gotten me into?” She decided to ignore the curious stares her goat gave her as she continued walking back and forth, muttering out loud. Greta tracked her until, finally, she came to a halt. “All right. I’ll keep my word … this time.”

Like Mrs. Wilhelm, Calista wanted to be fair, but to take on each ghostly request in the order she’d received them meant she’d have to start with one of the more dangerous ones and sneak into Farmer Kennewick’s cellar. She had no experience in helping ghosts, but it seemed prudent to begin with the easiest tasks and work toward the more difficult ones.

The rest of the day, she went about her chores as usual, but unlike other times, her mind wandered to Farmer Kennewick’s cellar and the chink in the wall where he said he’d hidden the locket and a considerable number of scolas. She thought of the mantel and the box that concealed Minnie Wakefield’s diary—the diary that her daughter must not read. And how could she tell Widower Lakeshire of his wife’s love for him?

She pulled up her milking stool and sat next to her

goat. Greta bleated and nudged her leg.

"I'm late. I know. Sorry," Calista murmured, setting the pail under Greta and taking the warm teats into her hands. "I've had a distracting time of it."

Ida Lakeshire's had to be the easiest request to attend to.

Perhaps a note.

She expelled more milk.

Yes, a note. Slip it under the Lakeshire door when the Widower Lakeshire is in the fields. That would be one request done.

She paused in her milking. Setting out to help departed villagers was no small decision. It opened up a new path in her life, one that might lead her into danger. "Nonsense. Mother's making much of nothing, I'm sure. The villagers are mean of spirit, but I can't imagine any of them actually hurting me." But then the image of Micah and his friends came to mind.

Greta bumped her head against Calista's leg, reminding her to return to her milking.

She wondered if she should make her decision to help the ghosts the first entry in her book of magic. But perhaps a decision didn't count as magic. On the other hand, she wondered if everything she wrote in that book had to be magical. All of this was far too confusing. She'd explore more of Amara's book that night. She hoped it would tell her how to proceed.

Now, about that last ghostly plea for help. None of the ghosts had burning hatred radiating from them the way young Squire Nielsen did. When she thought of him, the word murderer pierced through her, and she overshot the pail, squirting goat milk past her and onto the barn wall. At the same moment, the earth shifted like a restless animal. Just in time, she grabbed the pail and kept it from tipping over.

The goat shuffled, uneasy under her hand. “I’m sorry, Greta,” Calista said in the soothing voice she always used with her animals.

“You might not squeeze quite so hard, Mistress.”

Calista sat back on her stool. Now Greta was talking to her? She’d never become used to these new and very odd exchanges. Well, she’d have to, wouldn’t she, or forever be shocked and on edge. She tucked some stray strands of hair behind her ears and straightened her back. “Yes. You are right.” Patting Greta’s side and easing her grip, she concentrated on filling the pail with frothing milk.

When she’d finished, she stored the milk in the spring house, then fed the chickens. Still mulling the ghostly requests, she spread fresh straw in Flower’s stall. Her mule always greeted her with a friendly nudge, making the chore seem like a favor that was greatly appreciated. She gave Flower a scratch behind her ears, almost expecting a thank you, but the mule remained silent. “Thank you for just being Flower today and not speaking to me,” Calista said, stroking the mule’s damaged leg. She needed some things to remain as they should.

Before finishing her chores, she took time to visit her favorite place near the pond.

In March when the first promise of apples stirred along branches in small green bumps, frogs sang to her, and she smiled to think that when that season came again, she might hear the words in those songs.

But now winter was ready to bear down on them. She looked to the mountain. Already the clouds grew thicker and darker than just the week before. By nightfall, the first storm was sure to blow into the village. The Wrath of the Giant, the villagers called it, and even if she didn’t believe in a giant— let alone a wrathful one—that myth was so much a part of Stone Haven, it had become a part of her as well.

"So, Giant," she said. "Why are you so angry? Why—"

The roll of thunder came before she finished, and the sudden sting of sleet on her cheeks sent her fleeing to the cottage, her heart drumming at the sudden and unnatural onset of the storm.

Chapter Nine

By the time Calista burst into the kitchen, she was shivering with tiny rivers of melting ice tracing down her face and arms. So much for mocking old myths. She'd best not be so quick with her judgments.

"The Giant has his back up this day," her mother said. Smiling, she handed Calista a towel. "Dry your hair and stand near the stove."

Calista welcomed the warmth, but she didn't settle into the safety of the cottage the way she usually did. The onset of this storm had jiggled everything in her. Wind prowled just on the other side of the walls, its sharp claws prying at the shingles. She'd known storms in this cottage, but not one this sudden or this fierce.

Later that night, when she lit her candle and sat at her small writing table, she had to force her attention away from the howling wind. The non-stop rain must have swollen the river that ran along the backside of the farm because the roaring of high water pounding at the banks came through her closed windows. Taking a small piece of paper from her letter box, she poised her pen, ready to write the note she'd composed in her head while milking Greta.

My dearest...

Oh no. What is his given name? She'd always thought of him as Farmer Lakeshire, then Widower Lakeshire. She tapped her finger on the note, thinking, and then started again.

My Dearest. I penned this note so that you would know of my love in the event I could not tell you in person. I was to blame for that silly argument, and I want you to know I am so very sorry. Bless the person who carries this message of my true feelings. All my love, Ida

Calista ended by drawing a heart, hoping that if her words were feeble, the message of love would still reach him, and he wouldn't question how it happened to arrive under his door long after Ida's departure.

"Well done," Mrs. Wilhelm's voice whispered in her head. "Ida will be much easier to talk to for eternity. She is such a fidget." The ghostly figure materialized beside Calista's chair.

With only a slight jump, Calista tried to look unperturbed and set down her pen with a hand she couldn't stop shaking. "Mrs. Wilhelm, how did you come to me? Why not … oh, I don't know, someone else?"

"Excellent question. We'd hoped your grandmother would lend a hand, but she'd closed herself off from helping with her magic. Then Miriam came, and we waited for her, but she didn't have the Moonwater strength."

Calista stood up quickly, ready to confront Mrs. Wilhelm and defend her mother.

Mrs. Wilhelm placed a cool, calming hand on her arm. "Miriam is a delight, and we all love her, but we couldn't ask her. It would have been unfair."

Calista understood. Her gentle mother would have wanted to help, but she would have been in torment because she wasn't up to it. It was better that Mrs. Wilhelm hadn't burdened her.

"It was your heart that reached out to those without hope, Calista. Your great-grandmother had that quality, too, and like you, she listened with it. She helped so many before she moved on."

It made Calista feel proud to hear how alike she and her great-grandmother were. Her mother and grandmother had often told stories about Amara—how she was a master baker and brought forth a good harvest even in the worst of growing years. Her animals were always the healthiest, and no one healed creatures or humans faster than Amara.

Now someone not of her family was telling her that she and Amara Moonwater shared another admirable quality.

Pride goeth before the fall.

Her mother's warning rang in her ears.

Calista's cheeks flushed, remembering her mother's frequent admonition.

But she shouldn't be thinking about that. She needed to understand more about her situation at this moment. "Why now? I mean, suddenly you arrive with pleas for my help. Why not last year?"

Next year would have been even better. Or never.

"Very simply, the *magyk* awoke in you. For generations, it has happened to all of the Moonwater women when they are fully into their teen years. That *magyk* called to us, and that's when we knew you had the talent. You were the witch we'd waited for."

"I see." Calista choked. "So everyone knew about—"

"The Moonwater witches? Of course. Everyone in the village did at one time. And most were jealous nincompoops. Jealous and scared witless because they harbored evil thoughts, and their hearts held malice. A Moonwater witch could sniff any of that out in a thrice. I'm sure some elders remember the old stories from their youth, but their memories are dim and unreliable enough that today the younger villagers would either pay them no mind or—worse—panic if the old ones chose to bring up that history."

"It seems the people of Storm Haven have always disliked the Moonwaters, so they shunned us, even though they didn't know why."

Mrs. Wilhelm nodded.

"At least I know they didn't single out just my grandmother, my mother, and me. And my poor father, too. Just associating with one of us was enough to turn the village against a person. They were equally impartial in their mistreatment of *all* my family." She didn't try to hide the bitterness in her voice. "Please tell me about my great-grandmother."

"She and I were friends. I suppose you can say that we still are." Mrs. Wilhelm smoothed her hair. "But we have no contact" —the woman thought for a moment— "because of the curs … rules."

Calista started to ask what she meant when Mrs. Wilhelm said, "Once the community caught the scent of you and your power, all those more recent spirits wanted to apologize for the way they treated you." She shook her head. "The cemetery's full of regret, you know."

"And what about my great-grandmother? If she knew I was being treated like a … a witch all these years, why didn't she step up to help me?"

Mrs. Wilhelm heaved a testy sigh that in life must have set anyone nearby on edge. "I would like to explain, but I simply can't."

When Calista tried to object, Mrs. Wilhelm stopped her with a sad shake of her head. "I have to go. Mind that storm. It's going to be a fierce one, it is." She vanished, and Calista was again left with only the deafening wind.

Once she'd folded the note for Widower Lakeshire in half, she sealed it with a drop of wax inside an envelope. She'd planned on exploring more of Amara's book, but her body yearned to sleep and, for a time, forget all of the unsettling experiences of these two days.

Yawning, she climbed into bed and pulled her quilt to her chin, then fell back onto her pillow. Cupping her hands over her ears, she forced her eyes closed. She'd never been so tired.

In time, her weariness blotted out the cruel noise, and sleep bundled her into itself. At first, she floated undisturbed and peaceful, but slowly a troubling dream threaded its way into her slumber and made her restless.

She found herself being urged by the gray hare to follow him. She kept pace with him back to the cemetery, where she stumbled over the low stone wall and fell onto the sour-smelling earth that held the ancient settlers. Hands stretched up from below. They clawed at her, grasped her arms, and dragged her underground. She screamed. Her mouth filled with a black, tar-like substance, and she gagged, unable to breathe.

"Come!" A hand grasped hers and wrenched her back to the surface, where she stood, soaked with sweat and miserable, confronting another ghost, a ghost wrapped in a ragged shroud, pleading. "Make her tell the truth. Make her pay."

"No!" Calista broke free from the ghostly fingers and awoke on the floor next to her bed, gasping for air. Whose ghost was that, and where had that nightmare come from?

Chapter Ten

The next morning, the storm had vanished, and the only remnants of it were puddles and ruts where small gushing rivers had cut into the earth. Calista found porch chairs several feet away from where they belonged, their backs plunged into the flower beds, their legs shot stiff into the air.

She helped her mother restore order and then tended to her animals. They'd been safe and dry in the sturdy barn her grandparents had built. Like the cottage, it was old but crafted to withstand the storms that blew down through the pass. After breakfast, she retrieved the note for Widower Lakeshire and, steeling her nerves to see her mission through to completion, tucked it into her blouse.

"I'm off for a walk to see what other damage that storm might have caused," she told her mother. That was truly part of her reason for trekking down the muddy road. The other was to deliver the note, but she had no idea if she could do it or how her mother would react, so she didn't share that part of her morning intentions. Wrapped in her winter shawl, she struck off toward the Lakeshire farm.

In half an hour, she stood surveying the acres of land the Lakeshire family had tilled for as long as there had been a village. A dark figure of a man, his hat pulled solidly onto his head and a thick wool coat buttoned over his burly chest, came down the steps of the house. Widower Lakeshire favored his right leg, and Calista remembered the day her grandmother had set that leg. It had been such a bad break that the village Healer had predicted the man would never walk again.

"Well, that wasn't true," she said to herself,

thinking how it was that people always came to the Moonwaters when they had no hope, but never before.

She waited as he trudged across a fallow field that, come spring, would sprout new corn and wheat.

When he circled to the back and entered the barn, Calista rushed toward the house and quickly slipped the note under the door. Once the piece of paper disappeared, the porch creaked and moved underfoot. She grabbed onto the railing to keep from tumbling down the steps, but her hands began tingling, making it hard to keep a tight grip. Just when she thought she might land on the pebbled walkway below, the earth quieted, but the feeling in her hands intensified.

Believing it must be the excitement of doing a dangerous thing, she stuffed her hands into her pockets. Her heart pulsed in her throat, and instead of quieting, she felt as if dozens of bees were buzzing in her fists. Since she'd accomplished her first mission, she had a right to be excited—just not so much.

As she walked to the road and past the farm, she withdrew her hands, which were now almost painful, and clasped them together until they quieted.

Relieved that she had finally dampened her body's reaction to the success of her mission, she took a deep breath and relaxed. But on her way home, she had to admit the next two tasks on her list were much more challenging.

She'd already decided to remove Minnie Wakefield's diary next. The house was still empty, so she stood less chance of anyone seeing her. The best day would be the Sabbath. Almost everyone in the village clustered in the church far from the Wakefield house. Yes. Sunday it was.

****

The next week passed quietly and without any

ghostly visits, but Calista caught her mother fixing her with probing looks. Miriam may not have been a powerful witch, but she had a keen maternal sense when something was off about her daughter.

Calista kept busy and out of her mother's sight as much as possible. She didn't want to lie, and she didn't want to reveal her plan. It would only upset her mother to know Calista had decided to break into one of their neighbors' farmhouses.

The day before she planned to retrieve the diary, Calista finished the last batch of pumpkin muffins for the season. She put away the clean bowls and was about to untie her apron when her mother caught her hand and held it.

"I've waited long enough for you to tell me what you're up to. Now is the time."

Calista tried for surprised innocence. "I'm not sure—"

"This is your mother you're trying to hoodwink. Don't."

There was no way to avoid revealing her plan any longer. Choosing how to explain and not alarm her was the trick. Calista told the truth, but she only touched on how she planned to help the community of ghostly neighbors. Without mentioning Wallace, she used the hare's subtle wording, "I said I'd do what I could."

Her mother had drawn back in small surprise at the mention of the ghostly favors, but then she shook her head. "No. I won't have it. We can live in Storm Haven safely as long as we remain separate from the village. You cannot venture into their homes or, most certainly, their basements."

"You must trust me. And I think you do or you would never have opened that chest and given Amara's book to me."

Miriam sank onto a nearby chair, her head bowed. "I had no choice but to give you the book. Once the true Moonwater power expresses itself, there's no ignoring it. It must be supported."

"But your mother didn't support your gift."

"She had a valid reason. When I felt the first stirrings, I was only fifteen—too young by Moonwater standards—and a sign that something was not quite right. Then, of course, my mother still had vivid memories of a terrible loss." Miriam brushed back her hair, flushed and clearly upset. "I simply didn't have the true gift." She looked up. "About trusting you. Of course, I do. I do not trust the villagers, the ones who still draw breath. The others"—she tipped her head in the direction of the cemetery— "are another matter."

"I'll be careful." And saying that, Calista recognized just how anxious she was. Being caught on another's property without permission meant time in the stocks. For a Moonwater, it might be much worse.

Late that afternoon, Calista took the path to the side cemetery gate. And as he always did, the hare met her on her way past his home.

"Another visit?" Wallace asked.

"Yes. I've managed one favor. I thought I'd tell Widow Lakeshire. Although I'm sure Mrs. Wilhelm has already. She knows everything, it seems."

"The personal touch is always best." Wallace hopped ahead and dove under the gate.

Word was out about her visit because white vapors streamed from almost every plot except the dark area inside the low stone wall. She and the hare made their way down a ghostly gauntlet toward Widow Lakeshire's. But before they reached their destination, a bosomy figure whisked her way into their path. Calista knew that face. That full-bodied woman. "Eleanor? Mrs.

Pinehurst?"

It had only been a few days since they'd run into each other at the bakery. The church bell hadn't rung a death knell since old Thomas died. But here she was, Eleanor Pinehurst, dead and fuming.

"I am she," the ghost said. "I am Eleanor Pinehurst."

Calista stood, her mouth open in shock, thinking that indeed she might be losing her mind.

The day she'd accidentally pressed up against the bulk of this woman at the bakery, she'd seen her smiling over a lifeless body draped in a sheet and lying on a bed. That smile was so filled with contempt that it had stopped Calista's breath. She'd been unable to back away, magnetized by the vision of Eleanor rummaging through a wardrobe and changing her clothes. Then after mussing her hair in the mirror, she'd held a piece of onion to her eyes and fallen to her knees, clutching the bedsheets. Her cries had rung loudly in Calista's head as the door flew open and Mr. Pinehurst rushed to her side. He was easy to identify since he was the biggest man in all of Storm Haven.

"I don't understand. I just spoke with you the other day."

"Not me. My rotten sister."

Chapter Eleven

Calista, trying to make sense of what she'd just heard, stood facing the agitated ghost who claimed to be Eleanor Pinehurst.

"My twin sister is the one you spoke with," the ghost said.

Calista gasped.

"And I can see you already understand what happened."

Of course. Now Calista remembered the twins. Twins were a rare occurrence in Storm Haven, so it was remarkable, but she'd not seen them together since she was a child. One sister lived in Scrawly Springs, and the other was married to Mr. Pinehurst.

The vision Calista had seen that day took an even darker turn. One sister had killed the other. That was truly horrible. "She exchanged places with you. But why—"

"Property. Pure and simple. Matilda wanted my house and my land. I think she also wanted that husband of mine just to spite me. Matilda never did snag a beau, and for good reason. She was one sour human. How we were twins never made any sense—to me or my poor parents who had to deal with her." The ghost of the real Eleanor Pinehurst looked to the far corner of the cemetery. "My husband's over there. Matilda slowly poisoned him as he came to suspect she wasn't me." Eleanor harrumphed, and her bosom expanded. "Took him long enough. Big over-grown dolt."

"I'm so sorry."

"Not as sorry as I am. Look." The ghost pointed at the tombstone behind her. "They've chiseled the name Matilda! I am Eleanor. I don't even have a proper resting place." She swirled back to face Calista. "I was wrong to shun you and your family. For that, I am truly sorry. Please accept my apologies, and please help me."

Yet another apology. Calista would never become used to hearing these, but the old adage of "Better late than never" came to mind.

"Eleanor!" Mrs. Wilhelm bustled between them. "I told you yesterday that you had to wait your turn."

"Piffle. I want my sister to pay now, and I want a tombstone with my proper name on it."

Calista looked out over the hundreds of markers and imagined each of them with a plea for help. She couldn't do it, not for all of these people. She swallowed. All of these ghosts. Checking off one mission from her list suddenly seemed like no accomplishment at all.

Wallace glanced back at Eleanor Pinehurst who was in a head-shaking contest with Mrs. Wilhelm. The hare tapped Calista's leg with the tip of his ear. "We should back away now before they notice. No need to tell them about the Lakeshire note at this moment."

Calista took the hare's advice again and returned through the gate. "Wallace, I don't see how one witch—namely me—is going to manage to help all of those ghosts."

"One at a time. That's all you can do. They'll understand."

"I hope you're right."

"Of course. So do I. After all, my reputation as an effective familiar is at stake. I want you to succeed."

"What?"

"I want you to succ—"

"Not that. What you said about your reputation. What is a familiar?"

"Oh, yes. I forgot that you're new to the practice. Sorry." He sat on his hind legs, his long ears pointing straight up. "Think of me as a guide, a spirit that's here to lend any help when you need it."

"Well. That's a comfort."

"Good. I'm pleased to hear it."

Calista thought he might have smiled before he disappeared under the bush, but to herself, she wondered how in the world a hare was going to help her accomplish any of these favors. With her head down and filled with thoughts about being overwhelmed by hundreds of ghostly requests, she walked home.

Her mother met her at the kitchen door. It was clear she'd been waiting for her daughter and had questions.

Calista didn't give Miriam time to ask those questions. "I did the favor for Ida Lakeshire. Nothing happened. No one saw me, and so there's nothing to worry about."

Miriam dipped her chin in a short nod and went to the stove without a word. She stirred the bubbling pot with a bit more vigor than usual and splats of gravy sizzled on the hot iron grate. At dinner, they skirted anything to do with ghosts and magic, but Calista was quite sure her mother would continue to be upset about the promises her daughter intended to keep.

I'm upset as well, Calista thought. *I'll be ever so grateful when I'm done with all of this.*

****

That night, Calista set Amara's book on her writing table. Once again, she read the beginning to be sure she hadn't missed something important. First, she wanted to know what to include in any book of magic she might choose to create, and then she had to understand how *magic* differed from *magyk.* But the same warnings she had read twice were all that became visible on the page.

The warning about danger stopped her as it had

the first time. Danger was her mother's biggest worry, and if Calista faced the truth, it was hers as well. Amara had written that the earth would send messages to guide her. She wondered if that storm might be one. It still troubled her. Its sudden descent and fierceness were unlike any in her life. And if Earth intended to set her onto the right path, she wished it would do so without trembling under her feet. She was tired of being tipped off balance.

She re-read the part about paying attention to the creatures. Well, she was listening to them. She didn't seem to have a choice in the matter. And Wallace was counseling her. "Thank heavens for that."

Amara had foretold of the ghosts having needs. "They have enough of those to keep me occupied my entire life." When she came to the line about The Vengeance, she paused as she had the first time. It must be important because Amara had capitalized the words.

"So what is it?" Surely not the mythical giant she'd heard of all her life. She closed her eyes and tried to imagine what else Amara could be warning her about, but she couldn't come up with any ideas.

All right. If that giant did exist, and if he decided to exact revenge, what was it for? She considered the next message. *Harm no one.* The witches had the right way of thinking about life. She liked the idea of not harming others. She didn't like the one about taking revenge.

She'd missed nothing in these first pages, but the messages still confused her. She thumbed through the others—all blank. She wished Amara had written more. It didn't make sense that she'd set down all of these warnings and then give the reader nothing else.

It had been an exhausting day again, so Calista set aside the book and blew out the candle. She'd have to give it more thought, and perhaps after a good night's sleep, she'd be able to figure out the mystery of the blank pages.

Chapter Twelve

The church bell rang early the next morning, and as soon as Calista was certain the villagers had filled the pews, she slipped out of the cottage, determined to complete her next task.

One at a time, she reminded herself. Wallace was right about that. Today, she'd remove Minnie Wakefield's diary from her house. How hard could that be?

The Wakefield property was small in comparison to most of the other farms in the village. Mr. Wakefield had sold off much of his land to others on either side of him. Rumor was that he hated farming, and the less land he had to till, the better he liked it.

Calista made her way along a back path near the river, avoiding the road in case some villager was late to church or trying to dodge his godly duty. The storm had made the ground mushy, and no matter how carefully she picked her way across the boggy field, mud sucked at each step of her boots and slowed her progress. It had been a good thing she'd pulled on her work boots for this journey. They were already sealed against the wet by barn straw and muck.

If she didn't get into that house soon, Pastor Garrison would be done with his fire-and-brimstone sermon, the doors of the church would fly open, and out would flee the congregation.

She stepped through a small wooden gate at the rear of the property and onto a stone path that led to Minnie's back door. A nightgown, dingy and rain-soaked, hung from the clothesline. The wind gusted and the nightgown snapped at her with a "*Go away, trespasser!*"

Calista crept past the forlorn bit of laundry and up

to the door.

Locked. She tested the kitchen window. Also locked. She was about to walk along the perimeter of the house and try each window when she spotted an iron pot near the bottom step. An odd place for a pot meant to be on a stove. She lifted it aside and underneath lay a single key.

"Thank you for this, Minnie."

Calista removed her muddy boots and placed them on the step by the door. She didn't want to leave a telling trail of footprints inside the house. It only took a single turn of that key in the old lock and she stood in the kitchen. How bare it looked. Only a small table sat in the center with two chairs. The old stove must have come from another century. It had been well used over many lifetimes, for sure, but now it was dusty with disuse. For good measure, she turned the lock and tucked the key into her pocket.

There was no mantel over the kitchen hearth, but there was one in the sitting room, and on it, the box with Minnie's diary. She made her way through two chairs draped in white sheets like plump, vigilant ghosts and was quickly at the back door, diary in hand, when the sound of footsteps came from the front of the house.

No! Church could not have ended so soon. Yet, when she looked out the front window, there stood the baker, Mr. Bennet, and his apprentice, the twitchy-eyed Jones Boy, who couldn't bake a snowball so it would melt properly.

"Go round the back," Mr. Bennet said. "Just do a quick check of things. I'll take a look inside."

Heart pumping, Calista locked the back door again and rushed on tiptoes—not an easy feat—into the bedroom. The front door of the house swung open, letting in a stream of cold fresh air at the same moment she slid under the bed on her belly.

Mr. Bennet's footsteps clomped through the kitchen. The kitchen doorknob rattled. Thank goodness she'd locked that door. From her hiding place, she peeked at the large black boots entering the bedroom.

Boots! Hers were outside on the back stoop.

Please, don't let that boy see them.

She held her breath and clutched Minnie's diary closer to her as if that would soften the drumming sound coming from her chest.

Mr. Bennet must be keeping an eye on the property for Minnie's daughter, making sure all was secure until Selena arrived.

If she got out of this mess, she'd tell all the other ghosts of Storm Haven she could not risk helping them. She imagined what her mother would say if she could see her shaking under Minnie Wakefield's bed. Maybe nothing, but "I told you so" would be all over her face.

Please don't check under the bed skirt.

She felt the stocks clamp around the back of her neck.

The diary! What if he notices the box missing? Theft.

Calista's eyes watered from fear. They flogged people for stealing.

Something brushed along the edges of her mind. At first, it was a faint ruffling of air like a comforting warm breath on a winter's day, but it slowly took shape and became a word, a word more felt than heard, but it was as clear as if a person were lying next to her, whispering in her ear.

"Courage." The air around her warmed and her heart slowed.

Mr. Bennet's black boots circled the bed. She heard the jiggling of the window latch, then the clomp of his heavy footsteps followed by the quick closing of the bedroom door.

"All is well here," Mr. Bennet said loudly. "Best get back to the bakery before the church social hour is over."

Calista didn't breathe until Mr. Bennet's footsteps had faded into the distance. Then she waited for the church bell to stop tolling. She waited until the last sounds of the parishioners' footsteps passed Minnie's house. She waited for what seemed a very long time until she was sure all of the villagers had made their way home before she crawled from beneath the bed. Tucking the diary under her shawl, she peered out the windows, checking that no one was at the front or the back. Once outside, she searched for her boots. They weren't by the kitchen door. They hadn't fallen onto the ground.

The Jones Boy must have taken them.

Why on earth would he want my muck-coated barn boots? I pray he doesn't recognize them as mine. He's seen me often enough in the village.

She'd have to come up with a story if anyone asked how her boots came to be on Minnie's back porch.

Tentatively, she put one foot on the ground, squishing icy mud through her socks and between her toes. "Eww." Another step. "Eww. Eww." Walking home was going to be miserable. Very, very miserable. Hurrying as best she could, she talked to herself as a way to forget the torture of her cold, sore feet. "Never leave your boots outside like that again. Never."

A squirrel halted on its way across her path, and staring up at her, twitched his bushy tail.

Calista shook a warning finger at him. "Don't you dare mock me with that look!"

She was relieved when it bounded away without a sassy retort. She didn't want to have conversations with every animal she encountered.

Chapter Thirteen

"No. No. No." The next day, Calista stood in the cemetery, her arms crossed. She emphasized each no with a sharp shake of her head. "I've brought the diary. I've dug a deep hole and buried it at Minnie's tombstone. Its secrets are forever safe from prying eyes."

Mrs. Wilhelm's determined fists were set firmly on her hips. "And what of the others? You promised—"

"I said I would do what I could, Mrs. Wilhelm. I was almost caught inside Winnie's house. Do you have any idea what would have happened if Mr. Bennet had dragged me from under that bed? And I can't tell you the misery of walking home in stockinged feet through the mud!"

Mrs. Wilhelm looked up. "Why? I mean … the stockinged feet."

"The Jones Boy went off with my work boots. That's why."

"Oh dear." She made that small, perturbed sigh again. "All right. But *you* tell them you're quitting."

Calista dreaded turning around. She didn't have to see the mob of ghosts at her back—the powerful cold of their presence was already making her spine ache—but turn she did.

Farmer Kennewick was at the front alongside Squire Nielsen, their mouths open with unspoken demands, their lips turned down and such anguish in their eyes. Those two faces would haunt her forever.

"Look, I'm truly sorry, but I'm new at being a witch, so I do all of my own fetching and carrying. I can't risk any more house break-ins. You've—"

The hare hopped next to her foot. "Ask for more time, you know, to work on your magic."

She bent to speak to him. "I have no idea where to start, Wallace, so that might take forever."

"They have forever."

She straightened and looked out over the cemetery. He had a point, but still, she was reluctant to make any more promises, even if they could be fulfilled in the vague future. She took a while to consider his proposal, but as she did, at least a hundred more spirits clustered together with the others. "All right. I … I need more time. Then, I'll see if I can help you."

The ghostly *huzzah* blew over her and stirred the solemn trees that dotted the cemetery into jubilation. She had to get away before Mrs. Wilhelm added more tasks to her list. On their way through the gate that opened onto the farm, she muttered to Wallace, "How did I let you talk me into saying that?"

"I have a very persuasive personality?"

She stomped away, leaving him at his thicket without a goodbye.

Hare with a philosophy. Hare with advice. Perturbing. More than that. Unacceptable.

She should be able to think of appropriate replies without help. She was, after all, an intelligent human. And a Moonwater witch. That alone had to count for something.

That night when Calista lit her candle and opened Amara's book, the page was unreadable, as it always was when she first looked at it. It took a while before it sorted the runes out into words she could read. She wondered if the book would forever behave in this manner to make sure she wasn't an enemy.

At this pace, she'd never solve the mystery of the blank pages. She tapped her fingers, impatient to start. But it wasn't long before the familiar welcoming passages appeared again. She imagined her great-grandmother as a young girl, sitting at a writing table much like the one she sat at, penning these words.

She flipped through the pages she'd already studied several times and turned to the first blank one. She waited, tapping her foot, willing words—something—anything to appear before her. But when nothing did, she said, "Is *this* all that you've left me? A list of duties, and then not a single thing to help me carry them out?"

The book rose a few inches from her writing table and hovered there.

"What?" Calista sat back in shocked surprise.

Its cover snapped closed, and then it settled back into place with a light tap.

For a moment, Calista kept her distance, then slowly she sat forward and reached out an unsteady hand. At that same moment, the book cover flipped open again. She yanked her hand back, and the pages fluttered, fanning her face. When they stopped and lay flat, a thinly inked script flowed onto the page.

Today the pond was sheeted with thick ice, and I peered down into the water seeking some stir of life. What I saw was a world suspended for a time. Waiting for the spring thaw.

Calista turned another page and another. Each had a small story about the farm and the village and a young girl's dreams for her future.

Thunder rolled through the pass and down Vengeance Mountain today. Someone in Storm Haven must have challenged the [giant]. The [giant] will have none of that. Foolish villagers.

She paused at the bracketed word, giant. "Curious."

With a sigh, she leafed forward to more entries, enchanted by the short stories they told. She ran a finger across one spidery line of writing, then another until she came to the word *fetched.* This was exactly what she needed. If she could make the locket leave Farmer Kennewick's cellar and come to her room, there'd be no need to venture down there and risk being caught.

Eagerly, she read.

If I hadn't fetched all of those eggs from their hiding spots before nightfall, that wily fox would have feasted on my lovely hens' bountiful gifts. As it is, that sly she-devil made off with my prize rooster. Fetching those eggs early and securing my coop will be priorities from now on.

This was a nice bit of caution, but really no help at all. Calista needed a book of useful charms, not memories of lessons learned. "Why didn't you leave me the *magyk* you promised?"

A tingling at the tip of her finger started—tiny at first, like gnat wings. But that tingling grew until it was as strong as the day she'd slipped the note under the Wakefields' door. The buzzing on the skin of her palms was just this side of painful.

Calista stared at her fingertips. They glowed with heat. Blowing on them didn't help. Waving her hands in the air only seemed to make her fingers hotter. She pressed them back onto the cool paper of Amara's entry. Suddenly between the lines of the story, another set of words in dark red ink flowed across the page. A thicker, more serious pen had been used to write these words.

"What is this?" She stared at the book. Tentatively, she drew her finger down the page, and more dark red words filled the lines between Amara's entry about the thieving fox.

Calista giggled with excitement. "There you are." How clever. The story themes were tied to the spell hidden inside them.

The Fetching Spell: To bring items to you from other places...

She read the spell. *One inch of hair, your own.* Easy. Snip. *Four drops of boiling water.* She ventured into the kitchen, moved the kettle over the still-hot stove top, and when the water boiled, measured it into a small cup. On the way back to her room, she recited the spell, all the time swirling the lock of hair in the water. "Hair a beacon. Steam a trail. Heat the seeker. Bring the locket from Farmer Kennewick's cellar."

She closed the door and held out her hand, waiting for the locket to fall into it.

"What is it at this hour that calls me from my family?"

Calista jumped back from the direction of the voice. When she looked down, she was staring into the alarmed eyes of the gray hare. "You?"

"Yes. I believe so. Last I checked."

"But … but—"

Wallace hopped onto the writing table. "You didn't want me, so who did you want?"

"Not who. What. I was trying to fetch that locket." Calista sat heavily on the bed. "I'm not good at magic."

"Hmm. How many spells have you tried?"

She looked up at him perched next to the candle and Amara's book. "One?"

"Well then, best get on with some practicing. Try it again. You might not have said it just right. Spells can be fussy in the way they're delivered, you know." He jumped down from the writing table and onto the windowsill.

"Wait! Please stay. I'll try it again, but what if—"

"What if, indeed. I'd have hopped all the way to my nest only to be whisked back here a second time."

The hare settled onto the sill, prepared to wait.

Another inch of hair. *Snip*. She'd better get this spell right soon, or she'd have no hair left. Calista returned from the kitchen, and this time, she read the words from the book very carefully. Wallace twitched his nose, Calista closed her eyes and held out her hand, and they waited together in silence.

Waiting.

Waiting.

Clunk.

She opened her eyes, and at the end of her bed sat a sewing machine, one she'd seen many times through the tailor's window.

Chapter Fourteen

"Oh, no!" Calista stood trembling, staring at the tailor's sewing machine. How out of place it looked in her bedroom—how terrifying the implications of its sudden appearance were.

"Dear me," Wallace said. "This is a great deal more serious than fetching me from my home." He pointed at the sewing machine with one long trembling ear. "That will be sorely missed tomorrow morning."

"I must return it. Immediately. How do I do that?" With a touch of frenzy, Calista flipped the pages in Amara's book. Her hand halted when she came to a place where the story was about returning a borrowed tool.

Once again, her fingertips throbbed, and when she slid them over the story, the Returning Spell appeared in dark red lines.

Calista rolled her shoulders and bent again to the task. This time, the spell didn't require more of her hair. For that, she was grateful. It asked for spit. Easy. It did ask for some twirling and trust. Fine. Done.

It wasn't exactly a *poof*, but close. As soon as she did the last twirl, the tailor's sewing machine vanished.

Calista collapsed into her chair. "I'm not made for this."

"Well," the hare said, rising and butting the window with the top of his head until he had space to hop through, "what comes too easily to us is often not appreciated." Before he leapt out, he looked at her. "I have family matters to attend to tonight. I hope you won't call me back."

"No fear of that. I'm done with practicing spells." Calista went to him. "Thank you. It was a comfort to have you here."

"Of course." And he was out the window and across the yard.

****

The morning came with tepid sun and drizzle. Calista didn't look forward to the barn chores, but she wrapped herself in warm clothes and her father's sleek coat that he said shed water like a duck. She smiled, remembering the way he always told her that on his way out into the weather. Now it was she and Miriam who did the chores. Rainy. Snowy. Sunny, hot days. A farm needed working and someone to work it. Now, that someone was her or her mother.

Greta gave her milk without much conversation, except a tidbit about hearing a pesky hare out and about last night. "Probably looking to steal stored cabbage from the cellar," Greta said.

Not that her goat was above that sort of thing. Calista grinned thinking about the accusing side of Greta's nature.

She finished her work and trudged back to the house. Before she could open the kitchen door, it swung in, and her mother stood clutching her shopping bag, her face the color of fine-milled flour.

Something was very wrong.

"The bakery," she said as if that conveyed her entire message. She pushed past Calista and sat heavily on a kitchen chair.

"What about the bakery?" Calista knelt in front of her mother.

"I was on my way to buy dry goods from the general store when I came to a crowd outside Mr. Bennet's." Her mother pressed her fingers against her temples. "Such a babble. I stopped to see what the stir was about."

"And?" Calista took one of her mother's hands,

wishing she'd hurry up and tell her what was so upsetting.

"The tailor's sewing machine." She stopped to swallow. "Up to its treadle in frosting. All four legs buried deep in Mr. Bennet's cakes."

Calista sat back on her heels. She'd meant to return the machine to the tailor's shop. If she couldn't do a simple fetch or return spell, did she have any hope at all for more complicated magic when she needed it?

"Do you have something to tell me, Calista?"

"I did it." She never lied to her mother. In fact, she was a very bad liar. She explained about how she'd found the spells and how the first one hadn't gone well and… "But I worked the spells exactly as Amara said to."

Her mother stroked Calista's hair, and her eyes glinted with the promise of tears. "In the old days, so many of our family suffered if the villagers only sniffed the tiniest hint of witchcraft."

"Suffered?"

But her mother looked away, ignoring the question in that word. "Right now, they're talking about it being a prank or a disgruntled customer, but if anything else unusual happens, I fear the elders will turn their thoughts to the Moonwaters. That will soon spread among the younger ones who haven't heard the old stories. Another generation might be stirred to distrust or worse."

As much as Calista wanted to know what made her mother so fearful, she didn't press for an answer. Talking about the family's past always seemed to upset Miriam, and Calista had done enough to upset her already.

"I wish I had the power to help. I simply do not."

"I'll find out what I'm doing wrong," Calista said. "And I'll fix it."

Until she figured it out, she'd go back to fetching and carrying on her own. She was in danger either way.

Chapter Fifteen

Almost overnight, the season transformed from crispy autumn into a time for banking logs in the fireplace—a time for long nights and short snow-filled days.

One early morning, Calista baked the first batch of winter muffins. The heady aroma of dark brown cinnamon mixed with sugar, flour, and fresh eggs filled the kitchen and filtered through the cottage. When the muffins were ready, Calista bundled them snugly into her basket and set out.

Her walk into the village was cold, but she moved at a fast pace, and with the still-warm muffins clutched at her middle, she didn't feel the chill at all. Since she had so much to consider—her next task, her failed magic, her mother's mounting fear—the time between her cottage and Mr. Bennet's bakery passed quickly.

Mr. Bennet's bell clattered as she opened the door and stepped into the warm and deliciously fragrant space.

He stopped her before she could close the door behind her back. "I'll need no muffins."

"But—"

"I have a new baker, and I've set him to making all the muffins I need. He'll be doing the job from now on." He swung the door wider and waited for her to leave.

Stunned to silence at first, she stood unmoving. She couldn't have heard the man correctly. Then anger exploded inside her, and she jutted her head forward, forcing the him to look up into her face. "Who is this new baker?"

Mr. Bennet cleared his throat. "The Jones Boy. Showed promise, so I promoted him. Good lad." He sniffed the aroma rising from her basket, pungent with cinnamon, and from his expression, he wanted what Calista carried. Very much.

"Will you be buying any of what I bake ever again?"

He shook his head, his white cap shuddering, his nose twitching the way her goat's would near a cabbage patch.

She stepped closer to him, forcing his gaze to stay with hers. "And can you tell me the reason?"

He backed away, clearly not wanting her near him, his lips pressed together.

"Then I will leave you with this to mark the end of our agreement. I'm very sorry you have been dissatisfied." Calista placed a single warm muffin in Mr. Bennet's hand and stomped away. She glanced back to see the baker standing at his door, inhaling the steam rising from the warm morsel in his palm.

On her way down the street, Calista stopped the stinging in her eyes by brushing them fiercely with the back of her hand. "The Jones Boy. Ridiculous!" She trudged ahead, punishing the dirt under her boots. She narrowly missed bumping into the green grocer and instead, knocked against his fruit cart. Two apples tumbled onto the ground.

"He bakes muffins that taste of sawdust!" She said this loudly at the same time as she scooped up the apples and stuffed them into their bin. As she whirled to leave, the greengrocer quickly ducked back inside his store.

A village dog scrambled to its feet and darted out of her path. She dodged the tailor on his way to his shop. As she rounded the boulder to leave the village, she ran into three men who barred her way, but they quickly walked to the side of the road under the glare of her amber eyes.

On her way home, a wind funneled down through the mountain pass and swept into Storm Haven, bitterly cold with the promise of the first snow. As soon as she stepped onto her front stoop, it let loose with a howl like an angry beast and unleashed a torrent of rain that quickly turned to sleet. All the storms this season seemed bent on destruction. How lucky for her that she'd beaten this one home and was safe inside the cottage. Now, she had the very unpleasant task of telling her mother about Mr. Bennet.

She didn't have to. Her mother spied the full basket and knew. "Mr. Bennett isn't buying our muffins anymore, is he?"

Calista shook her head. "He's hired a new baker and put him in charge of muffins."

Her mother smiled, but it wasn't an expression of happiness at all. Her lips turned up at the corners, while her eyes drew down in resignation. "No. I'm sure the stir of suspicion has begun. We will have to be very careful from now on. You must not go near the village alone. We have sufficient provisions for a few weeks, so neither of us will leave home." She paced. "Let us hope that the story about the tailor's sewing machine will grow dim, and that chatter about the old days won't become widespread."

Calista wound her arms around her mother, stopping her pacing. "I'm so sorry. I'm not a gifted witch after all. This is all my fault."

"No. You are not to blame. I should be stronger. I should be the Moonwater to step up."

For the first time, Calista understood how much her mother wished she'd been given the gift her ancestors had. It must have been painful for her to know how powerful Amara had been. A failed witch was how her mother saw herself.

But maybe she was a failed witch, too. So far, she'd done everything wrong. And now she may have put them in danger by her mistake. She was the reason their income was diminished.

That night, sacrificing another chunk of hair, Calista planned to practice fetching an item to her from across the room. She should have done this in the first place, but she'd been so eager to complete Farmer Kennewick's favor that she had not used good judgment.

This time, she spoke the words more carefully.

"Hair a beacon."

Breathe.

"Steam a trail."

Breathe.

"Heat the seeker."

Breathe. Breathe.

"Hairbrush yonder, come to me."

At her command, her hairbrush flew off the dresser, but it hurtled past her outstretched hand and slammed into the wall.

She retrieved it from the floor. "Not exactly where I asked for you to go." She shook her finger at the brush the way she might at a naughty child.

She had made an object move from one place to *almost* where she wanted it! But it was going to take a lot more practice before she was ready to search out things from a distance and have them come to her. The ghosts would have to wait.

She pulled her hair out like wings on each side of her head and studied the ragged ends in the mirror. "What a mess I've made of everything, including this."

Chapter Sixteen

The snow came thick and steady and lasted almost two weeks, so Calista and her mother stayed inside the cottage, only making quick dashes to the barn to care for Greta and Flower and to gather the few winter eggs.

After this lengthy isolation, there was no baking to do. Between the two of them, they'd made the cottage spotless. Both had tired of card games, and nothing needed mending. She preferred to study Amara's book when she was alone in her room at night, so the days seemed endless.

When the storm finally ended and all was a silent white outside the windows, Calista longed to stretch her legs.

She cleared the path from the door to the road. The exercise felt wonderful, but it increased her appetite, and their provisions were dwindling. They'd dug out the last of the rutabagas from their straw bed in the cellar. The last onion. The last apple. Greta's milk and the hen eggs kept them full, but how long could they live on those? Even their flour bin was close to empty. They'd eaten the last of the rejected muffins the first week.

One morning when her mother counted their scolas into a stack on the kitchen table, they agreed they had enough to buy supplies for two more weeks. Then they'd have to find someone who would buy goat milk and eggs or trade those for staples.

"I'll make a trip into the village for flour and perhaps some potatoes or carrots from one of the farmer's root cellars," her mother said.

"Let me. I'm a much faster walker, and—"

"No, Calista. I want to get a sense of what the villagers are thinking."

"Then let me check Flower. Her leg looks less swollen. Perhaps she's healed enough to travel to the village."

Her mother shook her head. "I could use the walk. I've been confined in our cottage long enough."

Neither spoke of what was evident. No one would buy anything from them. Even before her disaster with the tailor's sewing machine, the general store balked at taking their summer crops, but Miriam's jaw was set with determination, and Calista knew better than to think she'd change her mother's mind.

Calista hated watching her mother make her way down the road, the snow as high as her boot tops. With these conditions, it would take her over an hour in the cold to reach the village, and then an hour back. Calista looked to the sky. It was clear overhead, but bloated storm clouds heavy with more snow hung above the mountain. If a wind came up from the west it would blow those clouds into Storm Haven. As her mother disappeared behind the first turn in the road, Calista whispered, "Hurry back."

Two hours came and went. Then another two. Calista had to stop herself from pulling back the front curtain with each tick of the mantle clock. As it was, she did push that curtain aside to peer out every few minutes. Her mother should have returned by this time.

To keep her mind from calling up all kinds of disasters, she tended the animals, dug through the root cellar straw again just in case they'd missed a turnip or some other edible vegetable, and stoked the fire.

Night came before she'd added another log. That was as long as she could bear waiting. She lifted the lantern down from the hook by the kitchen door and checked to make sure it was fueled. Bundled in the warmest garments she could find, she pulled on her good fur-lined boots, lit the lantern, and walked into the darkness.

No new snow had fallen, so her mother's trail was still clear and easy to follow. With each step, Calista grew more fearful. Her mother had never failed to return from the village before dark. It was an unspoken rule that all of the family should be safely inside the cottage before the sun went behind the mountain. There were too many dangers lurking outside in Storm Haven. Wolves. An occasional bear. But Calista was beginning to understand that perhaps her parents had feared the people of the village might do one of them harm under the cover of darkness. Now she sensed that in the old days the villagers had done something terrible to her ancestors, and her mother was too fearful to tell her the details.

She had to stop thinking that way. Her mother was safe. Only delayed. She'd be coming around one of the bends in the road. They'd meet, and with the lantern light, they'd find their way safely home.

"Please make it so." Her voice had pleading in it, so she stopped talking out loud. Pleading was not something she wanted to do, not even to herself.

The snow had turned to ice along the ground, and it crunched under her boots. She kept her head down, watching each step. She couldn't risk falling.

What if? That phrase popped into her head and wouldn't go away. What if something serious had happened to her mother? What if someone had robbed her? She had the last of their scolas in her purse. What if they hurt her? Killed…

"No!" The loud sound of her voice broke the silence and her heart faltered, making her painfully aware of how terrified she really was. She stopped to breathe and calm herself, but the stillness that settled around her was thicker than before. The small yellow circle of light from her lantern made the night beyond its reach seem more dangerous.

Holding the lantern higher, she peered ahead, knowing she had to continue. She couldn't stay here unmoving much longer or she'd freeze to death. And with that thought a sudden warmth came over her. It was the same feeling she'd had while hiding under Minnie's bed and trying not to panic.

"Courage." Again, the word brushed along the edge of her mind. Not a voice, and yet so clear.

"Who or what are you?" There was no answer, but she'd forgotten her fears and the cold and all the doubts about finding her mother safe. She'd met a sizable number of ghosts recently, so it could be any of them who was speaking to her. They wanted her to survive so she could help them with their afterlife requests. Or perhaps her great-grandmother had decided to lend a hand after all.

"Well, thank you. Whoever, whatever you are."

She walked on, this time with more determination.

The boulder where the sharp turn in the road would take her into the village should be on her left, but everything surrounding her was mounded in snow. More people had walked in this area, and her mother's tracks weren't as clear anymore. Calista had to rely on her sense of direction, and that sense told her she'd missed the boulder and was heading toward Vengeance Mountain, not the village. She hoped she hadn't missed the turn.

Then, there it was, the boulder—her guidepost. In the night, concealed with a thick white shroud, everything had become unfamiliar. Sure of the way now, she continued forward, away from the mountain.

The village was dark, except for a small fire that crackled outside the blacksmith's shop. Next to the fire sat a huddled and wonderfully familiar figure.

Calista ran and wrapped her arms around her mother. “I was so scared!”

“I knew you would be.” Miriam pointed at her ankle. Even in the dim light, it looked swollen and dark. “I caught my foot in a rut and fell.” She bit her bottom lip. “Now I understand how Flower must feel.”

“How did you manage the fire? How—”

“The blacksmith took some pity on me. He made me a fire, and he brought me hot tea and some bread.”

“No one else came to your aid? No one offered to help you home?” Calista’s voice shook with anger. *Is this village filled with nothing but unfeeling beasts?* She’d never thought so many people with such horrid natures could live in Storm Haven.

“They’re afraid.”

“Because of a stupid sewing machine and a few cakes?”

“No. There’s more.” Miriam pulled Calista close and spoke in a whisper. “Someone has been found dead.”

“What? Another death in the village?” Calista shuddered more from what her mother had just said than from the cold.

“Murdered, they say, and there are rumors that he died in the same place as young Squire Nielsen.” Miriam lowered her voice even more. “I could sense that witchcraft is on everyone’s mind. I overheard the name Moonwater twice. The second time is when I misstepped and twisted my ankle.”

Calista sat heavily on the ground next to her mother. “So the villagers think we’re to blame for the squire’s death?” She thought about the squire’s plea for help in finding his murderer and how she’d put his request at the end of her list. She might have to rethink that plan. “Who has been killed?”

"Mr. Bennet's new assistant, the young Jones Boy."

Chapter Seventeen

ith the last of their scolas, Calista convinced the blacksmith to take them home in his cart. He dropped them at their gate and quickly left before they'd taken a single step down the path. She and her hobbled mother had terrified one of the burliest men in the village.

Slowly, her mother leaning heavily on her shoulder, they made their way into the house and her mother's bedroom. After wrapping Miriam's ankle carefully in a strip of herb-soaked cloth and helping her into bed, Calista sat next to her mother. It was time to learn the history she had hinted at but never wanted to share. Calista set her jaw in a manner that she hoped would make it clear she wouldn't take any more evasive answers. This set of the jaw was something she'd learned from her mother, so she was sure Miriam would understand. Calista wanted the truth, no matter how difficult it might be.

"I know you said there was danger for our family and that I had to be careful if I created my book of magic, but you never were clear about what happened to the early Moonwaters."

Her mother frowned. "It's not something I ever wanted you to know."

"But I must. It's time."

When her mother turned back, tears glistened in her eyes. "Yes, I know. You're no longer a child I have to protect, are you?" Taking Calista's hand, she held it tightly before letting go. "The Moonwater witches of the old village were…" She reached for a handkerchief on her bedside table and blotted her eyes. "They were burned along with their books."

The horror of that surged through Calista like

flames. She felt the lick of fire at her feet. It rose around her, hot tongues flicking upward and toward her face. In a hoarse whisper, she asked, "Amara, too?"

"No." Miriam swallowed and cleared her throat. "They … hanged Amara and buried her somewhere on Vengeance Mountain." She'd held in this ghastly truth for a long time, but now that she'd set it free, the past horrors swept into the room and stunned Calista. "Unfit to lie with the good people of Storm Haven, they said. They humiliated my mother's family and drove them from the village. That's why we live here, almost at the end of the road and next to where they bury their dead. That's why no Moonwater ever steps into the church. We were banished."

Now Calista understood so much—why her grandmother had not created a book of magic and why she'd cautioned Miriam not to create one. She'd been terrified of what might happen to them if a book like that should be discovered. Now Calista understood why the Moonwaters stayed at their cottage on the sabbath and never ventured into Storm Haven's church.

"I can't forbid you to practice witchcraft," Miriam said. "I wish I could. For me, it wasn't difficult to set it aside. I didn't have the talent, but" —Miriam gripped Calista by the arms and pulled her closer to her— "you do, so it will be impossible to step away from such a strong calling."

"I'm still not sure I have the talent that you think I do. I'm not getting the spells right."

"And I should be helping you, but I can't. I'm so sorry, my sweet."

"You are helping me by telling me the truth and being here for me. I'm just a slow learner." She smiled, then after kissing her mother's cheek, snuffed out the candle and left the room.

She closed the door behind her, and for a moment, leaned against the rough-hewn wood to sort out what she must face in the days ahead.

They were out of money. Since nobody would buy muffins directly from her in the past, she was quite sure no one would do so now. She and her mother would have to be frugal and clever to survive until a new vegetable crop. Even then, she was certain that the greengrocer wouldn't buy enough of their produce so they could replenish their scolas.

Her mother was right. The village was numb with fear, but if they came together and if they talked about the untimely deaths … it wouldn't take long before the old stories about the Moonwater witches became fresh again. Witchcraft and spells would be common topics in the village square. There'd be talk of what the village did to rid themselves of her ancestors in the past. And after today, they'd have much to say about the Jones Boy—a fresh horror that would be connected to her family, especially herself. And since his death seemed to have happened in the same location as Squire Nielsen's…

She pushed quickly away from her mother's door, fiercely annoyed at how unfairly the villagers had always treated her family. She'd had no connection with the young squire except an occasional chat along the road, but she did have reason to dislike that Jones Boy. The greengrocer and the tailor saw her storm away from the bakery, and it wouldn't have taken any time for the villagers to find out that Mr. Bennet had stopped buying her muffins. They would piece those clues together, and all fingers would point at her. They'd say she'd gotten rid of that new baker for spite.

"Stuff and nonsense," she muttered, but with all she now knew about the Moonwater history, she couldn't dismiss her worry so quickly.

Once inside her room and with her candle lit, she scoured Amara's book for more, maybe simpler, spells. Maybe a spell that would help her retrieve the locket from Farmer Kennewick's cellar. One of the short stories that caught her eye was about a spotted fawn that Amara had come upon hidden in the foliage.

Such a perfect disguise nature had given this little fellow. Hidden in plain sight. Invisible. I sat, waiting for his mother's return, and when she did step into view, I backed away. She seemed to know I'd stood guard over her babe while she was gone.

Calista drew her finger between the lines and The Spell of Invisibility appeared just as the others had.

"Perfect." Being invisible would get her in and out of that cellar in safety.

After that horrid experience with the tailor's sewing's machine, she'd continue to be cautious and test each spell. She'd only try to make something in her room invisible. She had few choices and settled on her writing table. She'd need a mirror. One cinnamon stick. Two drops of water from new snow or clear stream. No hair required.

"Thank you for not repeating that bit, Amara."

It didn't take long to gather the items and place them in front of her. Once she had them collected and arranged, she closed her eyes and aimed her finger at her writing table. Carefully, she repeated the words her great-grandmother had written.

"Concealed from eye. None will see. Vanish now. Cease to be."

This spell had an easy cadence to it. It had to work. She'd done everything exactly as Amara had set down. Excited and yet anxious, she opened one eye and then the other.

"No!"

Her writing table was where it should be. She stomped her foot in frustration. Once again, she'd failed. Her mother was so wrong. She hadn't inherited any of the family's talent.

Calista picked up the mirror to return it to her dresser and glanced into the glass. There was no reflection of her face. She let it slip from her fingers onto the bed. For a moment, she froze in place, then with a trembling hand, she retrieved it and stared into it. The mirror only held the image of her room—not one bit of her except her plain woolen work dress floating in the air.

When she aimed it at the candle, the candle's flame danced in the glass, but no matter how many times she turned it toward her, she wasn't there.

She held out a hand to examine. Gone. Foot also gone. She held the mirror at arms-length and looked into it again, hoping that a larger view would improve the situation. Nothing.

"Now what am I to do?" She hadn't thought ahead at all. Well, she hadn't expected to make herself vanish. She hadn't even thought that might happen. "There's a lesson in all of this. I'm simply not ready to work magic in the manner of my great-grandmother."

"Twiddle-twaddle." Mrs. Wilhelm misted her way into Calista's bedroom. "You're ready. You're just overwhelmed. Look at the state you're in! Well, no. That's not possible at the moment, but you've worked one of Amara's most challenging spells. I'd say that's a huge step in the right direction."

"If only you knew what was afoot in the village, Mrs. Wilhelm, then you'd not think of this as a huge step in any direction."

"We all know what those ninnies are about, my dear. But you forge ahead with diligence, and we'll be next door patiently waiting."

"Don't leave yet." Calista held out her hand, hoping it was where she aimed it. "I want to thank you."

"For what?"

"For helping me twice when I needed it. You know, coming to give me encouragement when I was sure Mr. Bennet was about to discover me under Minnie's bed and again tonight on the road to the village."

"I'm sorry, but I don't know what you mean, dear."

Calista had thought Mrs. Wilhelm was the one she'd sensed and drawn courage from. "Then it must have been my great-grandmother."

Mrs. Wilhelm shook her head. "No. I'm afraid that's not possible."

"Why?"

Mrs. Wilhelm shifted uncomfortably. "She's not accessible the way the rest of us are, and even *we* must be asked if you want us to intercede. And you must do it in the right manner."

"But how do I find the 'right manner'?"

"When it is time, you will. Of that, I'm quite sure. At the moment, you have so much to focus on." She cleared her throat. "Those spells and the tasks." Mrs. Wilhelm sighed, and then broke into tiny particles, but before leaving, said, "Have faith in yourself."

Having faith in herself was going to be hard. Either her spells failed or they almost worked or they worked far differently than expected.

Unsettling as it was, she undressed her invisible self and pulled on her nightgown. It hung eerily above her unseen feet, and when she held the mirror up again, the tiny violet pattern on the material mocked her with its cheery promise of spring.

"I want to see myself right now!" The angry

impatience in her voice snapped like static around the room.

And there she was. In no more time than a quick command, Calista reappeared.

Gratitude and relief flooded through her, and she made herself a promise to be even more careful before she practiced again. And if she did start her own book of magic, she'd be sure to include more details about how to work spells.

For now, she had to keep herself and her mother safe until she mastered Amara's magic. She would not try any spells beyond the cottage until she was sure she could work them exactly right. She'd fetch Farmer Kennewick's locket the old-fashioned way and take the scolas he'd promised. The food they could buy would last until summer. By then, the villagers' fear and superstition would have subsided.

She doused the candle and curled under her blankets.

"I hope."

Chapter Eighteen

The sliver of a moon made it a perfect night to sneak into Farmer Kennewick's basement. Who was she trying to fool? There was no perfect time to do something so dangerous, but it was the best time she could choose.

She waited until the sky was its darkest, and using her memory of ruts and crevices, crept her way along the road. She hadn't wanted to risk lantern light, so she could only hear the stirring of night creatures around her and sense their eyes following her.

An owl called out from a towering oak. "Who is this thief on the road?"

"For pity's sake, don't screech like that." Calista's voice came out in a throaty whisper.

The owl swooped down and perched on a nearby fence post. "You're not very stealthy for a Moonwater witch."

She wished every creature in Storm Haven didn't know who she was and have some comment about her abilities. "I'm new at this. Why don't you help instead of criticize?"

"Hmm. Not stealthy, but sensitive, I see." The owl flicked its head and then fluttered to her shoulder. "I'll be your eyes since your human ones aren't up to the task. No offense intended, of course."

Calista wanted to come back with something sharp, but the owl had only stated the truth, and she could use some help, so she thanked it, and the way became much easier with its guidance.

In a short time, they arrived at the Kennewick's. A low wooden gate stood open, but not like an invitation, more like a careless hand had forgotten to close it properly. *Micah.* He was never one to pay attention to details. In school, he was the boy with mussed hair or a partly untucked shirt. His homework almost done, but not completely or with mistakes. And there was a restless danger about him. He hunched his shoulders, so he always looked ready to lunge. He put her on edge any time he was near. He reminded her of a mistreated dog on guard against being hurt, ready to attack and unpredictable.

The house was dark, so Micah was either gone or asleep.

The owl flew off to a tree branch. "Are you sure you want to be here? Kennewick's is not a good place for anyone since the old man died."

"Is it because of Micah?"

"Indeed. He's an armed human with little judgment."

"It would be better not to leave me with that thought, but thank you for your help."

"My pleasure." The owl flew off but lit onto a tree limb overhead.

She should go home. This wasn't a good idea. But they desperately needed the scolas, and crossing off another mission would prove she was trying to keep her word. She felt her way across the yard and to the side of the house. The cellar door was closed, but when she fingered the handle, it didn't have a lock.

At last, a good omen.

She grasped the handle, praying that the hinges didn't creak, and she was about to pull when a whispered voice behind her said, "Those hinges will make a very loud noise."

It was fortunate that Calista was not given to screaming. She fell away gasping as her friendly hare hopped into view.

"Sorry. But I thought I should warn you," he said,

again keeping his voice low.

"What are you doing here?" She sounded as if someone had a hand around her throat.

"Following you. Keeping an eye on that ravenous owl. As soon as your predator assistant left, I came out from hiding to see if you might need my help."

"What? Are you feeling guilty for talking me into saying yes to all those ghosts?" she hissed.

"Somewhat." He hopped to the cellar door. "Now, my advice is not to yank, but to pull slowly. Test how much noise these rusty hinges will make."

Once again, she leaned over the cellar door and very slowly lifted. The creaking wasn't loud, but in the silence it seemed so. She stopped. The house remained dark, and she didn't hear any movement from inside. She tugged the door higher. This time, the hinges complained even more, but the screech of the owl buried the sound. Calista looked up. The owl now sat on the roof, peering down at her.

She waved a thank you, and the owl's wings beat steadily into the night until it settled among the tree branches farther away.

"Sneaky owl," Wallacc said, poking his nosc from under a bush. "Not to be trusted."

"He helped me get this door open without detection, so I'm very grateful." She crept down the steps, fumbling for the wall and trying to remember exactly what Farmer Kennewick had told her. Near the door on the left about a foot to the.... She stumbled, knocking over something. It landed with a crash.

An eternity condensed into a few panicked seconds while Calista, on her hands and knees, held her breath, listening. Any minute she was sure she'd hear footsteps overhead. But none came, so she got to her feet and began breathing again.

"You are not very good at thievery after dark," Wallace said.

"And you are not very good at helping."

"I'm here for moral support. You should be grateful."

Calista swiped her forehead, surprised at how damp with perspiration it was. "I am. I'm just so—"

"Nervous. I understand."

Outside, the owl hooted.

"Now would you please hurry?" Wallace said. "That owl's lurking nearby, and he's still hunting for his supper. I'd like to be safe at home as soon as possible."

Calista reached out her hand and ran it along the stone wall near the door. High. Low. Middle … then she found the chink. She slipped her fingers into it and prodded until she touched something that wasn't stone. A small box.

This must be it.

She pulled it to her and opened the lid. While she couldn't see the locket, she could feel it. A heart with a tiny hinge and a tracery of design on the surface. She had Grace Kennewick's locket. Underneath was a leather purse drawn closed and heavy in her hand when she took it out of the box. The scolas.

She replaced the lid, then tucked the box inside her blouse and started toward the steps. She'd set one foot on the board when sounds of laughter stopped her. A faint glow of light came through the opening. Someone was here.

"What's the door to the cellar doing open, Micah?" asked a male voice.

"Don't know. I was down there this morning, but when I come out, I shut it up tight." Micah had a distinct voice. It sounded like grit in a grinder. Calista had heard it throughout the years that they'd sat in Parson

Garrison's schoolroom. She at the front. Micah at the back, slouched in a seat far too small for him. He should have been done with his schooling before Calista entered the highest grade, but as her father said, Micah didn't reach the top shelf when it came to learning.

Heavy footsteps approached, and the light grew brighter. Micah shouted into the cellar, "Who be in there?"

Calista ducked and backed away, hurrying while trying to avoid bumping into something. She hid behind a shelf and peered through the stacks of preserved food.

"Give me that light," Micah growled, and his bulky form came down the steps.

Another figure, taller and skinnier, followed Micah into the cellar. "Here. Take the rifle." The voice was familiar and stirred a sense of dread in Calista.

Micah shook his head. "I got this." He slid a knife from inside his jacket and crouched, scanning the shadows.

"You must of forgot to shut the doors."

Now Calista knew who the second one was. Micah's cousin. The one with a cocked eye who delighted in setting fire to beetles or other harmless creatures by filtering the summer sun through a glass. Gossip had it that Mr. Pinehurst's brother had sent him to Storm Haven to escape the law in his village after fire destroyed the schoolhouse.

"I don't forget that kind of thing, Colton. So hush your mouth." Micah kicked a box out of the way and, holding the light overhead, turned in a slow circle.

Calista made herself into a small bundle on the floor. If she could draw up any tighter inside her skin, she would. She bit down on her lip.

From across the cellar came the soft landing of tiny feet. Then again. And again.

Micah sprang like a coiled snake and grabbed up her hare by the neck. Poor Wallace twisted mid-air and kicked his hind legs, but there was no escaping Micah's fist.

"Hey, Colton. Look at what I got us. Rabbit stew."

"Let me break its neck. I been aching to kill me something all week." Colton reached for Wallace. His one good eye was on his prey and wide with excitement, the other one staring off to the side, fixed like a dark pebble.

"Let him go." Calista rose up from the floor and came from behind the shelf.

"Well, and who is this tall, ugly thing? Couldn't be that freak of a Moonwater girl from next to the cemetery, now could it?" Micah pointed the knife in her direction and grasped the hare more firmly.

Calista held back her anger. Tall. Ugly. She'd heard that her whole school life. Now the word freak came at her, and she felt it plunge into her almost as if Micah had thrust his knife into her chest.

Wallace squirmed. He wasn't dead yet, but he would be soon if she didn't make Micah loosen his grip.

"I'm not about to let a tasty stew escape my pot any more than I'm about to let a trespasser get away."

Micah turned the knife on Wallace.

"Stop!" Her voice carried authority and magic stirred behind her eyes, so that Micah forgot the hare for a moment.

Wallace wriggled free and scampered up and out of the cellar.

"Now see what you done!" Micah took a step toward her, his arms flexed. His face was hot with anger. "But you. You stay put. You're not going anywheres."

Chapter Nineteen

If she were invisible, she could escape. The problem was she didn't have a cinnamon stick, a mirror, or two drops of water to work the spell. And she couldn't go up against Micah's knife or the deranged Colton who yearned to kill something. She'd have to try some other way. Micah might be muscled and gripping a knife. Colton might have a rifle, but neither were sharp thinkers. She had to lie, and do it convincingly, not stammer and stumble the way she usually did when telling falsehoods.

"I saw your cellar door open, and I was about to close it for you. But that … rabbit jumped inside, so I came down to make sure he didn't gobble up your stored vegetables." She was sure neither of them knew that Wallace wasn't interested in their cabbages and carrots. They didn't even know he wasn't a rabbit. "I was about to shoo him out when you scared me with your sudden light, so I hid."

Micah looked confused. She'd thrown him off by telling him she was planning to do him a favor.

"Now, you can close up your own cellar, and all will be as it should." She edged toward the steps, but Micah thrust out his arm.

"No. Something's not right with you being in here."

Now wasn't the time for Micah to think clearly. It was time for her to do that.

"I was on my way to help Widower Wakefield with … a sick horse." Now the lie stuck in her throat, and even she couldn't believe her story.

"She's a liar." Colton stepped beside his cousin and holding his rifle out, blocked her from escaping.

"And a thief," Micah said. "Trespassing's a crime.

I can say I caught you sneaking around my root cellar fixing to steal from me. Nobody's going to care about a dead thief who's a Moonwater, too."

Dead? He was ready to kill her? Colton, yes, but Micah had always just been a mean, clumsy bully.

"You'd best take me to the magistrate, then, if you think I've done something wrong. You don't want a Moonwater's blood on your hands, Micah Kennewick."

When she spoke his full name, he lowered his knife.

"Do it," Colton said, and he nudged his cousin.

Micah slowly raised the knife point at her again.

She had to take a chance and say something now, or it was going to be too late. She'd have to try a different tactic. Her words came out in a rush. "Think of your reputation. I can hear the village tongues now. 'Micah Kennewick couldn't best a girl without his knife. And that was with his cousin, Colton, holding a gun at her! Imagine that! Two Kennewicks couldn't outfight her even when they both had weapons.' Colton's already a disgrace, sent away by your uncle. Do you want the whole village laughing at you, too?"

Colton turned his dead eye on her. It was never clear if he saw out of it or not, but nobody liked it cast on them. She so wanted to punch it hard with her fist, and take a chance she'd shock them enough to give her time to run away.

Before she could raise her arm, Micah shoved Colton aside. "I decide what happens in this family now that Pa's gone." He grabbed her arm and took the first step up, so he was eye-level with her.

She blinked at the unpleasant jolt his touch sent through her. Overwhelming anger. Mistrust. Hate. Memories of jealous rage. His emotions were an invasion of everything foreign to her. How could anyone see the world in this way? Everything inside Micah was dark and full of fearful thoughts. At the edge of this darkness and this fear was something else, something she couldn't let enter her consciousness. She twisted away, trying to break their contact, but he tightened his grip. If she couldn't set herself free physically, she had to stop the flood of these miserable images mentally. But she didn't know how. As more and more of his ugliness flushed through her, she remembered how, in the darkest time after her father died, she would think of the beautiful stories he told her, and that shifted her thoughts away from the pain of her loss. Maybe if she concentrated on happy memories, that would help her now.

Calista turned her mind to Greta and her nourishing milk. The wise hare and his philosophy. She made herself recall the March song of the frogs, her father's voice as he told the stories of the goddesses. The aroma of spices baking in sweet dough. And with each memory, Micah's miserable ones grew fainter until she experienced them no more. She could stop being connected with people's thoughts and memories if she went to her own. What a wonderful discovery.

"You want to go see the law. You got your wish." Micah yanked her up behind him, and she stumbled along. It was better to get out of that cellar and as far from Colton as possible than to resist. Her life to Colton Kennewick was worth no more than a stick of kindling. She'd seen the dead look in his eyes up close—no one's life had worth. One thing she knew for sure was she never wanted to touch him, to take in what he concealed in his twisted mind.

"Then you go right on ahead, Cousin," Colton shouted at their backs. "I'm off to track down that danged rabbit and turn it into something I can eat." He walked into the darkness, and Calista shuddered at the sound of him cocking his rifle.

With Colton gone, she might have a chance to escape. Micah would never be able to catch her if she started running. She'd wait until he wasn't paying close attention, then she'd slip out of his grasp and head back to the cottage and her… But he could follow her, and if he did, she'd be putting her mother in danger. She couldn't do that. She'd have to take her chances with the magistrate.

She only hoped that she could trust the magistrate to treat her fairly. Before she knew about the Moonwater history, she had some confidence in the ways of the village. Now she didn't. Now she feared she might be another of her family lashed to the stake and set on fire. Or she could find herself with a rope around her neck. With that in her mind, she held her hand to her throat.

His lantern swinging and casting distorted shadows into the night, Micah clumped ahead with her in tow. They came to the last turn in the road, when the earth shook under their feet. It shook so hard that both of them toppled.

Micah dropped the lantern and let go of her arm to grab onto a nearby tree trunk. She crouched on her hands and knees, waiting for the shaking to stop.

A rush of howling wind swept down the mountain toward Storm Haven. The sound crashed over them. Deafening. Terrifying.

Micah let go of the tree and buried his head in his arms.

Calista ducked and clapped her hands over her ears.

"Courage."

The sensation of that word came stronger this time, and it felt as if streaks of lightning shot through her entire body. Mrs. Wilhelm could never do this. None of the ghosts she'd encountered could—even Squire Nielsen, who was an inferno of rage.

She didn't know how to ask for Amara to come to her aid, so she still had no idea of who or what was instilling this feeling of power and resolve in her. The trembling earth could well be a sign that the myth of the vengeful giant was true after all. She might have been wrong.

The answers to these mysteries would have to wait. Right now, all she knew was she wasn't willing to be dragged by this oaf anymore. She'd present herself to the magistrate for judgment.

Calista climbed to her feet and, picking up the lantern, shoved Micah aside. "I know the way to the magistrate as well as you, so come with me."

Still looking dazed, he didn't argue but stumbled along, darting looks this way and that like a nervous weasel. While the heaving earth had fortified Calista, it seemed it had rattled Micah.

When they came to the magistrate's door, Calista raised the iron knocker and brought it down with two solid whacks. It took some time before the door swung in, and a dimpled-cheeked Mrs. Lowery, the magistrate's wife, stood before Calista. She was dressed in a sleeping cap and long robe knotted at her middle.

"And why have you called me from my bed?" Mrs. Lowery spoke crossly.

"I've come to seek justice," Calista said. She stressed the word, justice.

"At this time of night?"

"Justice does not sleep, does she?"

Mrs. Lowery shook her head in irritation and dragged the door open. "Come."

She settled the two in a room with shelves of books along two walls and an imposing desk, then left to fetch her husband. It wasn't long before the spry Mr. Lowery shuffled toward them, his slippers making a soft sound on the smooth plank floor, the ends of his white hair curling from under his sleeping cap.

He lowered himself into a chair behind the desk. "Who is asking for justice at this late hour and why?"

Micah started up from his seat, but Calista spoke first. "I do, Magistrate Lowery. I set out to do a favor for Micah Kennewick, and he's accusing me of trespassing. I'd like you to set things to rights, so I might go home to my mother."

Calista told her story, choosing her words with care, and ending with, "So I was about to chase that hare out of the cellar when he arrived."

"Was anything missing from your cellar, Micah?"

"Not that I seen, but—"

"Well, then I see no reason to keep all of us from our beds. No harm was done. Good intentions. Misunderstanding." Mr. Lowery dismissed them with a wave of his hand and rose from his chair.

Calista stood up quickly, ready to leave as soon as she could. But she moved too fast and out tumbled Farmer Kennewick's box onto the floor. The locket spilled from inside along with the leather purse and several glittering scolas.

Chapter Twenty

No matter how her mind raced to find a way to explain the locket and the bag of money, anything she came up with was going to sound preposterous.

The ghost of Farmer Kennewick pleaded with her to return the locket? Not likely. She couldn't say that Micah's sister asked for her to find it. That was too farfetched, and they could easily prove it a lie by asking her.

"I … uh. This isn't how it seems. I didn't—" She had to stop talking. She sounded like an idiot. No. She sounded like she was guilty. Which of course she was. She'd taken the locket and the money. She couldn't deny that.

"I told you she was thieving from me." Micah scooped up the locket and the bag from the floor. He dropped the loose scolas inside and drew the top closed. He was about to put everything into his pocket when the magistrate held out his hand.

"That is evidence, Micah. I'll take care of it until after the trial."

It was on Micah's face to refuse, but Magistrate Lowery continued to hold out his hand. "You may have it back afterward."

Micah's expression turned sullen, but he dropped the locket and the bag of scolas into Magistrate Lowery's palm.

The magistrate locked both in a drawer of his desk, and then looking more like an undertaker than a man of the law, he said, "I regret this, but, Calista, you must stay until the hearing."

"No. Please. Let me return home tonight. I'll promise to come back. My mother will be frantic if I'm not home in the morning." Calista already imagined her mother's alarm at finding her bed empty, the chores not started.

"It's the law, I'm afraid." Mr. Lowery took up keys from his desktop. "You are bound over for a hearing by the elders tomorrow, Calista Moonwater D'White."

She'd never forget the gloating expression on Micah's face as the magistrate hauled her to the stocks on the village square and thrust her legs and hands into them.

"I'm sorry, but I can't put you into the jail. There's a Tidwell already there and too drunk to stand."

He draped a thick fur around her, and he didn't force her head through the top hole. For those two kindnesses, she was grateful, but she'd already known from his touch that he planned to offer some comfort. The magistrate wasn't unkind, and from the memories she'd glimpsed at the press of his hand against her back, Calista was sure he did strive for justice.

He waited with her until Micah was out of sight, then mumbled a goodnight and returned inside his house.

How was she going defend herself before the Elders tomorrow? The locket and the scolas would be proof enough of her guilt. She couldn't tell the truth or they'd surely lock her away as insane. Nobody talked to the dead. Worse yet, with all the gossip about strange happenings, they might do as her mother feared and condemn her as a witch. The only thing left for her was to repeat the story about finding the cellar door open with a *rabbit* foraging for stored vegetables. But she didn't have any idea how to explain that locket and those scolas that tumbled from under her blouse.

She shivered while running through the possible defenses. She'd found them on the cellar floor. She was about to hand them to Micah when he dragged her off.

She couldn't believe that story. How could she expect the Elders to?

In a few hours, her legs grew numb, and her hands ached with the bitter cold, so she stopped appreciating the small measure of kindness the magistrate had shown her. She was being treated in a most cruel manner, the way her ancestors had been treated.

Anger and not a small bit of fear roamed freely through her, and when it threatened to break her resolve not to cry, she dreamed her way inside her cottage. Her father was alive, telling her stories and soothing the jibes of the villagers into the shadows the way he used to.

"The giant has always lived in the mountains," he'd say. "He waits for the villagers to acquire the wisdom to be tolerant and treat each other fairly. Until that day, the West is closed to Storm Haven, and none are allowed through that pass."

From across the room, her mother would glance up at this part, the look on her face a mystery to young Calista. "That is an old myth that should be put to rest," her mother always said.

But her mother's look was no longer a mystery. Calista understood she had fought to hide the worry about her daughter's future, and so she'd become irritated and even angry whenever there was mention of the *villagers* and *wisdom* in the same breath.

"Now, Miriam, the tales may be old, but they're good stories, heh?" Her father always squeezed Calista tight before shooing her off to bed.

She missed her father and his easy ways. He often forgot important things like mending a leak in the roof, but he never forgot to sing to Greta, so her milk would be sweet. He never forgot to thank the March frogs for their arrival, and he always placed upside-down pots along the side of the pond, so they'd have shelter from the owls and other predators. A lot of his time was spent spinning tales, and he harvested stories like other farmers harvested corn.

Calista remembered a comment her grandmother often made while peering out the window at him. "His head is more in the clouds today than usual, Miriam."

Her mother would nod and smile, and being the practical one, carry on with whatever chore she was doing.

A thought came to Calista as she shivered in the predawn, a thought that hadn't occurred to her before. Could her father's impractical nature have washed her mother's magic away? She had to be in charge of so much when her husband wandered into the woods in search of stories to share at the table that night.

Blinking into the sunrise, Calista recalled how carefully her mother counted out the scolas, measured the remaining flour, and set the fresh eggs to the back of the cooler to make sure the older ones were used first. Her lists of maintenance never ended, while Calista's father might manage to repair a broken hinge on the chicken coop, and then become distracted by bees nuzzling deep inside honeysuckles.

When he came home so late after a day working for one of the farmers, he sometimes had forgotten to collect the scolas they owed him, scolas her mother counted on to provide…

Calista was suddenly fully awake. "When did my father start working for the farmers?" She calculated the passage of time. "I had thirteen years when that happened. That was five years ago." She remembered the shock of having Mr. Kennewick appear at their gate. Of course, he stayed on the road while talking to her father for several minutes before hastening away. Now that she was attending to this change in her father's circumstances, she had no trouble recalling that day vividly.

But there was another memory pulling at her, one she hadn't thought important. Not until now. That year in early fall she'd walked around the corner of the barn where her mother stood, her arms raised shoulder height, her hands spread wide over a shock of wheat. Her eyes were closed and she was muttering something. Calista had remained silent, listening to the monotonous sounds. Sounds that were like a… "Chant."

Since she'd learned the history of the women in her family, Calista now understood what was happening that day. Miriam Moonwater D'White was working a spell. A week later Mr. Kennewick came to their gate.

What had her mother said about the arrival of her magic? "When I felt the first stirrings, I was only fifteen—too young by Moonwater standards—and a sign that something was not quite right." Perhaps her mother's magic coming early didn't mean it was defective. It could well have been a sign of an impressive power.

Despite the misery of her hands and feet locked tightly inside the stocks, Calista smiled. Her family story had just been rewritten. Because her mother cast an effective spell, Farmer Kennewick hired her father. She sighed and the love for her parents warmed her head to toe.

Samuel D'White may not have been one to mind the clock carefully, but from that day forward, he did provide for his family with odd jobs at the Kennewick's. And when Mr. Pinehurst saw no harm came to the Kennewicks by associating with the husband of a Moonwater woman, he asked Samuel D'White for help. The two often drank tea or ale after the work was done, and she remembered how that pleased her father greatly. Finally, he had another man in Storm Haven to share time with in pleasant conversation.

Calista adjusted her position a bit to ease the discomfort in the stocks and then settled again into her thoughts.

The closing of a door jolted her back to the square and the numbness in her arms and legs. In the gray light of morning, the magistrate was coming toward her with a bundle of keys rattling in his hand.

"Come," he said, releasing her. "Mrs. Lowery says you are to wash up and have tea before the hearing."

Calista tottered on feet she could barely feel as she followed after the man whose white hair, now released from his nightcap, fluttered around his head like an irritated goose. The air inside the house warmed her, and she gratefully washed away the night's misery with a cloth and a hot basin of water. Mrs. Lowery gave her tea and a biscuit, but didn't sit with her at the table. The woman didn't treat her badly, but she kept her distance. Calista was used to that, so she sipped the tea and savored the biscuit as if it were her last.

She swallowed. That might be nearer the truth than not.

The church bell tolled, calling the villagers and all elders to hear a case, and soon a stir of movement came from outside. Voices, at first muted, grew louder until Calista imagined the entire village gathered in front of the magistrate's house.

The magistrate signaled her to follow him out the door. She thanked Mrs. Lowery for her kindness and got a curt nod in return.

But no matter, she thought. She wouldn't be remembered as rude, just as a trespasser and a thief. And a witch. She couldn't stop the tight smile. What an unseemly combination of crimes.

When the magistrate opened the door, the crowd's

uncontrolled excitement blew back over her. It seemed she'd been right. The entire village stood pressed tightly together. Her first impression was of a large, hydra-headed animal ready to surge forward and trample her with its feet. In the center, the fraudulent Mrs. Pinehurst stared back at her, a grim smirk on her lips. Micah stood with Kip Delany and Bailey Phelps, and they all wore the same smug look of satisfaction. They didn't have to lift a hand against her. This time they'd get to watch while others did.

Chapter Twenty-One

"Everybody step away!" the magistrate shouted. "Not you, Horace. Or Caleb," he said to two of the older men. He peered into the crowd. "Where's Jonathon? Nicolas?"

"Here." Two other elders pushed forward.

"Then we are convened." The magistrate read the charges from an official-looking scroll, but when Calista looked over the man's shoulder, it was blank. "Micah Kennewick, are you present?"

Micah left the company of his two friends, Kip and Bailey, to push through the crowd. "You bet I am."

"Tell us the particulars of last night."

Micah, his shoulders hunched, his head jutted forward, faced the villagers. "I come home and found my cellar door open. Inside, I seen something unnatural creeping along the stone wall. Then I spotted them two red eyes down in the corner. Kind of mad-like, you know? That's when I took out my knife and had at the devil what was with her." He pointed at Calista.

When he said the word, devil, there was a collective intake of breath from the crowd. Micah drew himself up taller, encouraged by the way everyone stood spellbound.

Calista stared at him more fascinated by the exaggerated story than scared. How could he make what happened in the cellar sound as if Wallace was some huge evil beast? Unfortunately, calling her hare the devil had changed the mood of the surrounding villagers. That word had a lot of power in this crowd.

"When I had that critter by the neck, she"—he jabbed a finger in Calista's direction— "come at me with her claws."

Calista made fists. She'd love to wallop the dolt in the jaw and stop him from continuing his wild tale. From the rapt expressions on faces in the crowd, he was convincing them she was a threat to the community.

But he was a dangerous dolt, so she'd not strike out at him. She'd keep her mouth sealed, and hope this would all end soon. She took a deep breath. Then came the last and the most damning part of his story. "My sister's locket! Yes. She'd snatched it all right. And my poor dead father's purse of scolas, too."

That brought gasps from everyone, and the nervous herd in front of her pawed the earth, uneasy at the mention of the locket and the scolas. She might have imagined it, but it felt as if there was a small trembling along the ground at the same time. Some of the villagers lifted one foot, then another and looked down, but what was happening before them was much more riveting than what was happening underfoot.

Of course, she was guilty. Even the magistrate was witness to the evidence tumbling from her under her blouse. It took less than two minutes of the elders shaking their heads and nodding to decide that, and only a few more to decide her punishment.

"Flogging. Five lashes," the magistrate pronounced.

"Only five lashes? But she's a witch!" Micah yelled.

The crowd gasped. He'd shouted the one word nobody Storm Haven ever said out loud. He'd called her what had once been damning in the old stories.

"And maybe a murderer," he said even louder.

Witch. Murderer. There were no more alarming words in their language, and said together in such a highly charged moment, was sure to cause panic. Already the air vibrated with unease.

She spied Mr. Bennet off to the side, his baker's hat at the back of his head. She was sure he was thinking about the Jones Boy. She prayed he wouldn't remind everyone she'd had reason to kill his new baker because he'd stopped buying all of her baked goods. That would only add fuel to this fire that was threatening to ignite. The tailor fiddled with the measuring tape thrown around his neck. He'd seen her angry that day. He'd have a lot to say about her behavior, given a chance. The green grocer bit into a large apple and chewed, his eyes wide with excitement. He was another villager who could speak against her if the word murderer took root. She'd almost knocked over one of his vegetable stands when she stomped her way from the bakery, her basket still brimming with unsold muffins.

Now she looked more closely at the others staring back at her. They all had the same expectant, yet fearful look.

"Hang her." That came from the back, and Colton Kennewick glared at her until she looked away at the nervous, shifting crowd.

Calista sensed the surge before anyone took a single step forward, but when those in front moved toward her, the magistrate held up his arms, "Stop! There will be only a flogging this day. That is the penalty for theft."

The crowd eased back, but embers of ancient fears and superstitions flickered among them, and it wouldn't take much to fan those embers. The old stories of witchcraft were ready to flame up again. Her mother's greatest fears were coming to life. Calista blinked away images of a Moonwater tied to the stake, of a noose dangling from a limb. She touched her throat before she realized her hand had moved from her side.

The blacksmith was the one chosen to unleash the

whip against Calista's bare back. The man didn't look at her as he marshaled her to the whipping post, and then tied her hands to the rusted chain. He had the shears ready to cut her blouse up the back when he set them down.

At his touch, she'd quickly read the nature of the man. Steady. Honest. Simple in the way he thought about life. His one ambition was to care for his forge and shoe the village horses well. He took pride in his work, but he didn't want anything to do with using a whip against her, and his mind was churning with ways to avoid it. He was about to lie to the magistrate and the crowd.

"The whip's gone missing," he announced loudly to everyone.

Disappointment rumbled through the square.

"Then go and buy another for the village," the magistrate said. He rubbed his hands together for warmth and shook his head. Impatience in his every move.

The blacksmith set off to the general store with the owner, and at the same moment, tiny white flakes sprinkled onto the ground. From the gathering clouds, Calista was sure that they were about to see a heavy snow.

Mr. Bennet took advantage of the break and offered hot muffins to the hungry crowd. "Special price today," he said. "Only three scolas each." He moved among the villagers, passing out the muffins and collecting the coins.

This was a carnival. A cruel entertainment. And she was at its center.

From deep in the crowd, Kip Delany choked and spat. "What in the name of the giant is this?"

"Euuu! There's grit in this." A woman in front wiped her mouth with the back of her hand.

Bailey Phelps hurled a muffin and hit Mr. Bennet

in the chest.

"The witch is trying to poison us!" Mrs. Pinehurst stepped forward, shaking a crushed muffin in her fist.

This second use of witch didn't evoke the same fear and awe as when Micah used it. Now she sensed hatred. How quickly that old word had crept back into the villagers' vocabulary. How quickly it had attached itself to her.

The magistrate held up his arms, and the elders pushed everyone back. The door to the general store slammed, and with a slow, but steady tread, the blacksmith returned holding a new whip. He opened it so the tail dragged along the earth. Once again, he picked up the shears and this time he cut Calista's woolen blouse up the back.

Flakes of snow settled on her bare skin and quickly melted into tiny streams trailing along her ribs. The cold made her shoulders ache, but it might also block some of the sting of the whip.

The hushed crowd drew around her in a circle. While she waited for the pain to begin, Calista looked into their eyes. When she did, each person glanced away. But not Kip. Not Bailey. Not Colton who stood at the front, arms folded, licking his lips. Mrs. Pinehurst busied herself dusting muffin crumbs from her chest.

Micah grinned and mouthed, "You will hang next."

Chapter Twenty-Two

Calista clenched her fists, waiting for the first sting across her back. Staring down at her feet, she counted out five slow beats. It wouldn't take long for him to deliver those lashes once he started. It was going to be the first one she'd have to brace against to keep from yelping in pain. The second would come quickly and not too hard. She was sure of that because the man didn't like dealing blows against people. He especially didn't like to do so against a woman. She'd read that from his touch. Behind her, the blacksmith's every move was hesitant and slow. Calista almost yelled at him to hurry up, but she refused to show any emotion while all of the village watched, eager for her to plead for mercy or cry out in fear.

Shivering, she silently urged him to get on with the whipping. Her lips were numb now and she had trouble keeping her jaw from trembling with the cold and the fear she couldn't push away. The snow came down heavier each minute.

"Do not touch my daughter!" Miriam's voice cut through the air like a thunder peal.

From over her shoulder, Calista watched the approaching figure of her mother. Miriam charged forward like a towering force of nature. Her hair flared out like long dark flames, and even from a distance, her eyes flashed rage. Nothing about her, except her familiar cloak, resembled the sweet and quiet woman who lived in the last cottage next to the cemetery.

It took some moments for her to cross the square, and all that time, none of the villagers moved to stop her. Miriam blew into their midst, and a hurricane couldn't have scattered them more quickly. She shoved aside the blacksmith like a pesky fly and snatched the whip from his hand. Then, with her finger aimed at the crowd, her voice rolled over them in a low and dangerous rumble. “You! All of you bring shame on Storm Haven. You are superstitious, evil people. Your hearts are full of darkness, and you should hang your heads in shame for the way you behave toward my family. Each of you is a sniveling coward who would punish a girl for being a Moonwater. I challenge any of you to stop our leaving this wretched place.”

“She’s a thief,” Micah shouted.

“And you’re a lout and a bully, Micah Kennewick. And perhaps much worse,” Miriam said, drawing another collective gasp from the crowd.

“Whip them both.” That was Colton, and he broke the spell that gripped the villagers and kept them back.

They pushed forward at the same time that the elders disarmed Miriam and returned the whip to the blacksmith.

Shouts from the angry crowd were deafening. It wanted to hear the snap of the whip and see blood. Nothing was going to prevent it from having the satisfaction of a good beating.

Nothing that is, except the sudden shake of the earth. It had been unsettled all morning, but now it brought silence to the square as villagers clutched at each other to keep their footing.

Miriam ignored the unsteady ground and released Calista’s hands, then she wrapped her cloak around Calista, holding her tightly to her side.

Micah recovered his balance and lunged for the whip, but the blacksmith held him away.

“No. Keep your distance,” the blacksmith said, placing himself between Micah and the two women.

“If you won’t use that whip, somebody’s got to do

it!" Micah's neck bulged with thwarted satisfaction.

The crowd regained its solidarity and its footing at about the same moment. Shouts came around the square.

"Micah's right!"

"Get on with the whipping!"

"She broke the law!"

They drowned out whatever else the blacksmith was saying.

Kip and Bailey followed Colton. Together, they jostled their way through the villagers to stand next to Micah in a challenge to the blacksmith.

"Get on with it. It's your job. Beat the witch," Colton shouted.

"Yeah. Time to do this." Kip jutted a fist into the air and Bailey did the same.

The magistrate, who'd landed on his backside, struggled to his feet and raised his hands, trying to bring calm, but no one took heed.

Mrs. Pinehurst brushed him aside the way she would a smelly old dog. "Witches both!" she declared. "Storm Haven should not be a haven for the likes of them."

One of the men in the crowd grabbed Calista from her mother. Another re-tied Calista's hands to the whipping post, and then tied Miriam's in a second ring so they faced each other.

"Wait!" the magistrate shouted, but no one paid any attention to him.

Several others held back the blacksmith while Micah spit on his palms and hefted the whip.

"You won't be thieving from a Kennewick any time soon, witch." He drew back his arm, dragging the tails behind him, then cracking the whip in the air.

Calista flinched but held tightly to the post. She wouldn't scream. She wouldn't cry out for mercy. She stared into her mother's eyes. "I'm so sorry."

"You have done nothing to be sorry for."

"I brought this horror upon us. I shouldn't have—"

"This is not your doing, my sweet. The old stories were always here, waiting to come to life. These people want to see us suffer, but they don't even know why."

"Shut up, witches," Colton said. "See what they do?" He looked out over the villagers. "Spells is my guess. You can't trust a witch, and you sure can't trust two of 'em together."

That brought some laughter. Nervous energy spiraled out from the crowd and hung over the square.

Micah leaned close to Calista and whispered. "Did you hear that nice crack in the air? The next time you'll feel it clear across that ugly back of yours."

"Get on with it, Micah, or give me that thing, and I'll take care of business here with this one." Colton ran his hand along the whipping post and briefly touched Calista's.

Small, maimed animals. Pranks that weren't humorous but hurtful. All of that was in his touch. And something else.

"Poison," Calista gasped before she could stop the word.

Colton jerked his hand away, and for a moment, paled.

With only the brush of his hand against hers, Calista had seen Colton burying a bottle, a skull and crossbones on the front. But she had no idea what these brief images meant. All she knew for certain was that the word poison scared Colton.

"Give me that damned whip, Micah!" Colton grabbed for the whip, but Micah yanked his hand back from his cousin's grasp.

"Back away! I'm doing it. Sometimes the wait is what makes the pain go deep, and I want this pain to go right down to her innards."

Micah had always disliked her, called her names, made fun of her in school. Calista was just beginning to understand that he truly hated her, and that was a puzzle. She'd never done anything to harm or embarrass him. She'd thought "lout" and "bully" but never called him those names or said them to anyone else.

Micah cracked the whip twice more.

The magistrate protested, but not very loudly this time. Calista understood that he needed to be done with her flogging, so he could go back to the warmth and comfort of his cottage. He was honest yes, but not a very forceful magistrate, and he wouldn't be one at all if he hadn't inherited the position from his father.

Mrs. Pinehurst clasped her hands around her belly, clearly eager for what was about to happen.

"Ready?" Micah said, his voice shaking with expectation.

Despite being bound tightly at the wrists, Miriam managed to reach Calista's hands and touch them with her fingertips.

With only that slight contact, Calista was filled with the warmth of her mother's love. The cold against her bare skin lessened and her heart settled into a steady rhythm. Her mother's own special magic rivaled any that the other Moonwaters possessed. Now Calista knew she'd survive the pain of the whip and the humiliation of being treated like a common thief. Once she was free, she'd see to it this village never mistreated another one of her family.

The crowd drew closer. And that's when Calista sensed something else besides the power of love stir inside her mother. This new energy came like spring melt from crystal clear icicles. Gentle, yet persistently increasing. A trickle that promised more.

In the complete silence that hung over the square, the gentle patter of snowflakes settling onto the ground increased and came down faster and heavier. Then from the distance the sound of rapidly approaching hooves cut through the air.

Chapter Twenty-Three

A lone rider galloped around the last curve in the road, and the horse that had to have been eighteen slowed to a trot. The man himself was massive. The closer he came, the more it became apparent just how tall and muscular this stranger was.

When he reached the knot of people, he dismounted and stared at the clutch of villagers now frozen more by the shock of his arrival than the cold air and the anticipation of the whipping. His wide-brimmed hat shadowed his eyes, but Calista felt their intensity. He was dressed in leather. His coat strained at the fasteners, and his chest heaved under the supple animal skin as if it were his own. Now that he was so close, Calista saw how young he was, not more than a year or two beyond her.

"And what have we here?" His voice was big in keeping with the rest of him. It carried far beyond the gathering and down the street.

Mrs. Pinehurst, her chin tucked inside her shawl, scurried across the square toward the road. She didn't glance back until she was at the landmark boulder, and then she quickly disappeared behind it.

Two town dogs slunk between the buildings, their tails between their legs, and a hushed whisper flitted from one villager to another.

"He's almost as big as his horse."

"Could he be from Vengeance Mountain?"

"No one comes through there."

"A giant might."

"That's no giant."

"Mighty close to one, I'd say."

Mr. Lowery must have suddenly remembered he was the magistrate again because he stepped forward.

How strange the two looked facing each other. Mr. Lowery, a person of ordinary size, appeared to be one of the wee folk of fairy tales. He stood looking up, his neck at a painful angle.

Clearing his throat, he said, “I am Magistrate Lowery. What is the nature of your business in Storm Haven?” He’d regained his political face, but his voice only carried a touch of shaky authority.

“First, what is the nature of this business?” The man pointed at Calista and Miriam.

“They be witches,” Micah shouted over the heads of the villagers, and everyone stepped aside, clearing a path from this strange man to the whipping post and Micah.

“Mind my horse.” The man dismounted and handed the reins to Mr. Lowery, and then, pushing past the magistrate, he strode directly to Micah. “And who are you?”

As burly as Micah was, he too seemed to have shrunk. “Mic … Micah Kennewick.”

“Well, Micah Kennewick, what makes you think these two are practicers of witchcraft?”

Micah must have been casting around inside his small brain for an answer the way his eyes darted here and there without focusing on what was in front of him. “That one … she …she thieved from me,” he finally managed to stammer.

Next to him, Colton nodded with too much energy until the man looked in his direction. Colton froze, blinking. He pressed his lips together and worked them like nervous worms. Bailey and Kip melted into the crowd and then trotted down the street.

The man brushed Micah and Colton aside and went to stand next to Calista. A hush fell over the crowd.

“Did you steal from Micah Kennewick?” he asked

her.

"I was doing his father a favor."

Nervous murmurs rose from the villagers. They drew back as if they suddenly feared being too close to her.

Micah shouted, "Lie! My pa's been dead for years."

"It was an old favor," Calista said quickly, and her half-truth sounded whole. After all, it honestly was an old favor, one Farmer Kennewick had put off asking until the right time.

The man scooped up Calista's shawl from where it had been tossed. He shook it free of snow and gently settled it around her shoulders.

"In my experience, it's always better to hear all of the story before meting out punishment." He looked between Miriam and Calista. "Did you explain this favor?"

Calista shook her head. "I did not."

"Can you now?"

She took a moment, then nodded in cold, jerky movements.

Without asking permission, something Calista believed he never did, the man unbound her hands, and then her mother's. He took the whip from Micah without Micah so much as squeaking out an objection and handed it to a nearby elder. "I'd hang this where it will remind others of consequences. Something as simple as seeing a whip often prevents misdeeds."

The elders trudged away, mumbling to each other about whips and consequences of misdeeds. Micah and Colton dodged around him and fast-walked across the square to where Micah had tethered Squire Nielsen's horse. Once it had been a sleek mare with head high and ears alert. Now, under Micah's careless hand, the horse's head drooped, and the tail hung limp, a disheartened beast.

When Micah mounted and yanked the reins, it moved with the weariness of a plow horse.

"The Kennewicks were often cantankerous but never mean of spirit." The man made the comment like a thought expressed out loud.

"Who are you?" Mr. Lowery handed back the reins to the horse.

"Simon Pinehurst. I've come to see my parents."

Calista swayed, unsteady on her feet. The cold. The near flogging. Her mother in danger because of her. And now, this.

"Oh, Calista!" Miriam steadied her daughter, but Simon let go of his horse's reins and lifted Calista into his arms before she fell. "Mr. Lowery," he said. "See that my horse is taken care of."

"Yes. Yes. Of course. Straight away. I'll do that, Mr. Pinehurst," Mr. Lowry said before scurrying toward the blacksmith's barn with the horse in tow.

"You need a warm fire and some hot tea," Simon told Calista, and he didn't wait for the magistrate to return to lead the way into his own house. At the door, he shouldered it open and walked inside as if he lived there.

Simon carried Calista to the couch and set her in front of the crackling fire.

Miriam took a seat next to her daughter and rubbed the numbness from Calista's hands.

Calista was still dazed, and while in his arms, she'd only managed to learn two short yet shocking things about this man's past. She'd avoid any contact with him in the future. It was safer for both of them.

An astonished Mrs. Lowery came into her parlor to find three people she hadn't invited.

"Mrs. Lowery," Simon said in the commanding

voice of a king. "Please fetch us some hot tea and toast."

She didn't question him and turned immediately to leave the room.

Miriam, her face a map of worry, drew even closer. "You're so cold. So terribly cold."

"I'm all right," Calista said, but her jaw quivered in spite of working to control it. It would take a while for her body to recover from all that time in the weather.

Mr. Lowery came into the room in time to see Simon Pinehurst stoke his fire and thank Mrs. Lowery for her hospitality.

Calista turned her attention to Simon Pinehurst. She remembered the rugged young boy she'd often seen tilling the Pinehurst fields with his father. He'd never noticed her, but it was so usual for people to ignore her that she'd never thought much about it. Besides, she much preferred being ignored. The alternative in this village had always been ugly.

She'd never thought about him after he left Storm Haven. Since then, he'd grown far beyond rugged, but for all of his mass, he had a refinement about him. She noted the way he settled onto the stiff-backed chair as if testing its strength before trusting it to take his full weight. The delicate way he held Mrs. Lowery's fine teacup between his thumb and finger and lifted it to his lips. Simon Pinehurst was nothing if not aware of his size in small spaces and how to move to avoid collision with delicate objects. Calista interlaced her fingers in her lap until they turned white. She was far too aware of his physical presence as well. That was absurd. She had to stop this … this ogling.

Finally finding her voice, she said, "You have done me a great kindness today. I'm very grateful, and I'm so sorry that I have to be the one to tell you of your" —she hesitated— "your father's death."

Simon set his cup on the table at his side. "When?"

The magistrate stepped between the two. It was as if it had come back into his head that this was his house, and he was the elder in charge of all things legal in Storm Haven. "It was winter last. He suffered on and off with bouts of sickness, and then he died of a sudden. The Healer did all that he could, but he'd never seen such an ailment. Nothing could have saved him, I'm afraid."

Calista shivered, but this time it wasn't from the cold or the threat of a lashing. This time it was from the memory the magistrate's words had brought back from three years ago when her father died.

Like Mr. Pinehurst's, her father's sickness came in fits and starts like a cruel canker to steal him away one bit at a time. He had some good days, and when he did, he'd return to work. But then in the following days, he'd bend over, gripping his stomach in pain and take to his bed. His head, he told them, throbbed.

That went on for some time. Good days. Bad days. And then he died.

With that memory hammering at her, Calista gripped her hands and refused to let her grief show. She returned her focus to Simon.

"And my mother?" he asked. "What of her?"

The magistrate rubbed his chin in thought. "She was in the square today. I'm sure she was. Did you not see her?"

Simon shook his head. "But you must be mistaken. My mother would have come to me if she'd been among the others." He grinned like an oversized imp and pointed at his chest. "She never could miss me, now, could she?"

This was a conversation that Calista did not want to have. Not here. She'd seen Mrs. Pinehurst rush off before Simon spotted her, and Calista knew why, but she couldn't tell that to anyone. Not yet. The weight of secrets grew heavier inside her every day. Minnie's diary had seemed a challenge, then Farmer Kennewick's locket along with his scolas had almost put scars across her back. Now she had murders to deal with. The Pinehurst one was already solved, but she couldn't tell what she knew about that. Besides, they'd never believe her story, and they'd put her into the stocks forever if she muttered one word of what she knew because of *visions*. Or they might do much worse. She shuddered thinking of what had happened to her ancestors in the village square when they'd been convicted of witchcraft.

She hadn't considered tackling Squire Nielsen's murder yet, but it nattered at the back of her brain, so she knew she'd eventually have to find out who'd done the poor man in. Of course, there was also the Jones Boy.

She covered her face with her hands. Oh no. He might well meet her in the cemetery with a plea for help, too. Yet another poor spirit asking for her help.

"Are you ill?" Her mother put an arm around her shoulders.

"I'm only tired. I need to go home." Calista looked up at Mr. Lowery. "I did take the locket, but Farmer Kennewick told me where it was hidden, and he asked that I take it to his daughter, Grace, and apologize for secreting it away from her. He offered half the scolas for my service. The other half was to go to Grace." She stood to face the magistrate. All of that was true, and her telling of it sounded convincing. She simply left out *when* Farmer Kennewick asked for the favor. "I am no thief."

The magistrate considered her story for a moment before he went into his study. He returned holding out the box to her. "Complete your task as the good farmer requested. It is more important now that he's no longer with us, and I'm sure it will bring him peace."

Calista took the box. "I hope so." One fewer restless spirit needing her help would be a relief.

Chapter Twenty-Four

Magistrate Lowery abandoned the warmth of his hearth again, this time to take Calista and her mother to their cottage. Calista knew his act of consideration was because of Simon Pinehurst's powerful presence.

Simon rode alongside the wagon until they came to his family's farm.

Calista thanked him again, wishing she could warn him about his aunt. But he'd have to discover the truth about that woman on his own, and she was sure he would very quickly. A son would recognize someone masquerading as his mother no matter how much her twin looked like her.

Calista had only met Matilda a few times before that unfortunate collision at the bakery. Once in a while, she'd come to Stone Haven for short visits with her sister. Side by side, it was easy to tell them apart. Matilda's mouth always drew down, and there was a tightness at the corner of her eyes, the look of a myopic mouse. Eleanor, on the other hand, was always cheerful. Now Calista knew Matilda wasn't only sullen, but evil at her very center.

As the wagon pulled away, Calista followed Simon with her eyes. He walked with an easy gait that reminded her of a noble figure from one of her father's tales. Here was one man taller than she. If she wanted to see his face, she had to crane her neck, and what a strange feeling that was. She was used to looking down on the tops of people's heads.

With his broad back straight, Simon mounted the front steps of his home. He paused at the door and knocked. In only moments, it swung open.

It was all she could do not to call out a warning at

this last minute because that woman could be dangerous. But Calista held back. He could take care of himself. She'd detected that at his touch. There were some benefits to being able to read other people's thoughts.

The last glimpse she had of him, he was doffing his hat and stepping inside. Oh, what she'd give to see that meeting. She was certain the real Mrs. Pinehurst was about to be revenged when her sister's crime was exposed. Finally, Eleanor would have her name on her tombstone. The best part would be that, for a change, she had to do nothing to right this wrong.

After the magistrate drove away from their cottage, Miriam busied herself brewing some calming tea, and Calista made for the thicket. She had to know if Wallace was safe. But he didn't appear when she called him, and she returned home fearing the worst.

Poor dear Wallace, was he alive or did Colton or the owl catch him?

Although she gulped down several cups of her mother's calming tea before going to bed, Calista's dreams that night were all about flight from danger. She and Wallace fleeing. Micah and Colton chasing them. The next morning, she was out of bed at sunrise, still shaking from dreaming about the near misses of Micah's knife and Colton's deadly threats.

She went to the thicket again, this time kneeling to shout into his nesting place. Still, he didn't answer or poke his head out to greet her.

Worry chipped away at her. She was so tied up with concern for the hare that she forgot to put Greta's milk into the spring house and had to return to the barn to fetch it.

"You have something heavy inside you today, Mistress."

"Yes, Greta. It's Wallace. He's gone missing. I'm

afraid something terrible has happened to him."

"That one's too cunning to be trapped, if that's what you're thinking."

"Traps are only one of the dangers he might have encountered. But I hope you're right. He's a good friend." Upon saying that Calista understood how much Wallace had come to mean to her. *Please let him be safe.*

On the way from the barn, Calista gathered a few dried lavender sprigs she'd hung from the rafters last October. She wrapped them in a small leather pouch and tucked them into her skirt pocket. Before starting on her errand for Farmer Kennewick, she took some time to brew tea and make toast, so it was mid-morning when she set out on Flower to deliver the locket.

It was half a day's ride to and from Scrawly Springs, but the snow was light and the mule moved easy and steady under her. Flower's leg had fully healed and she seemed eager to take the journey. Calista was eager, too, and looked forward to seeing her father's home village.

She'd only been there twice before, once with him when he had some family business. The last bit of property that the D'Whites owned had been sold, and he had gone to sign papers. Calista remembered that day as one of the happiest with him.

She'd often thought about that time. It helped to remember when they'd been together before his illness came and before he was in such distress.

He would feel better than he had in days. So much better that he looked forward to his work with Mr. Pinehurst, and that spring morning he'd set off early. His cheeks had a glow and his laugh, the one she always remembered, was robust and filled her with happiness. It was the last sound she heard before he swung his leg over Flower and rode toward the Pinehurst farm.

At the end of that last day when he made his way from the road to the barn astride the mule, she paused kneading the bread, and looked out at him from the window. Usually, her father sat tall. Not that night. He hunched forward over the mule's sturdy neck. Before he reached the barn, he slid to the ground and staggered up the back steps. She remembered how she quickly washed the dough from her hands, panic pumping through her body, and rushed to the door.

Nothing her mother tried helped him. Her healing tea. Her herbal compresses. All had failed.

Calista's second visit to Scrawly Springs was with her mother, taking her father home to be buried with his kin.

She shook herself out of those memories. It was better to concentrate on what she had to do after this errand was finished.

Of course, she'd tell the ghosts of Mrs. Wilhelm and Farmer Kennewick that she'd managed another favor, but she dreaded facing any of the others who still waited for her to help them. "Well, one step at a time," she said to Flower, patting her along her bristly neck. The mule was one animal that didn't talk to her.

She still worried about Wallace, and wished he were along on this trip. She'd love to have someone to discuss these matters with. Flower was sweet but obviously disinterested in her affairs.

She wondered if Wallace might have any ideas about how to handle Squire Nielsen's request because she had none, except to ask for Amara's help. That's what Mrs. Wilhelm said she must do. The question was how.

She rode into Scrawly Springs, and since it was almost as small a village as Storm Haven, the cemetery was only a short ride to the other side. Her father's grave was in a large plot surrounded by an iron fence. A plaque with The D'White Family engraved across its face hung on the gate.

Calista withdrew the leather pouch and poured the lavender sprigs into her palm. Inside the gate, she knelt next to the marker that was inscribed with Samuel D'White, Beloved Husband and Father.

Lavender had been his favorite flower. He always said purple was a royal color meant to be worn by kings, queens, and, of course, goddesses. She didn't place the dried flowers on the grave, but instead ground their richly scented buds between her palms and sprinkled them over the snow-covered ground. Their summer fragrance rose and filled her with longing for those warm days and her father. Her chest grew tight with the pain of her loss, but something like a gentle hand smoothed that pain away, leaving a sense of well-being. This was the way she'd always felt when he'd held her, told her stories, and made her feel so special. She stood, almost expecting to find him at her side, but when she glanced around, the space was hers alone.

"I wish you'd come to me like the others have." She waited, hoping he might hear her, hoping he might arrive.

But no. And so it was time to leave. Time to finish this favor.

Calista easily found Grace Kennewick's cottage. It was nestled in a grove of pine trees with an inviting path leading from the road. Calista slid from Flower's back to make her way to the house and tapped on the glass pane of the divided door. A wavy form of a woman approached, and the top half quickly swung open. Grace was as Calista remembered—sunny and smiling, but when she saw Calista, she frowned.

At first, Calista thought Grace might close that door and bolt it against her, but she didn't.

"Calista? What brings you here?" Grace's voice sounded strained.

"I've come to do a favor for your father."

Now anger sprang onto Grace's face. "That is just cruel. You know my father is dead."

Hurriedly, and with the same partial truth about an old favor long delayed by the loss of her own father, Calista delivered Farmer Kennewick's apology and handed over the locket and the scolas. "In truth, I have half of the money. Your father asked that I keep it, but I wouldn't if my mother and I hadn't fallen on such difficult times."

Grace stared at the heart-shaped locket, looking stunned at first, but then she broke into sobs. Swiping her eyes, she opened the bottom half of the door and came out onto the stoop. Reaching up, she threw her arms around Calista. "Thank you so much. I have nothing of my mother's, so her locket is a treasure to me."

This was the first time Calista had felt someone's gratitude, and it shocked but then delighted her.

Grace stepped away and with her head down and said, "I'm so sorry. I always meant to tell you how I regretted treating you as I did, but my friends—"

Calista stopped her. "Friends are a powerful influence on us when we are young. I hold no ill feelings, Grace." In saying that, she understood the freedom of forgiveness. It lightened her heart, and she returned home with less dread of the next favor she had to do for one of the irritated spirits.

At the Scrawly Spring market, Calista stopped to buy a few staples and fresh fruit and vegetables. Silently, she thanked Farmer Kennewick for the scolas that would see them through a few more months—perhaps long enough for their garden to come in.

Although she didn't return from Scrawly Springs

until dusk, Calista bedded down the mule, and since her mother had tended to the other chores, she hurried to see if Wallace might have returned.

"You must be back at your home by now," she said as if commanding him to be safe would make it so.

At the thicket, she called to him and waited, praying his head, topped with those remarkably alert ears, would pop out of hiding to greet her. She knelt, patted the earth, and called to him again. It had been three days since Micah had snatched her hare up by his neck. And then Colton had set off to track him down. He must have caught him. He'd turned her friend into—

"Who is this at my front entrance?" Wallace hopped into view.

Calista sat back, overwhelmed with relief. "I was so worried."

"Thank you for that, but no need. That lumbering brute couldn't catch me if he had four legs. Legs can only do so much without cunning." He hopped closer and stared up at her. "How did you fare with that beastly Micah Kennewick?"

Calista told him the story, and he listened, only interrupting with a flick of an ear and what might have been a harrumph at the parts about the whip and the horrible mob of villagers.

"And I've delivered the locket to Grace Kennewick."

"I'm impressed, Calista. Truly."

When she mentioned Simon Pinehurst, he sat up on his hind legs.

"Now that is very interesting. What are you going to do about him?"

"Nothing. Absolutely nothing. And why should I do … or think about doing something about this, uh, this person?" She felt her cheeks flush hot and rubbed them with her fingers. "I'm going to let him discover the deception and set things to rights with his aunt on his own."

"Hmm. I wonder if his mother knows he's here? And you seem a bit perturbed. Do I sense an infatuation?"

"What? No! Of course not. I was worried about you."

"What was I thinking? Calista Moonwater D'White couldn't possibly succumb to such a trivial notion as love."

"I have much better, I mean, much more important, things to think about than Simon Pinehurst."

"Of course. Of course. How are those other favors for your neighbors coming along?"

"Well," Calista said before standing and brushing off her skirt. "Not the way I would like them to. I'm going to ask Mrs. Wilhelm to clarify why my great-grandmother can't appear to help me when all the others in the cemetery can come to me to ask for my help. And then I'm going to set myself to improving my magic." Calista shook her head. "I simply do not understand how it works, and I must. I'm sure I could take care of all those ghostly needs with a few effective spells."

"Absolutely. Based on what you've told me about the mad mob and its penchant for taking pleasure in whipping fellow villagers, I'd say you have the right idea, but we should visit Mrs. Wilhelm first thing in the morning. I'm not keen on entering that smelly section of the cemetery this late in the day." Wallace quivered from his nose to his tail. "Something's amiss over there."

"Agreed," Calista said. "As venerable as those graves were, it troubled her to be near them any time, but in the twilight, they became a sinister presence.

Chapter Twenty-Five

That next morning Wallace was already waiting at the cemetery gate when Calista arrived. They walked past the stone-edged section, and even Wallace stayed as far from it as he could. "I never like this spot," he said, hopping faster. "And lately I like it less. It has a sickening smell to it."

Calista, who had pinched her nose, nodded in agreement and picked up her pace.

They came to the newer section, and today the cemetery was being ordinary—silently sacred and only a bit eerie in the early shadows. She looked around for the spiraling ghosts beseeching her help, but there were none. How unusual.

She stopped and Wallace went ahead several hops before he also stopped and faced her. "Are you coming?"

"Where are they?" Calista asked.

"Probably conferring. They do that in stressful times. They must have sensed you were in trouble. Or maybe word's out about Simon Pinehurst's return. Then they do have a new member who, I hear, has caused a stir. They're deciding how to manage him. That's my guess." He hopped ahead. "Come along," he said without looking back.

Calista walked after him, picking her way among the tombstones. She'd just come to Mrs. Wilhelm when the familiar chill wrapped around her.

"Poor dear." Mrs. Wilhelm's wispy voice blew cold near her ear. "We heard about your ordeal, and—"

"I was the one who ventured out and bore witness to that travesty of justice." Mrs. Pinehurst pushed past Mrs. Wilhelm in a poof of vapor. "I saw that imposter of a sister, bloated with excitement and pastries. And I saw my son rescue you. That is indeed my boy. He's magnificent, isn't he?"

She'd answered Wallace's question. Eleanor Pinehurst knew very well that her son was in Storm Haven, but Calista wished she'd lent a hand, even a ghostly one. "I could have used your help that day," she said.

"I wanted to help so much, Calista, but I'm not permitted to do any physical intervention without your asking. You didn't do that. You will when you're ready. Of that I'm certain."

When I'm ready, Calista thought, guessing that would be when she finally mastered Amara's spells. But who knew when that would happen? Certainly, she didn't.

Farmer Kennewick glided between Calista and Mrs. Pinehurst. "You did it, didn't you? My daughter has the locket and my message?"

Calista nodded.

"I am eternal grateful for what you done."

"Yes." Calista smiled at the humor she found in that.

Wallace jumped atop Mrs. Pinehurst's misnamed tombstone. "See if he can offer you some information along with that gratefulness."

"What do you mean?" Calista asked.

"He's Micah's father and Colton's uncle. He might have something that will help you handle those two now that you've helped him."

Farmer Kennewick billowed closer to Calista. "Your hare is right in suggesting I help. I can only say that Micah's got poor judgment and he holds tight to any wrong done against him. He puts his back up at rejection. He can't manage any of that. My fault, you see." He looked away, a dejected slump across his shoulders. "I tried to make my neglect up to him, but by letting his bad behavior go unpunished, I only made things worse. So very worse. I have much to ask forgiveness for." He stroked his beard, suddenly lost in old memories.

"And Colton?" Calista asked, hoping to find out more.

"About Colton. He's real trouble. Something's always been off about him, so it's best not to trust him. He got the bad nature of his mother, you know. And I"—he frowned, considering his words before continuing— "I know he puts a lot of bad notions into Micah's head. I've never said what's in my mind about him because he is kin and my brother's only child, but…" Farmer Kennewick's face grew so sad that Calista thought he might cry.

When she reached out to offer comfort, he vanished.

"Wait!" she called, but it was too late.

She was sure he hadn't finished telling her all he wanted to about Micah or Colton. Calista had heard that in his voice. He'd said "but" and almost continued with more about those two. Perhaps she already knew the worst about Micah. And she was pretty sure Colton was capable of killing more than beetles and small animals. That would be an awful admission for his uncle to make.

Mrs. Pinehurst was at her side once more as soon as the farmer left. "So what do you plan to do about that deranged sister of mine?"

"I thought—" Calista started to tell the woman she'd decided to let Simon take care of the matter, but Mrs. Wilhelm broke in.

"That's enough, Eleanor. Let the girl be. She's just been through so much."

Mrs. Pinehurst bustled off to her grave, emitting impatient huffs along the way.

"Such a way to behave." Mrs. Wilhelm shook her

head. "Especially now with all the confusion Luther's arrival has caused. Tsk. Tsk."

Calista had never heard of a Luther in Storm Haven. "Who's Luther?"

"Luther Jones, the poor lad that was dispatched by some villain. So sad it is. He was just sixteen." Mrs. Wilhelm's lips turned down, and the creases between her eyebrows deepened.

Of course, Luther was the Jones Boy. He was the new member Wallace said was causing a stir. "There's a problem with him because…?"

"He's not settling in as he should. He's restless. Those kinds of spirits are the most challenging, usually young ones who've met with a bad end. And he and Squire Nielsen are at each other every moment. None of us can find the peace we're supposed to have here." Mrs. Wilhelm, her face swarming with worry, waved her hand over the cemetery. "The Squire by himself was a handful, but now—"

"I've not looked into the Squire's request, and I'm afraid to do so. Not for me, but for my mother. I've already caused her so much anguish."

Mrs. Wilhelm sighed. "Of course, dear." She started away, a ghost burdened by responsibilities. That confused Calista. She'd always thought those on the *other side* left behind the worries of the mortal world. It seemed that was not the case. All of the ghosts she'd met had carried their worries and regrets with them.

Wallace eyed Calista from his tombstone perch, reminding her why she'd come here today.

"Wait." Calista trotted after Mrs. Wilhelm, who had already dipped halfway into the earth. "I want to help. I do. But I need help myself. Mrs. Pinehurst says I have to put in some kind of request if I want one of you to come to my aid in any way. Is that true?"

"Yes," Mrs. Wilhelm said. "We can visit and we can ask for your assistance. We just can't intervene in the world of the living unless asked, and by someone possessing true *magyk.*"

"*Magyk*?" Why did that very familiar word sound so different when Mrs. Wilhelm said it with that stress on the last part of the word? "So when do I know if I have this … this true *magyk*?"

"Oh, you'll know, and from what I've seen, you are mighty close, dear."

Well, that sounded hopeful. Calista wished she understood what *mighty close* meant and when she could expect her true *magyk* to arrive. "Then what about Amara? How do I ask her to come and show me the ways of her *magyk*?"

Mrs. Wilhelm twisted her hands, looking worried. "In Amara's case, to bring her to you and enlist her help is a bit more challenging."

"Why?

Mrs. Wilhelm cleared her throat in the way nervous speakers do when they're not prepared to answer questions.

"Please tell me," Calista said.

"It will take courage, and you must be strong, more than ever in your life." Mrs. Wilhelm's face flushed with fear. "And to ask for Amara's help, you must" —again that nervous clearing of the throat— "go to Vengeance Mountain."

Chapter Twenty-Six

Calista stood as unmoving as the tombstones surrounding her.

"I know how shocking that idea is to you, dear, but going up Vengeance Mountain is the only way to call Amara to your side," Mrs. Wilhelm said.

"Why didn't you tell me this before?" Calista didn't know if she had a right to be angry, but she did have a right to be frustrated by Mrs. Wilhelm's hesitant answers.

"Because there is some danger. A great deal of it actually. But after Luther Jones was dispatched and that mob had at you, I believe you'll soon be in as much danger in Storm Haven as on the mountain." She hovered half-in, half-out of her grave.

Although Calista always doubted the story about the giant, she didn't want to ignore any possible threat. She needed to arm herself with as much information as possible. "Is the danger due to the giant? If so, how do I take it on without it destroying me the way the stories say it destroyed others?"

"Those are questions that are at the heart of Stone Haven's tragedy, Calista." Mrs. Wilhelm pressed her fingertips to her temples. "I want to tell you what you need to know, but I fear I can't."

"Can't or won't?" she said sharply, her frustration set to boil.

"A bit of both, my dear. But trust me. There is good reason I hold back this information." She sighed. Then she spoke so softly that Calista had to lean close to hear what the woman was saying. "It's about the … uh … the—"

Calista was out of patience. "About the what?"

"The … curse." Mrs. Wilhelm whispered the word, but the sound it made was ominous. "I'm dreadfully sorry."

"What curse?" When Calista asked her question, the earth shifted underfoot. The stench from inside the stonewalled section of the cemetery rose like a foul cloud into the air and was so strong that Calista had to gulp back the bile in her throat. "All right. If you can't help with those questions, then at least tell me what to do when I get to the mountain. How do I call Amara to help me?"

But Mrs. Wilhelm had already slipped from sight, leaving Calista and the hare alone. All was quiet again.

Calista barely held back from pounding on Mrs. Wilhelm's kneeling angle. "Why does she avoid answering me?"

"She's obviously quite frightened," Wallace said.

"It was when she mentioned the" —Calista leaned down to whisper in Wallace's ear— "curse."

He nodded. "But now you know that you must seek out Amara if you want her help. There's no waiting for her to come to you."

Calista looked toward the mountain and shivered.

"It's only a place after all," Wallace said. "Just a bit of land that juts higher into the sky than Storm Haven."

"Wallace, it's a place where no one ventures." She used to doubt the tales, but she couldn't anymore. The sudden and fierce storms. The upsetting shaking of the earth. The mystery of the hushed encouragement that came at the exact moment she needed it. What had just happened when Mrs. Wilhelm mentioned some curse. These kinds of unexplained happenings could be real, why not other farfetched ones? She now believed those myths about the giant might come from something other than addled minds.

They returned through the side cemetery gate, and at the thicket, Calista said, "If I go there, am I to face a giant full of rage? What do you think?"

Wallace considered her question before answering. "I believe there's something more powerful up there."

"And what is that?"

"The Moonwaters."

Calista looked down at Wallace, stunned. "My ancestors? But they're—"

"Sadly, yes. They're dead."

Calista wrapped her cloak more tightly around her, considering what Wallace had just told her. If his version of the story was true, she had more ghostly confrontations ahead, and this time they'd be with family.

The wintery sun hung above the mountain, and she looked toward the East at the early light of day. Even bathed in sunlight, the mountain jutted cold and threatening into the sky. Snow clouds clung to the summit like dark wraiths.

"I wasn't expecting to climb up there, Wallace. That complicates things a bit."

Wallace said nothing. He never volunteered information, it seemed, only advice. Maybe he knew more about the mountain's secret that might help her, but from his continued silence, she'd guessed she'd have to ask for it.

"My great-grandmother writes of The Vengeance. What do you know of it?"

"Only what has been passed down in stories from past generations of my family."

"Can you be a little less cryptic?"

He nodded. "Yes. It seems you're ready to hear the other version of the stories. In our thicket, it has been said that when the villagers condemned a Moonwater witch to the flames, the fire burned so hot and so fast that it drove the villagers out of the square. Those who dared peer through their windows swore that the ashes—still red with fire—swooped like a swarm of insects into the air and flew off to the mountain. The evidence of village guilt scattered far and wide, but with each burning, the fires grew fiercer and the mountain more threatening for those who ventured to climb it. Finally, no one felt safe to come or go through that pass. Some went missing. Some had what they said were narrow death experiences. That's when the really bright minds decided hanging Moonwater witches was so much better." He looked up at her. "I hope this isn't too distressing."

While it was hard to hear the grim details of her ancestors' murders, she said, "I asked for a clearer explanation, so I appreciate it, Wallace. Please go on."

"Our stories say that with Amara, they had a little more work to do to hide their wickedness. A few volunteers trudged up toward the pass and dug her grave at the base. One came back crazed, the story goes. Someone found him huddled in the church, wild-eyed, jabbering nonsense and going on about being attacked by fiery swarms of winged insects. They landed on his two friends, he said, and they burst into flames. He barely survived by running off, but death chased him all the way to the church.

After that day no one climbed the mountain. Our legends say that the ghosts of your ancestors prevent passage and bring death, not any vengeful giant. Talking about a giant became a way for the guilty villagers to avoid using words like witch or Moonwater. The old stories said when someone uttered them in the same breath, their hearts became stone, and they fell dead where they stood."

"That's dreadful." At the same time, she thought it was even more dreadful how quickly this generation of villagers had overcome that fear and leapt to hate her once Micah had shouted not only witch but devil for all to hear. "They seem to have forgotten that superstition."

"Yes. I heard." Wallace said. "Too bad. I prefer a healthy state of fear in this case."

"In the thicket, what do they say about these unnatural storms and the shaking of the earth lately?"

"We believe it's your ancestors who send the storms and the tremors.

"What?" Calista hadn't expected that.

"They remind us of their power and the injustice they found in Storm Haven. The Vengeance has only been a threat in old stories, but it could happen. I've heard speculation about when it will happen since I was very young. The villagers set out to destroy those who possessed some powerful and dangerous *magyk*, but they didn't have the sense to think about the consequences."

"You said magic, but it sounded strange, the same as it sounded when Mrs. Wilhelm said it earlier. Why?"

"I've been told there's a difference between magic and *magyk.* And it's an important difference, but you might want to ask Amara about that."

She'd never considered there could be two kinds of magic. She hadn't expected to hear that or such a different version of the story about the giant. Then she remembered the strange marks around the word *giant* in Amara's book. Was she debunking that myth? In any case, if Wallace was right, those witches were indeed powerful and a force she might have to face. She thought about the strange message, c*ourage,* when she was in such danger. Mrs. Wilhelm must be mistaken. It had to be her great-grandmother who came in moments of crisis. There was no one else Calista could think of. Amara had to be looking out for her after all. To find out for certain, she'd have to go up that mountain.

"Those who destroyed the Moonwater witches are buried inside the stone wall." Wallace twitched his nose in the direction of the cemetery. "We believe that wretched smell is their guilt."

So guilt was the sourness she smelled each time she entered the gate. She'd always caught whiffs of it, but it had become more noticeable since her small collision with the fraudulent Mrs. Pinehurst. She'd been mistaken about the reason for the stone wall surrounding that section of the graveyard her whole life. It wasn't built to show respect for the early settlers. It was built to keep them separate from their descendants—people who hadn't murdered their neighbors. No wonder she instinctively gave that area a wide berth.

And now she recalled her dream with a shudder. Hands jutting from the graves, reaching for her. That might well be a warning. She had every reason to be cautious when making decisions. Anything she chose to do could lead to trouble, even death.

"Do you know what" —again she bent to whisper— "the curse is about?"

Wallace shook his head. "I'm sorry. That is new to me."

"I suppose I'll find out once I'm" —she swallowed— "there."

"If you want company on the trek up that mountain, I'm free tomorrow."

"Thank you." The hare was a good friend if he was willing to leave the comfort of his home and climb the mountain with her. "Mrs. Wilhelm's holding back something that I think she must tell me before we challenge Vengeance Mountain."

"She's scattered these days." When Calista didn't

answer, he said. "You should have laughed at that. Ghost. Scattered."

"I'm too worried to laugh at the moment. I need to know what she meant by 'there's some danger'. I'm afraid it's much more dreadful than she's letting on."

"Of course. I thought you might need some humor after all that I've just told you. Come by tomorrow. We'll see if we can pry that information from her together. Whatever you do, don't fetch me to your room the way you did last time. We hares do not fly. We are earth-bound creatures." He scuttled under his bush and Calista returned to the cottage thinking about Wallace's version about the myth of the giant.

Chapter Twenty-Seven

That night she studied more of Amara's book of magic. While reading her great-grandmother's entries, Calista became caught up in the beauty and wisdom of the words. The stories were simple, but eloquent, and slowly out of them the young Amara came to life.

A tower of a girl, she bent to care for the smallest creature in need but seldom bothered to meet the darting eyes of the villagers who scurried to avoid her. Her ears were tuned to cries of the hawk and the chirp of the cricket, but she kept herself deaf to petty gossip that buzzed like a cloud of wasps at her back. From her stories, Calista learned that her great-grandmother spent most of her time alone or in the woods with the animals.

Calista looked up from the book. *My great-grandmother was as lonely as I have ever been.*

The more Calista read of Amara's daily life, the more she came to understand how Amara's magic filled her and the world she lived in as naturally as the forest filled the hillsides or the mountain rose to the sky. Her breath, her heartbeat, her thoughts fell into the rhythm of the world around her. She disturbed nothing. She blended into everything. So unlike the heavy presence of the villagers.

She turned to another page of the book. "I am a stranger here—the other—just as all my family have always been. They will destroy me because they fear what they don't understand. I see how they think. I'm a witch. Witches are evil. Witches must die."

Calista ran her finger over the words and between the lines more writing appeared. She wondered what spell she'd find in this entry.

Consider carefully before you go to the mountain.

But if you do go, have courage and believe that you have the power to change the evil that thrives in Storm Haven.

This was no spell, and the writing looked different. It wasn't spidery with upright strokes. The letters were dark and thick and slanted far right. When she looked, her fingertip was smudged with fresh ink. But instead of drawing away with fright, that familiar warmth of comfort flowed through her. At this moment, the passage had fortified her with courage and a belief in herself. She hoped she'd have both when she needed them.

****

The next morning, while Miriam worked in the laundry shed, Calista quickly finished feeding Flower and milking Greta. On her way from the barn, she turned the bundles of healing herbs that hung from the rafters to keep them from mildewing. She gulped down a cold glass of milk before starting toward the thicket to fetch Wallace. He'd promised to go with her to the cemetery, and she'd like his company for this mission. It was important to find Mrs. Wilhelm and try one last time to have her explain how she went about asking for Amara's help once she reached the mountain. This time, she was armed with Wallace's version of the story. This time, she'd tell Mrs. Wilhelm she knew who presented danger up there and she'd demand to know what she should do about the mysterious curse.

As she rounded the side of the house, a shadow loomed over her, almost knocking her to the ground.

"What in…!" she shouted, windmilling her arms.

Strong hands grabbed her shoulders and kept her from falling. "I'm sorry." It was Simon Pinehurst. "I came around the back, because no one answered the door."

"Chores." Calista gestured in the general direction

of the barn, still startled. No one ever came to the cottage, that was part of why she couldn't catch her breath. The other was that he was still holding her shoulders and flooding her with a river of emotion and more secrets. She didn't want to know who he was or what he'd done, but it was all there. Such excitement and so many adventures—some not within the law. She pulled free and stepped back.

"Are you off somewhere, or can you talk for a short time?"

"Um. Well, yes. I mean, of course." She took a breath. "I … I have time to talk." What was the matter with her tongue?

"Can we sit somewhere?" he asked.

Her manners seemed to have vanished along with her composure. "I'm sorry. Please come in. I'll make us some tea."

He followed her into the house and she set the kettle on the iron stovetop. The task helped her regain some calm, after the sparks his touch had sent through her. There was a goodness in him, but he had a devilish streak a mile wide when it came to women. That much she'd read very clearly. He was only in Storm Haven for a visit, and then he planned to leave again. Business was the message she felt, but she couldn't see what kind. And there was something else—she must have made a mistake. No. She'd seen him in a darkened room, his hand scooping up gems and hiding them inside his coat. Simon Pinehurst was a thief.

He took off the hat that shielded his eyes, and for a moment held her gaze before setting his hat on the chair next to him.

Quickly, she reached for the tea canister, tiny needles pricking along her scalp. This unsettled state was annoying. She had to calm down.

"You seem fully recovered from that ordeal the other day." His voice sounded different inside the house. Not as loud or untamed. He seemed to know to speak more softly at her kitchen table.

"I'm fine. And thank you again for saving my mother and me from that oaf and the hysterical crowd he'd stirred up against us."

While she gathered the cups and started the tea brewing, she kept her back to him, but his presence was large in the room. Her father had filled this space with his smell of leather and lime soap, too, but Simon's scent was only a small part of what he brought into the kitchen.

She swiped the surprise of dampness that came so suddenly across her forehead before carrying the tea to the table. Before she sat down, she fetched the last of her cinnamon spice muffins.

He ate the first one in three bites, then ate the second one with more care. "I'm fond of muffins. My mother…" Without finishing, he lifted the teacup to his lips.

Had he discovered the truth? If so, why had he come to her?

"About my father," he said as he sipped more tea. "I wonder how he died. I don't have a clear story about that, you see. My mother … well, she can't seem to tell me about it, says it's too distressing. I hoped you might be able to."

How could she explain to Simon that his mother's twin had poisoned his father? And that she'd learned this from his real mother's ghost? She couldn't. It was impossible. That fact made her irritable. Holding back the truth was against her nature, but this truth would surely make him think she was unstable … insane, actually.

"It was just as Magistrate Lowry said. He died suddenly, but he'd been ill a few times before that."

"And no one bothered to find out what his sickness was?"

"You should ask your mother again." Calista hated the brittle sound of her voice.

"Of course." He finished his tea and stood, putting his hat back on. "I'll do that." Moving to the door, he said, "Thank you for the tea, and I'd have more of those muffins in the future."

He was gone before her voice returned and she muttered, "I'm glad you liked them." She slammed her hands onto the table and rattled the tea cups in their saucers. "Arrg!"

Chapter Twenty-Eight

Calista cleared the table and washed the few things in the sink, scrubbing a bit harder and a bit longer than necessary. Keeping the truth from Simon vexed her, and truthfully, it vexed her more that he hadn't detected his aunt's deception. He didn't seem dim. But what lay ahead kept her on edge as well. She still had to solve a couple of murders. Then she had to face venturing up the mountain if she was finally going to discover what those old stories were really about—a giant or Wallace's folklore of vengeful witches. And now there was this curse. What would come next?

She'd make a last effort to extract information from Mrs. Wilhelm. That woman must tell her what she needed to know once she arrived up there. If she didn't leave soon, her mother would be finished with the washing and would be asking her about her plans for the day. She didn't want to tell about her plans, which would only worry Miriam.

At Wallace's prickly bush, she tapped the earth. He popped out right away. "And are you on your way to see Mrs. Wilhelm one more time?"

"Yes. I'm up to finding a way to solve the squire's and Luther Jones's murders, and to make people understand that the Moonwater witches had nothing to do with either one. It's time to bring some sanity back to this village. I'm ready to climb the mountain, but I'm not sure what to do once I arrive. Mrs. Wilhelm has to tell me, and she has to explain what she meant about the curse."

"Better check in with her again then. You don't want to make mistakes up there, you being a Moonwater witch or not."

They entered the cemetery and went to the third tombstone on the right next to the main gate.

"Mrs. Wilhelm?" Calista called and waited. When the woman didn't rise to greet her, she rapped her knuckles on the stone, feeling like an idiot. "I'm readying myself to be off to the mountain. I must ask some questions before I leave."

Calista looked down at Wallace with a question that she didn't have to put into words.

"I have no idea why she refuses to appear," Wallace said.

"She's hiding something from me. I'm sure of it." Calista stomped over to Mrs. Pinehurst's grave. "Mrs. Pinehurst?" she called. The cemetery was behaving the way it had before the clamor of ghosts entered her life. It was quiet.

"I don't want it to be quiet," she said, sounding grumpy. Then, flinging her arms out to encourage the ghosts, she said. "I want it filled with your voices, giving me tips about how to get Amara's help. I could also use tips on how to survive the mountain, just in case those fiery winged insects take a dislike to me." She waited, tapping one foot. "Well?"

Calista finally propped herself against Mrs. Wilhelm's weeping angel. "All right. I'm trying to help you," she said. "The least you could do is try to help me."

The movement was very slight, but it caught her eye. She glanced down at Wallace. "Did you see that?"

He didn't answer. He'd seen it, and he'd gone mute because, like her, he knew someone was watching and listening. An eavesdropper had to be why the ghosts weren't here to greet her as usual.

"Who are you?" There was no sense in pretending she didn't know someone was lurking behind one of the monuments across from where she stood. "Come out from hiding and show yourself."

The broad-brimmed hat appeared first, followed by the grinning-faced Simon Pinehurst. "I didn't plan on eavesdropping, but you are an entertaining woman."

"I'm so glad I could provide a diversion for you." She made straight for the side gate with Wallace at her heels.

"Wait. Please." Simon stopped her before she could leave. "I was rude. I apologize."

He was so clever. But, she'd known that from what she'd sensed at his touch. Clever and beguiling. Love came easily to this man and disappeared quickly. How many young girls' hearts had he snapped in two? She didn't want to know, but she's already sensed several. And she wanted nothing to do with a thief, but he still blocked her from reaching the gate.

"What do you want, Simon Pinehurst?"

"Answers. Truthful ones."

She dug her toe into the ground, deciding whether to pretend ignorance or tell him what she knew. He was a rogue, yes. Polite, yes. Handsome, unfortunately. Trustworthy? Absolutely not. Superstitious? She hadn't made up her mind about that yet. If she did give him his honest answer, would he cry "witch" and fetch a noose?

Wallace hadn't fled. He sat quietly at her heels.

How would Mr. Pinehurst react to a bit of conversation between the hare and her, she wondered. She stooped and whispered into one long gray ear. "Can you let this one hear you?"

"If you like, but isn't that rather chancy?"

"Yes, but then we'll know where he stands."

"Carry on then," Wallace said.

Calista straightened, looking directly at Simon. "What's your opinion about giving this person the truth, Wallace?"

The hare didn't hesitate to speak up. "Test the waters. See what he does."

The surprise that crossed Simon's face lasted only a few seconds before he knelt and held out his hand. "Wisdom in a small package. I like that. And you are called Wallace?"

Wallace put his paw into Simon's spatula of a hand. "Indeed, I am."

"I assume you know of me already. Simon Pinehurst here, seeking the true story about my father — he glanced toward the cemetery— "and now perhaps my mother."

He knew the truth, or suspected it. And he accepted Wallace without flinching. He'd seen her knocking on tombstones expecting an answer and talking to the air, yet he hadn't told her she was insane, just entertaining. She found that annoying. She was accustomed to being shunned—she wasn't accustomed to being laughed at.

She decided she should tell him all. And do it quickly. Placing her hands on her hips, she looked up at him. "I'm sorry to tell you this, but both of your parents are dead."

He flinched at the news, but then said, "I knew that woman wasn't my mother. She was too much like my sour-faced aunt."

"I know your mother died at the hands of her twin sister. I'm fairly sure your father did, too." She paused, hoping she'd been right to be so blunt.

She waited for an outburst, but instead, Simon led the way to the gate and held it open until she and Wallace passed through. He remained silent on their way down the path.

At the thicket, Wallace hopped to his home and before diving under the prickly bush said, "Calista, I think we must postpone that trek up the mountain until Mrs. Wilhelm reappears."

"Agreed. Tomorrow, perhaps."

Wallace sat as tall as possible on his hind legs and stared up at Simon. "You've come to Storm Haven at the opportune time to do justice and help Calista." He disappeared from sight before either of them could reply.

"There's more to this story," she said to Simon. "Some I understand, but much I do not." She shared her worries about the sudden, fierce storms and the trembling earth. "These started right after my accidental and unpleasant collision with your aunt." She held back telling him how she could also read thoughts of others by their touch. Some things were better left unsaid.

When she stopped her story, he waited as if he knew she'd soon continue. Calista wished he'd say something to break the silence. She'd never been so uncomfortable.

"I sense there's more," he said finally.

"Yes." She looked past him as she stretched out that word because the next part was difficult to say out loud to anyone, let alone Simon Pinehurst. Then, with some caution, she told him about the ghosts and their favors. She did this slowly, watching for his reaction. He kept his eyes on her, but disbelief didn't cloud his face, and he didn't laugh, so she continued until he knew as much as she did.

"So you were really telling the truth about that locket and those scolas?"

"Of course." He hadn't believed her? He'd thought she was a thief like him? Intolerable. She had a mind to march away and leave, but as she turned, he stepped in her path.

"Sorry. Please, go on."

"Your mother wants her sister to pay for her

crimes, but she really wants her true name on her tombstone."

Again, she waited for Simon's reaction, but none came. And the silence hung between them like a thick curtain. She couldn't read his face, and she'd made up her mind not to touch him ever again, so she didn't have a single clue about what his thoughts were.

Standing in the cold, uncertainty mounting, she finally shouted at him. "I'd like you to say something, please!"

"I'm considering—"

"What? If I should be hanged like my great-grandmother because I'm a witch? Or maybe you'd prefer to light me on fire." She stomped her foot and immediately felt like a child having a tantrum. *Stupid. Stupid. Stupid.* But she was in a rage—partly due to the fear that she'd shared what she shouldn't, and partly due to this stubborn mule of a man who refused to set her mind at ease by answering her.

"No. I'm considering how much to pay the stone carver to change the name on my mother's tombstone."

Her rage sputtered out, leaving her cheeks burning from embarrassment. He believed her. Wallace had said he'd come at the right time.

"Twenty scolas," she said. "Based on my experience with the man a few years ago."

"The bigger issue is my aunt. How do I expose her without exposing you? I don't think the elders will believe I spoke with my mother's ghost, but they might believe you did. That wouldn't help you at all." He grinned. "Based on my experience with them yesterday."

He was repeating her words, taunting her, but she wouldn't rise to that bait. "What you say is true, but I have an idea. If you have Eleanor's name chiseled into that tombstone without anyone knowing, and then let the word spread through the village that a ghostly hand did the deed, you might scare a very guilty Matilda enough to confess her crimes."

He smiled. "You're not only very beautiful, you're very intelligent." He swept his hand to the side, bowing in an exaggerated manner, and before she could step away, he took her by the hands and pulled her closer. "I won't take advantage of any witch, especially one with eyes the color of gold. That's just too dangerous, but I will make my intentions clear. I plan to know you much better."

She was about to stop the flood of images coming to her the way she had when touching Micah, but something made her hold back. Underneath his touch was a gentle kindness she hadn't felt since her father's embrace. Yet Simon's was laced with an urgency very unlike her fathers, and that frightened her. Not because of his simmering passion, but because she was suddenly bound up by a deep enchantment that made her speechless. She pulled away.

"I'm serious," he said before walking toward the road. Over his shoulder he called to her. "But first we have to set things right for your family and mine."

She regained her senses once his hands weren't clasping hers, but where was her voice? Somewhere in her stomach, set to stammer. How…? The audacity! Insufferable man.

Wallace poked his head from his under his bush and stared up at her.

"Oh, be quiet!" She stomped away toward the cottage, her fingers once again tingling. She held them in front of her face. "Will you stop!"

****

That night Calista took up Amara's book again. As much as she feared testing more spells, she'd come to think that the tingling in her fingers was caused by something more than excitement. Perhaps it wanted her to be alert to danger. From the lumbering Micah or evil-hearted Colton, to the beguiling Simon Pinehurst. Still, she hadn't ruled out Amara. Her great-grandmother was a special witch, according to everyone, so Calista favored the idea that it could be Amara who sent those messages. *Be careful. Danger ahead. Pay attention.* It would be comforting if Amara were at her side. That might mean that when she did go to Vengeance Mountain her great-grandmother would be there to protect her from whatever danger awaited.

If she could only work Amara's spells without mistakes, she'd feel much more confident that she'd complete the journey safely. She scanned the pages, until she came to the story she'd read before about the pond suspended in time.

Now that she knew Amara's secrets, it was easy to pull up the hidden writing and the spells connected to the story themes. Running her fingers over the lines, she revealed the spell to stop time that Amara had so cleverly tucked between her description.

Sit with feet placed on the floor or— if possible— earth. Encircle anything outside yourself that you don't want to suspend in time, then press your right palm against your heart and cover that hand with the other. Close your eyes and breathe. Hold it for the count of four and exhale for the count of four. Think of balance and stillness. Become one with that moment and imagine it staying forever. The stronger your concentration, the longer the spell will hold.

To release time, raise your arms to the East and welcome time's return.

WARNING: You must never repeat this spell more than three times in a single moon phase.

Calista didn't have a clue what encircling things outside yourself meant. Well, this was only a practice, so she'd find out the answer later. She had no desire to place her feet on the snowy ground, so she sat on her bed and, trying to remember each step before she started the spell, counted.

"One, two, three, four," she murmured, wondering how many times she'd have to repeat that. Nothing seemed different around her. She'd best do it at least one more time. "One, two, three—" The change padded like an alert cat into the room. She risked a peek. Her candle flame cast a steady, unflickering light next to her bed, and a deep silence surrounded her as if she had mufflers over her ears.

When she took a step toward her door, her legs became mired in an invisible slurry, her feet cushioned by air. The distance between her outstretched hand and the door latch increased. She stepped forward. The latch receded. She was trapped in her room. She must have worked this spell in the wrong way, just as she had the others.

No. She'd left out the encircling. Now she understood how important that was. She could move forward because she wasn't trapped in the moment, but everything else had to remain as it was before the spell. She tried to open her window, but it wouldn't budge.

"Lesson learned," she said. She looked into the black night, where not a tree branch stirred, and where her keen-eyed guide, the owl, was silhouetted against the sky. It didn't perch on a branch or the peak of the barn. It hung suspended in the air.

"Oh, no! This is terrible."

Chapter Twenty-Nine

As soon as she saw that poor owl captured in flight by her spell, she raised her arms to the East and set her friendly guide free. The candle flame flickered. When she was able to open the window, she sighed with relief. Everything had returned to normal.

She scoured Amara's book to find the "Encircling Strategy" and studied it until she was sure she understood exactly how to suspend only the area she wanted to freeze in time. Finally, yawning, she curled up under her blankets, tired but feeling a bit more confident that if she had to, she could work this spell the right way.

"I suspended time," she whispered to herself, and hearing that out loud boosted her faith in herself. She still didn't know how that spell was going to serve her, but at least she'd done it properly. Now, if only Mrs. Wilhelm would pay her a visit, she'd be more fully armed when she tackled that trek up the mountain.

****

Chunk. Chunk. Chunk.

It was still early the next morning, so early that she couldn't imagine anyone visiting the cemetery. But the sound had come from there. Calista stepped outside the barn and listened.

Chunk. Chunk

Still, she couldn't figure out what the noise might be. It wasn't a shovel digging into the earth. That was all too familiar, so she'd surely recognize it. Shrugging, she returned to her work, curious about what could be causing it, but needing to do her chores before investigating. She finished raking the old straw and spread some fresh, then with the steady *chunk chunk* to lead the way, she set aside her rake and started toward the sound. The closer she came to the cemetery, the more distinct it became. She peered beyond the side gate. "Simon Pinehurst?" She pushed her way inside and walked toward him where he knelt with a hammer and a chisel.

He stood to meet her. "Good day."

"What are you doing?"

He pointed at his mother's tombstone. The first letter M was gone, so now it read atilda. "The only way I know to keep a secret is to never tell a single person. My work is not the best, but it will do until my dear aunt tells me who she really is and confesses to her crimes, then I'll have the stonecutter do a proper job."

Simon was right about secrets. The village thrived on them the way a horse did on fresh grass. Something told in confidence in the morning was fodder for the entire village before midday.

"How is it with your aunt?" She couldn't imagine living in that house with a woman who had done such horrible things to his family. It had to be miserable for him. And now that she noticed, he did have a pallor to him. Probably the stress.

"She avoids me as much as she can by pretending to be ill. I'm very impressed by her skill as a liar. It's as if she believes all she says." He removed his hat and swiped his forehead with a handkerchief. He folded it and stuck it into his pocket. With a wry laugh, he said, "This time she might be telling the truth. I think I've come down with whatever ails her. I have a slight fever."

"Are you sure you've caught something from her and not eaten food that's tainted? You do watch her carefully, don't you? I mean with the food."

"I haven't eaten anything she cooks. I take my meals at the inn. I tell her I have business there."

"That's good." Calista had it on her tongue to

invite him to the kitchen for some of her mother's special healing tea, but she held back. She wouldn't encourage his attentions.

"What do you know about Colton Kennewick?" he asked.

"Only that he has evil dwelling at the very center of his heart. He's best avoided."

"I don't remember him in Storm Haven when I was a boy."

"He came after you left." Calista told what she knew of him and what Farmer Kennewick had said. "I think his uncle knows that Colton is capable of many dreadful things, among them possibly murder. But even in death, the farmer's loyal to his brother, and won't say that about his nephew."

"I've seen him leaving from the back door a couple of times when I return to the house. He never comes when I'm there, so I'm sure he watches the door. My aunt hasn't mentioned his visits, so I let the matter be."

Now, that was suspicious. If Colton came and went from the Kennewicks, he was up to something, and it wasn't good.

"Well, I'd best get on with this." Simon knelt and returned to work chiseling away the rest of his aunt's name on the stone.

"Simon?"

He paused with his hammer raised and looked up at her.

"Beware Colton Kennewick."

"Of course. I know he's to be guarded against." He smiled at her. "Thank you for your concern though."

She wanted to tell him she'd be concerned for anyone in his situation, but he was concentrating on his work, so she backed away.

On her way from the cemetery, she looked out over the crosses and tilted monuments, hoping one of the ghosts would appear. She might be able to send word to Mrs. Wilhelm that way, but none of them were there, and she was beginning to think they'd given up on her. But that seemed unlikely. After all, she'd already accomplished three challenging tasks for them and with Simon's help, she was about to achieve a fourth.

Where are you, Mrs. Wilhelm? I have questions and you're the only one who has the answers.

At the low stone wall, she came to a quick stop. A black wooly mold spattered the ancient tombstones, slowly sealing the already sketchy names behind a thick fur. Each time she visited the cemetery this section became more repulsive and harder to venture past. She almost expected to see the dead rise full-bodied and putrid from their graves. With that thought, the smell became stronger. She covered her mouth and pushed her way through the gate.

Later that morning, she was putting the last of the mixing bowls into the cupboard when old Thomas Tidwell's family passed the cottage in their wagon on the way to the cemetery. She'd barely wiped down the counter before their wagon returned, the horse at a fast trot.

They hadn't stayed at their father's grave very long. But they had little reason to do more than offer some flowers and say a prayer or two. She doubted they chatted with the permanent residents the way she did.

Late that night, she'd just settled at her writing table to read more of Amara's stories when an insistent tapping came at her window. She pulled back the shutter and stared into Wallace's eager eyes.

She opened the window. "Wallace? Whatever are you are you doing here?"

He hopped inside. "Close the window."

She obeyed. There was an urgency in his voice that demanded she act quickly.

"Are your doors bolted?"

"I think so."

"Go and see."

Without questioning him, Calista ran downstairs to the front door and then the back. She also made sure all of the shutters were secure. For a moment, she held up her hands. Her fingertips weren't sending her any warnings. What was wrong with that hare?

Back in her room, he waited, his ears pointing straight to the ceiling, alert.

"Tell me what has brought you here like this," she said.

"There's unrest in the village. Talk of witchcraft isn't whispered anymore. It's an open topic, an angry one fed by fear. Old Thomas' family came to the cemetery to put fresh flowers on his grave. That's when it all started."

"What?"

"They found Matilda Pinehurst's name chiseled away and Eleanor's crudely put in its place. They're saying it's the work of witches. Moonwater witches."

"Why do they say someone from the Moonwater family would do something like that?"

"They say it's the beginning of The Vengeance foretold in the old stories."

Calista dropped onto her bed, her hands limp across her thighs. The old stories were full-blown now. They weren't even disguised in the myth of the giant. She could almost feel the fear at work, generating anger, inflaming the villagers to strike out at her and her mother. "What of Simon? He should be encouraging his aunt's confession."

"No one has seen him since early this morning."

A banging at the front door almost stopped her heart. She ran from her room colliding with her mother.

"Calista, what is it?" Miriam clutched her robe around her shoulders, her hair in tangles and her face bleary with sleep.

"I don't know."

The banging started again. This time Simon's voice came through the door. "Calista. Open. Please."

Chapter Thirty

Simon fell into the room as soon as Calista unlatched the door. He closed and bolted it behind him. Perspiration beaded his forehead. He leaned against the wall, gasping for breath, his ashen face the color of Greta's milk.

Miriam took Simon by one arm. Calista grasped his other, shuddering at the sensation of the dreadful pain coursing through him. Between them, they guided the staggering man to the hearth.

"Fetch blankets," Miriam said.

When Calista returned to her room, Wallace was there with his nose twitching, anxiously looking up at her. "Who was at the door?"

"Simon. He's very ill. Deathly ill." She pulled the blankets from her bed.

Wallace hopped to the window ledge. "Let me out. I'll try to gather more news from the village."

Calista opened the window. "Wallace, be careful. I sense danger everywhere."

He hopped off in the direction of the village without answering.

When she got back with the blankets, Simon lay shivering and saliva trickled from the sides of his mouth. Miriam and Calista glanced at each other. They'd shared this moment before on the night her father died.

They covered Simon with the blankets and placed a pillow under his head.

"Stoke the fire," Miriam said. "I'm making some of the healing tea."

Calista stirred the embers under the grate and added more wood. In minutes, the room became warm. Still, Simon shivered and his lips were tinged a life-threatening blue.

Calista knelt next to this giant of a man who had all the symptoms her father had shown. She feared that death would take him as it had taken her father three years ago.

Even now, she heard her father's fist thudding on the door, an echo of minutes ago when Simon arrived. Too weak to lift the latch. Too near death to take the last step inside his cottage without help.

She wiped tears of memory from her eyes. She needed to hold on to the picture she had in her mind of her father's strong back and the sound of his cheerful laughter.

Simon groaned and Calista returned her attention to the present crisis. She cushioned Simon's head on her lap as Miriam came from the kitchen with a steaming mug of healing tea and a spoon. "Lift his head."

Calista cradled Simon's head and held it higher, so her mother could spoon the tea between his lips.

He choked but then swallowed. Miriam's steady hand kept lifting the tea spoonful by spoonful into Simon's mouth. It took a while, but his lips slowly turned a normal color, and soon he swallowed the tea without choking.

How could her mother not believe she was a powerful Moonwater witch? The man stretched out on his back in front of their fire was coming to life, and it was Miriam Moonwater who was making that happen.

Still weak, Simon pushed himself up to sitting and leaned against the leg of the chair. With a low moan, he cradled his head. "I have no explanation for all of that."

They helped him into the chair and Miriam refilled the mug, insisting he finish every drop. "Whatever happened, you barely survived it." She pulled up the rocker to sit near him. "Now, Simon, remember everything that led up to when you first felt ill." She glanced at Calista. "I know what is in your mind, but set that aside and listen carefully."

Calista didn't doubt for a moment that her mother knew her thoughts. If the healing tea could save Simon from what seemed the same affliction, why hadn't it saved her father?

Simon drank the last of the tea and leaned back in the chair. Exhaustion lined his face, but his breathing was regular and his voice strong again.

"I was at the table. For once, my aunt said she felt well enough to cook and share supper with me. While I had no desire to be with the woman, I thought it might be a good time to plant the seed about the altered tombstone. I was going to say I'd visited my father's grave and happened to stop by dear Aunt Matilda's, only to find her name removed. I thought that if I started with the notion of a vandal, then ended with a hint about a ghostly touch on my shoulder, it would sound unplanned and make her nervous enough to confess."

"What are you talking about?" Miriam asked.

Of course, her mother didn't know. Calista had kept so much from her, but she couldn't continue doing that. She knelt next to the rocker and looked up into her mother's face. "I have a great deal to explain."

"More than your promise to help the dead?"

"Just a little more." Calista started by revealing the secret of Matilda Pinehurst all the way to the plan she and Simon concocted to force a confession from her. She even included Wallace.

"Oh my," Miriam said before falling silent, her forehead drawn into lines of worry. "You are indeed a Moonwater witch, and we are in extreme danger. All of us are." She straightened and said, "Did anything you ate or drank taste off tonight, Simon?"

"I didn't eat what she served. I only moved the food around on my plate. The ale was bitter—a cheap brew, I decided—but I was quite thirsty, so I thought nothing of it and drank the entire pint."

"Did you fall ill after you drank?"

"I felt queasy, but nothing too distressing. I'd heard of your remarkable tea, so I thought I'd come begging for some." He smiled and raised the empty cup. "It was as I walked here that I felt the first pains in my stomach."

"I fear you were given poison," Miriam said.

"Poison!" The word exploded from Calista's lips. "Colton Kennewick."

"What about Colton?" Simon asked.

Calista ignored Simon's question. She was staring at the fire, talking to herself. "That day in the square when Colton's hand brushed against mine. Of course."

"Calista, what—"

But Calista was intent on the memory of that day and the images she'd seen, so she wasn't listening to her mother. She got to her feet, pacing. "It made no sense until now. Then, Simon" — she looked at him— "you told me Colton visited your aunt when you were gone. You caught him sneaking from the back door of your house. Somehow, he's in part to blame for what happened to you."

Miriam got to her feet. "If Matilda wanted to kill her sister and later Mr. Pinehurst, what better way to do it than poison? Who'd ever suspect a gentle person like Eleanor Pinehurst of something that horrible? I certainly did not. If I'd known it was Matilda, not her sister in that house, that would have been different. Even as a young girl, Matilda always had an angry red aura about her." She frowned. "I should have noticed. I should have seen who she was, but I wasn't paying attention."

"It's about money, I'm sure of it," Calista said. "Matilda must pay Colton to bring the poison to her and get rid of the empty bottles." When she'd touched Colton's hand on the day of near flogging, she saw him burying a bottle with a skull and crossbones. "Of course." She whirled toward Simon and her mother. "My father. He drank ale with Mr. Pinehurst after their day of work. Father would have only had small sips. He never did drink as much as a full pint." Calista took a deep breath to keep herself as calm as possible and to think clearly. "Matilda didn't plan to kill him, but she did because she put the poison into Mr. Pinehurst's ale, and then he shared that with my father." Calista made her hands into fists. "Eleanor told me, but I didn't make the connection."

"She told you what?" Miriam asked.

"Matilda *gradually* poisoned Mr. Pinehurst because he was growing suspicious of her real identity." Calista's temples throbbed. She closed her eyes and pressed her fingertips to her forehead. "She did it slowly to avoid suspicion, to make it appear as if he had a mysterious ailment."

"And there is the answer to your unspoken question, Calista. Your father was slowly poisoned as well. When he worked at the Pinehurst's he'd drink it in small amounts, so it probably didn't do much more than upset his stomach. It was stored in his body over time until it became so strong even the healing tea couldn't overcome it."

Tears streaked Miriam's face, but when she met her daughter's eyes, there was something else besides sorrow. She brimmed with anger.

That look brought Calista up short. It was a side of her mother she'd rarely seen. There was so much about Miriam Moonwater D'White that Calista didn't know, but she sensed she was about to find out.

"Colton can't buy the poison in Storm Haven. He must go elsewhere," Miriam said. "Tomorrow I'm off to Scrawly Springs. Someone there might sell to him. Simon," —she helped him to his feet— "are you recovered enough to return home?"

"I can manage that." Simon kept Miriam's hands in his and said, "Your tea performed a miracle."

Miriam smiled at him. "It's an old family recipe. I'm grateful for the women who handed their wisdom down. Now, you must act as if nothing happened. Tell Matilda the story about the ghostly hand just as you planned to do."

"It will give me pleasure to see my aunt's shock. I'm sure she thinks I'm dead alongside the road." At the door, Simon glanced back. "I owe you my life. That won't be forgotten."

Calista felt the emptiness of the cottage as soon as he stepped outside. She busied herself gathering her blankets, but her mother stopped her.

"I see you think he's a fine person."

First Wallace and now her mother? "He's very … tall."

"And you, my sweet, are very observant."

Chapter Thirty-One

That next morning it was barely light, but Miriam was already up and dressed when Calista came downstairs.

"I heard you down here. Why are you up so early?" Calista asked.

"Sorry if I woke you, but I want to reach Scrawly Springs by the time the shops are doing business." Miriam pulled on her boots. Then, opening the kitchen door, she said, "Today I mean to track down where Colton bought the poison."

As Miriam led the mule from the barn, Calista walked alongside. There was danger afoot, and with each step, Calista wished she could keep Miriam on the farm. Yet she knew how important it was that her mother find the evidence about Colton's purchase of that poison.

"You'll be home before dusk. Please," Calista said.

"Far before that. Scrawly Springs is a small place, and your father had many friends and relatives there. They will help me." Miriam straddled the mule and then looked down at Calista. "Will you stop looking so worried? I'm not going away forever."

"I'm not worried. Really." And she wasn't. She was much more than worried, but she couldn't describe the feeling. All she knew was she wanted her mother nearby. Calista grasped Miriam's hand.

Miriam looked down. "Stay here until I return. Do not go near that village."

"I won't."

"I love you so much. I'll be back soon with some information that will make Storm Haven a safer and better place."

Once Miriam was out of sight, Calista rushed through caring for the animals. She needed to talk to Wallace and find out what he'd learned on his visit to the village. After she called to him several times and he didn't pop out of his thicket, she gave up, hoping he was just out scouting for news and not in trouble. These days she was always so quick to think the worst, but she had reasons for her fear. That fear doubled with her mother's leaving and now Wallace not being here. Perhaps he'd gone foraging. She stepped through the side cemetery gate.

But before she'd had time to search him out, an agitated ghost intercepted her. This was a new one, and when she looked closely, she recognized the Jones Boy. Even in death, his eyes twitched. Some things must stay with you for an eternity.

"You have to help me!"

Oh, no. Not another beseeching, troubled soul.

"I didn't do it, but he thinks I did, and he won't leave me be."

"I don't understand you. Who won't leave you be?" Calista backed away, but he kept after her.

"The squire." He glanced over his shoulder as if he expected an attack. "I couldn't tell nobody who done it. Nobody'd believe me anyways. It'd only be my word up against the one who done it, you see. And the others might have done me in when I said the truth. I'm in the same danger now because that one's here watching me."

"What a jumble of information. I can't make sense of what you're telling me. Who are 'the others'? What did they do? Who's watching you now?"

She wanted to tell him how ridiculous it was to hear a ghost tell how he feared danger from someone, but that might addle him more. She was of a mind to run home and never come here again, when another ghost, this one far too familiar, burst between them.

"There you are, you scoundrel." The squire's ghostly self shook with the usual anger, but this time his apparition sent sparks in all directions. "Tell me the truth."

"I didn't do it."

"But you were there. You know who did."

"It don't matter. If I tell, he might come for me sure as those others come for you."

Maybe the newly dead hadn't become accustomed to just how safe from harm they really were. That was the only explanation Calista had for the Jones Boy's unlikely fear.

"Preposterous. You're an imbecile. Nobody's coming for you, but I'm out to hunt down the miscreants who took my life. Speak. Now." The squire's ghost looked as if it would splinter into angry bits.

"I only thought they was planning on thieving from you."

"They? There was more than one, then! How many and who were they?" It's impossible to successfully shake a ghost by his jacket collar, but the squire tried. "God's blood. This is intolerable! Tell me their names!"

"Wait, Squire!" She'd have to do something to calm the man down. "If you don't give him a chance to answer, you'll never find out what happened that day."

But it was too late. The Jones Boy had vanished and Mrs. Wilhelm appeared, disheveled and more than upset from the way ghostly filaments spiked around her. "You see what I have to deal with?" she said to Calista.

The squire turned his fury on Calista. "If that boy won't give me the murderers' names, then you must find out who they were."

"Me?"

"Of course, you. You are the only one in Storm Haven who can."

"Oh, that's just lovely. I'm the only one in Storm Haven that everyone hates as well. I can't so much as walk into the village without people thinking how long it has been since they had a good hanging."

"I wish you both would calm down long enough to make some headway in this matter," Mrs. Wilhelm said, her hands out, pleading.

The earth shifted, and Calista steadied herself on the head of Mrs. Wilhelm's sleeping angel. Once again, her fingers tingled. The next jolt came much harder. The squire, who was swishing back and forth above the tombstones, didn't notice either of those things, but Mrs. Wilhelm gasped and pointed toward the old section of the cemetery.

The low stone wall that had surrounded those graves lay in rubble.

Calista let go of the angel. "What's happening?"

Mrs. Wilhelm couldn't turn pale, but she did seem to be close to evaporating. "The Vengeance."

The squire sped away.

Mrs. Wilhelm hovered over her grave, about to vanish.

"Wait! Have you seen Wallace?" Calista wanted to take hold of the woman and keep her there. It was very frustrating dealing with ghosts.

"No. And I assume you're about to challenge the mountain. Be careful, dear. There can be grave danger."

"You keep saying there's danger. Now it's grave danger? What does that…"

But Mrs. Wilhelm was gone.

"Fine. I'll figure out what I have to do on that mountain by myself." She'd done with the cemetery and the ghosts who should have left their earthly problems behind. "I am not coming here again. I am finished with all of you."

She'd come to the rubble that used to be the wall around the old section, and this time the stench brought her to a quick stop. She pinched her nose closed, trying not to be sick. The moss that had only flecked the tombstones now coated them, obliterating the names. Out of each grave oozed a thick, black substance that resembled old blood.

It seeped from the earth and slowly congealed, sending thousands of earthworms wriggling from underground and squirming away. But they were not quick enough. The ooze crept over them. They writhed, but couldn't escape. Their bodies shriveled and disappeared under the blackness.

The tingling in her fingers became small zaps of electricity, discharging under her skin and spreading into her palms. The intensity increased until she stood waving her hands as if to fling hot tar from them. This had to be Amara's way of warning her. Leave at once or be caught in this trap of painful death.

She stopped the scream that rose into her throat and ran, her heart pumping flight into her legs, the image of the writhing earthworms driving her toward the gate and escape. That horrible substance couldn't touch so much as the toe of her boot.

Whatever it was it had to be contained and quickly. Amara's *magyk* was the only way she could think to do that, so she had to find a spell right away. She had to work it and do so correctly.

As she raced around the back side of the cottage, she ran hard into Micah, who stood by the back door. Colton, a rifle over his shoulder and a bloody trap in his hand, stood next to him.

Chapter Thirty-Two

“Well. Well. Well.” With the smile of a coiled snake, Micah grabbed Calista’s arm and pulled her close, flooding her with such a vast reservoir of hate and fear that, if he hadn’t had a firm grip on her, she would have sunk to her knees.

The last time she’d touched him, she’d blocked all of these horrid sensations, but now she let them in. She needed a clue on how to stop him from hurting her. Why else would he be here?

In his touch, she saw her twelve-year-old self about to go into the school house. Micah stepped in front of her and offered her a flower in exchange for a kiss.

“No,” she said. “I don’t want to kiss you. Not ever.”

He dropped the flower and ground it under his boot. Rejection. So much anger. He shoved her aside hard, hurting her shoulder and smiling that same snaky smile he wore now. On his way inside the school house, he looked back at her. “Didn’t want no kiss from you anyways. I was joshing you. Ugly thing like you ought to go hide herself.” This was a memory she’d not clung to, but one Micah had.

She remembered what Farmer Kennewick told her. Micah couldn’t stand rejection, and she’d rejected him. Now she understood why from that time on, he’d hated her.

“What is it you want, Micah? To hurt me for stealing from you? You know I didn’t. I’ve done your father’s favor. Ask your sister. She has the locket from your mother and the scolas the way your father wanted.”

At the mention of his sister, Micah flashed images of jealous confusion. His father had favored Grace who was bright and pretty, a lot like Mrs. Kennewick. He'd ignored his son. Micah had been shunned by his own family, the same way Calista had been shunned by the village. She understood how being ignored and barely tolerated felt, but he'd experienced that from the people who ought to have loved him.

Calista couldn't help feeling sorry for him. Sad images of a young Micah came to her, and for a moment, she was sure he knew what was in her thoughts. He loosened his hold on her, so she spoke quickly while he was off guard. "Right now, I have a serious problem to take care of."

He let her go, and with his release, the flood of all things Micah stopped.

She stepped away, rubbing her arm.

"I'm not here about any of that thieving you done. It's my horse." He pointed toward the barn where the squire's mare stood tethered. "Dumb thing stepped in a rabbit hole and near broke its leg."

Colton held up the bloody trap. "It scared some of them long-eared rats into my traps though. I got me some good eating."

Calista looked away from Colton and the blood-smeared trap. She couldn't bear to think what poor creatures had suffered at his hands. She dreaded that one might have been Wallace. Shoving that thought aside, she went to the horse. She'd seen the mare from a distance at the square that dreadful day, but up close, her condition was worse than she'd thought. Her coat was dull, and each rib distinct. She stood favoring her left front leg which was swollen below the knee. "Poor babe," she said, stroking the slender neck and feeling the pain that radiated through the mare.

"You fix her up so as I can ride her, and I let you go. You can take care of that problem you say you got.

From all the hubbub in the village, I'd say you got a lot more of them problems coming anyways." He grinned.

"What's happening in the village?"

"You'll find out soon enough."

"Very well, but I need time to heal your horse. Leave her with me, and I'll see she's right by next week."

"Next week! No. I got work to do and I need that nag to ride. You heal it now, or I shoot it." Micah took the rifle from Colton. "The renderer'll give me enough to buy me a new one."

Calista stepped between him and the horse. "I'll do what I can. Put that gun away."

"How'd I know you was bluffing?" He shoved a finger at her. "The lie was in your face, that's how."

She didn't bother to answer him because that would only stir him up more. She went into the barn and selected one of the dried bundles of herbs. She could heal the horse with her poultice, but she needed some time for the herbs to take effect, and she didn't have any of that. But if she did have time, the horse's leg would mend and she'd be able to look for something in Amara's book to help with whatever was happening in the cemetery. The only way she could do either was to suspend time. She'd practiced the spell. She'd done it almost right the first time and she'd figured out the encircling part. At the moment, she didn't have another option. Ever since the day she'd collided with Eleanor Pinehurst's twin, she'd had nothing but crises—one after the other. It was time to stop putting out fires and begin preventing them.

Turning her back on Micah and Colton, she pretended to sort the herbs while she repeated the spell. She made sure to mentally encircle everything she wanted to keep outside the stoppage of the clock—the horse, the cottage and the path to the back door. As she worked the spell, she hoped it would also stop the black blood seeping from the graves.

Micah shouted at her. "What you doing in there? You best not be—"

"One. Two. Three. Four." She repeated the count and the breath and kept the moment in her heart. The hush of stopped time settled over her, and when she looked outside, Micah and Colton stood dumb as fence posts, Micah's last words still at his lips.

With the herbs in hand, she headed toward the cottage, pausing to talk to the horse. "I'll make you a poultice. You'll be out of pain quickly."

In the kitchen, she heated water, and while the herbs steeped, she brought Amara's book to the table and searched for anything to do with unstoppable black ooze the color of dead men's blood. But there was nothing. Maybe the only spell she had was the time spell. How long would it hold? When she worked it before, she'd been distracted. She hoped that if she concentrated, the spell wouldn't expire before she at least finished helping that poor horse.

It was difficult to tell if her herbs had steeped long enough when time was suspended, but the aroma of her brew seemed right, so she made the poultice and carried it to the barn. Careful not to touch either Micah or Colton on her way to the horse, Calista slipped between them. She knelt next to the injured leg and gently wrapped the poultice around it.

"You should feel the pain ease shortly," she said.

Although the horse didn't speak to her, she was certain she understood, and when Calista touched the swollen leg, already she could sense that the pain had lessened. "I wish I could keep you here and take care of you."

The horse nudged her.

"I'm sure the squire would be more furious than

usual if he could see you now."

She had no way of knowing how long she sat waiting for the swelling in horse's leg to go down, but when she looked under the poultice, the leg was normal size and the horse could put weight on it again. Still, it would take some time for this poor animal to recover fully, and she wasn't sure Micah, who had the patience and sympathy of a lightning bolt, would wait for the horse to heal completely before riding her.

A small tic of sound alerted her to the change first. Greta's gentle bleat and the stir of air said the spell was ending.

"—messing with me." Micah's gritty voice tore the last bit of silence with the words that had frozen at his lips, and time moved forward.

"I'm not messing with you." She pointed at the horse's leg. "She's almost healed, but you shouldn't ride her yet. Give her some—"

Micah yanked the tether free from the rail. "It's my horse. I'll ride it when I want."

"Fine. But if you wait, the mare will be good for years. If you ride her too soon, she won't be of use to you at all." She gathered up the herbs and the wrappings from the ground, pretending not to care. "Do as you like. As you say, she's your horse."

That must have been the right way to take care of Micah, because he led the horse off without mounting her, Colton at his side. Colton halted long enough to shoulder his rifle and take aim at a song bird.

Calista shouted at their backs, "Let me know how the leg is. She might need more treatment."

That was enough to distract Colton. He missed the shot and the bird flew off.

The horse looked back at her.

"I'll do my best to get you away from Micah," she

said, holding up her hand in a pledge.

The horse seemed to understand and ducked her head. A nod.

Chapter Thirty-Three

Once Micah and Colton became only specks on the road back to the Kennewick farm, Calista returned to her most pressing problem. She had to stop whatever was coming up from those graves. It must not spill onto the rest of the cemetery—or worse— into Wallace's thicket and her farm.

She ran to the cemetery. The ooze hadn't crept to the gate yet, but it had come closer. Even though the snow flurries were light, the air stirred with a promise of a heavier storm. Still, she couldn't postpone this journey any longer. She wound herself inside her shawl, pulled on thick mittens, and struck out with long, sure strides. She was headed to the mountain for help, and she could use a friend at her side, but Wallace wasn't at his nest, and her mother was in Scrawly Springs. She was fairly sure Simon would come if she asked him, but she could only imagine what terrible situation he was facing with his aunt about now. No. She was on her own.

With each step, she felt less certain. Her magic was better. It just wasn't the Moonwater level *magyk*, so when—if—she reached her great-grandmother, all she could do was hope that Amara would accept her and not send her packing or, worse, destroy her. In her head, the words interloper, fraud, failure looped around and around. She hadn't proven herself as a witch yet. If anything, she'd proven she hadn't mastered any of the spells.

She reached the boulder and paused at the fork in the road. To her left was Storm Haven Village. To her right the steep path that led to Vengeance Mountain rose up and vanished into the clouds. Wallace had told her the villagers were in a stir about Eleanor Pinehurst's tombstone and hurling accusations at the Moonwaters. The village was undoubtedly as dangerous as the mountain, so either path she took could mean she'd encounter misery, even death.

A quick glance up at the mist-shrouded summit made her shiver, but she clutched her shawl closer around her neck and started to climb. Now wasn't the time to let fear take charge.

"Witch!"

The screech came from behind her, and she whipped around to face Simon's aunt, her face wild—hatred shooting from her eyes.

Villagers who'd been hidden by the boulder charged from behind it.

Kip Delany, who was in the lead, yelled, "Now we got her."

They advanced toward Calista, some grabbing up stones. Their faces all bore the same twisted darkness.

Two men brandished scythes. Bailey Phelps broke off a tree branch and aimed it at her like a pointed shaft. The women had become Gorgons, those dreadful creatures her father often told of in his tales. She could almost see flailing snakes sprouting from the heads of people she once knew as wives, mothers, and storekeepers.

In her father's stories the goddesses conquered the Gorgons and defeated all of their enemies. His heroines showed no fear and never cowered in the face of danger.

Calista drew herself to her full height and in a voice even she didn't recognize, shouted, "Stay where you are! I am not a witch to play your games with."

There was a brief pause—shock perhaps at the hearing the word witch—then pain radiated from her chest to her shoulder with the sudden impact of a hurled stone. Another struck her on the side of her head, and she dropped to her knees with a warm trickle of blood down her cheek. More pain flared at her chest when another villager hurled something sharp, and she fell onto her back. A roar like a released flood of water filled her ears, and she blinked up at a sky of contorted faces all with mouths of jackals.

"Burn the witch!"

"Hang her!"

Calista struggled to get up, but hands grabbed at her and dragged her to her feet.

"Let me go!" This time her command came like the deep-throated growl of an enraged beast.

Whoever held her left arm released their grip. With her free arm she swung hard and landed a solid fist to Kip Delany's jaw. She jerked her knee up into Mathilda's stomach. The woman flew back into the crowd, toppling three of the villagers at the front. A hush fell over them.

Crouched and ready to spring, Calista fixed her amber eyes on those facing her. The earth trembled, and a warmth flowed through her from the wound in her head to her toes inside her boots.

"Courage."

The villagers clung to each other now. What had been rage, became fear, fear of the unsteady earth rocking underfoot, fear of Calista's fury that spun out from her, fear from the sudden and intense cold dropping from the summit of Vengeance Mountain. All of these conspired to freeze the mob into inaction.

She'd keep them frozen and away from doing her harm just as she'd kept Micah and Colton at bay while she treated the horse. She was about to utter the words when she remembered she could only work this spell three times in a single moon phase. Quickly, she calculated how long the moon had been dark. Three nights. It would be two more nights before the new cycle began, and she'd already worked this spell twice. She tensed her shoulders. What if … what if she needed it up there when she … if she met the witches? Well, she needed it now or she'd never reach her destination.

Slowly. Deliberately. Never unfixing her stare, Calista pressed her right palm against her heart and covered that hand with her other. She inhaled for the count of four and exhaled for the count of four, encircling herself and the path to Vengeance Mountain. Encircling Wallace, wherever he was. And Simon and her mother. They must be free to move through time. She remembered how Amara's words had looked on the page. *Balance. Stillness. Become one with that moment and imagine it staying forever. The stronger your concentration, the longer the spell will hold.*

Her thoughts narrowed with each breath. The widespread horror of the mad villagers in front of her constricted to the pain on the side of her head, and then that vanished, and she held a single focus. One breath. One exhale. And the silence of stopped time descended again, only unlike before, in this instance, it thudded down with a permanence. Nothing she'd frozen in time would return to life until she decided it should. That she knew. She felt a pulse in the center of her chest—*magyk. magyk. magyk.*

Pivoting away from the paralyzed mob, she started up the narrow path. One step after another, each one taking her into colder air, into the mist, into a danger she had no way of understanding, let alone dealing with. Yet, one word repeated like a song inside her mind. *Courage.*

"Have faith in yourself," Mrs. Wilhelm had said.

There was no other choice now, so she marched ahead.

The trail to the summit steepened and narrowed. She'd never climbed this high before, and nothing was familiar. She stumbled in ruts and tripped over tree roots that thrust their way above the snow-packed ground. Visibility became less and less the higher she went, and she slowed to be sure of her footing. She didn't want to misstep and break her leg or twist an ankle as her mother had done. Either accident would bring death. No one knew where she'd gone. No one would look for her until it was too late and she lay frozen on this mountain.

Always tell someone when you start out on a long trek. Those were her father's words. But there had been no one to tell, even if she'd bothered to remember his warning.

In spite of the frigid air, she became thirsty. How stupid to set out on this journey without at least some water. She licked her lips and immediately regretted it. They cracked and ached. She pulled her shawl up to cover her mouth. The warmth of her breath eased the pain, but now her eyes felt like chunks of ice set into her head, and she had a hard time seeing through the thick snow clouds that clustered around her. Blinking didn't help. Since she couldn't see where she was stepping anymore, she slid her boots over the snowy surface, so her progress slowed even more, and she grew colder.

She reached out in front of her, feeling her way, grasping low branches, jamming her numb fingers against boulders. *Go back*, her sensible self urged. *Find another way to deal with the black ooze and the superstitious village filled with hate. Find wise Wallace. Make Mrs. Wilhelm tell what she was holding back about Amara and The Vengeance.*

The tears that pooled at the corner of her eye spilled onto her cheek and froze. "Stop!" She was angry at this show of weakness.

"We can't stop now." The voice came from near her boots.

Shocked, Calista jumped back and tripped on a root. Before she could steady herself, she sat heavily on the snowy ground. "Owww!"

Chapter Thirty-Four

"Wallace!" She didn't know if she should be shaking him with anger because he'd almost stopped her heart, or hugging him in gratitude for being here and being safe.

"I came upon that tableau at the crossroads. They are an extremely ugly group, I must say."

"Where have you been? You are continually a worry, you know."

"It's touching that you worry for me. I was in the village doing a bit of eavesdropping. Very interesting, you humans. I was going from one chattering cluster to another, trying to gauge the mood, when suddenly everything in the village came to a halt. I assume you had something to do with that?"

Calista smiled. "I did." She got to her feet and rubbed her hands together. They were numb inside her mittens, and she was sure they would bear the marks of frost before long. "So what did you hear?"

"Matilda mostly. That woman has the lungs of a wild boar." He drooped an ear. "She accused you of all kinds of things—witchcraft among them, of course, then she managed to have Simon put into the stocks before charging out the square. That was something of a scene. It took four men to wrestle him down and lock him up. I imagine by now he's freed himself. Those stocks weren't made for the likes of him."

"What on earth did she accuse him of?"

"Her attempted death. He had two empty bottles of poison in his pockets." He cocked his head at Calista. "I wonder where those came from?"

Matilda Pinehurst had to be stopped. She was almost as vile as that black ooze in the cemetery. She hoped Simon had broken free. If so, he could escape Storm Haven since she'd encircled him before casting the spell.

"Come. It's time to find Amara and sort out this mess." Calista bent down to Wallace. "Shall I carry you? Your feet must be frightfully cold, and I could use some warmth in my hands."

"That's a perfect solution to both of our problems."

With Wallace cradled against her, Calista set out again. While she was still slow in moving forward, her hands warmed and her confidence increased. Wallace was a great comfort.

She had no way of knowing how long she'd been climbing, except for the increasing weariness across her shoulders and the soreness in her legs. She had to stop several times to rest, but she didn't consider turning back anymore.

After her last rest, she walked only a short distance before stopping again. The change in temperature was subtle, but she was sure the air around her was becoming warmer. How strange. She was still climbing, so it should be getting colder.

She sniffed. The tangy odor of old fire ash was unmistakable. "Do you smell that?"

"Best put me down," Wallace said. "I think we've arrived."

The question was, where? "Now what do I do?"

But the answer came before Wallace touched the ground with all four paws.

The heat became as intense as if someone had suddenly flung open huge doors of a fiery furnace. Calista and Wallace ducked behind a boulder, and even with the thick stone shielding them, Calista broke into a sweat.

"Who trespasses here!" It wasn't a single voice, but a chorus, an angry chorus.

Calista stared down at Wallace. "Mrs. Wilhelm said things like 'grave danger' then she held back telling me what she meant. Now I know why."

"Remember, Calista, these are your ancestors. You didn't harm them, and because you're related to them, you might be the village's next victim. Tell them who you are and remind them you aren't to blame for their horrible deaths."

"Great idea, but how do I do that without being incinerated?"

"Sorry. I'm really not sure, but you best do something, because my whiskers are already singed."

Wallace was right. His whiskers curled at the ends, and when he twitched his nose tiny black flecks drifted away.

Without showing herself, Calista called to the witches. "I'm Calista Moonwater D'White. I need your help." She thought by making the message short, she stood a better chance of them understanding who she was and what she'd come for.

The heat lessened, but nothing more. Should she stand up and let them see her? She was debating what to do when the chorus bellowed again. "Show yourselves."

She didn't think about her reply. "We're afraid of you!"

"And rightly so! But if you're who you say you are, you will not be harmed."

"And Wallace? Will he be safe as well?"

"We will decide that once we see this Wallace." The voices were still loud, but not as ferocious.

Calista rose slowly and crept around the boulder. Wallace hopped at her heels. Ahead of them, flames licked at the sky, and in each one, a woman was caught at its flickering center. All of their eyes were dark with hate and pinned on Wallace and her. The heat was bearable, but Calista knew it could increase in an instant, and they'd both be ash.

The roar of the voices had been terrifying, but now their silence was even worse. Calista was certain they were considering what fate the intruders deserved. She fervently hoped they wouldn't deliver death.

She stood mute with Wallace silent at her feet. When she glanced down, he didn't as much as move an ear. Where was her philosopher, her counselor? She could use some of that "wisdom" about now.

The change in the air was slight, but distinct, and she shifted her eyes away from Wallace and directed them once again at the flaming figures. They swayed, then parted, just as flames would when something non-flammable was thrust into their center.

A tall, slender figure slowly came toward her, and even though the fires licked on either side of this advancing person, there was no rushing or evidence of pain. The woman's hair shimmered blue-black like the feathers of a crow, and when she set her gaze on Calista, it was with amber eyes. They held a mysterious fire of their own. She walked with purpose, like a queen to her coronation. Stately. That's the word that came to Calista. And most certainly, this was a woman of power as well as grace.

When she was within touching distance, she held out her arms. "Calista. My lovely child."

"Are you Amara Moonwater?"

"Of course. I'm the one you seek, am I not?"

A single tear traced down Calista's cheek. She'd discovered Amara Moonwater, the most powerful witch ever, her great-grandmother. And Amara wasn't displeased with her.

Calista stepped into Amara's embrace and gasped at the intense delight she felt. "Oh, I've so wanted to meet you."

"I knew you'd make your way to me eventually. I sensed your power long ago when you were a child, and that power was only a small light of possibility. It made sense that, with time, you'd blossom into your full Moonwater potential." Amara stepped away, but held Calista by the shoulders. Inspecting.

"What are you looking for?"

"Me." Amara smiled. "What I'd hoped to leave behind."

"And?"

Amara nodded. "You are exactly as I wished. Your grandmother, your mother… Well, they chose another way." She released Calista. "No blame, mind you. I understand. Who would want to burn in torturing flames or feel the tightness of the rope choking life from their body? It was wise to walk away from the practice of witchcraft. And they lacked the power."

Calista wouldn't allow anyone to speak against her mother or her grandmother, not even Amara. "No. My mother is a powerful witch. She set that aside—"

"Because she didn't have the talent." Amara waved her hand, dismissing whatever else Calista had to say.

Suddenly angry, the words to defend her mother and grandmother were at her lips when she felt the gentle and furry nudge of Wallace.

"Oh, I can see you're ready to defend Miriam and your grandmother. Don't. That's not necessary. I don't care about them or the path they chose. I only care about you and your path, Calista." Amara leaned down to stare at Wallace. "And you are?"

"Wallace."

"An unusual familiar, but I approve. Cats only draw attention. Hares? Never."

Wallace didn't react to what Calista thought of as a demeaning remark. She was about to come to his defense when he nodded. "Exactly how I see it."

He was ever the diplomat, but she couldn't stop the uneasiness that this exchange was creating. Amara was her great-grandmother, but she had no right to speak against those she loved or insult her best friend.

"I sense your feelings, Calista," Amara said. "Set those aside and hear me." She held out her arms toward Storm Haven. "All of that is about to end."

"What do you mean, 'end'?"

"The Vengeance, my dear. The curse is now broken. Your ancestors have waited for the right living Moonwater witch to arrive and set their wrath free." Amara's grim smile sent shudders through Calista. "You have succeeded. You've freed us to descend the mountain."

"How did I do that?"

"You're here, aren't you? That is what is required, the presence of a powerful living witch like yourself who makes the trek up Vengeance Mountain. Amara smoothed her hair, shifting her glance away as if she didn't want to see Calista's reaction.

"I must seem dense," Calista began, then paused to form her question carefully so there could be no misunderstanding that she needed Amara to speak clearly, "but can you explain this curse so I can understand it perfectly?"

"Of course." Amara cleared her throat, an uncertain sound so unlike one Calista associated with her great-grandmother. "I set this curse in place moments before a horsehair rope brutally dispatched me. Since I was a bit … preoccupied at that moment" —with her hands on her hips, she stared into the sky before leveling her gaze at Calista— "I made a … small error." She held up her thumb and index finger with a tiny space between. "I'd meant to destroy those clustered around me, but—"

"You trapped the Moonwater witches on the mountain and prevented any Storm Haven villager from venturing through this pass. If they did, they died as your ancestors died, in fire." Her great-grandmother had made a very big mistake, and it had rankled for many years. That was plain from her expression.

Amara nodded and looked away. "Right. You have it. Absolutely correct."

"I understand that a mistake like that must—"

"That is in the past." Amara's voice snapped like an abruptly closed door, and then she turned in the direction of the clustered witches. "Now, all they're waiting for is my signal to begin."

"Then what happens?" Calista tried to damp down her fear, but it was quickly overtaking her. She dreaded Amara's answer.

Amara spread her arms wide enough to encompass all of Storm Haven village below. "Fire. Death and destruction."

Chapter Thirty-Five

In spite of the heat generated by the gathered witches, Calista went cold at her center when Amara said "Death and destruction". The words were terrible, but the way her great-grandmother delivered them was apocalyptic.

"What ... what do you mean?" Calista stammered.

"A firestorm like no one has ever seen. Incineration of the detestable remains of our murderers. They're pouring forth from their sinful graves for this moment. You must have seen all that's left of their hideous black hearts coming up from beneath the earth." Amara lifted her chin toward Storm Haven. "That will perish—the village, those farms with their smug houses and predictable fields. Every man, woman, child. The town will be nothing but ashes once I give the signal and unleash the Moonwater witches."

Calista stood stunned at what Amara had just said. It was true. Some of the villagers were cruel. She thought of those she'd frozen in time on her way up the mountain. And, yes, most of the villagers treated her family badly. Mr. Bennet paid her too little for her muffins. The tailor always eyed her with suspicion, and the greengrocer looked away when she stepped into his store. But these people had never struck out at her. They were only merchants trying to make a living, and befriending her might have kept the villagers away from their shops. The magistrate wasn't among those calling for her to suffer because of her name. He was only trying to uphold the law, and when he'd heard her story about Farmer Kennewick's request, he'd ruled fairly. The blacksmith hadn't even wanted to unleash the whip across her back. And what of Simon and Farmer Lakeshire? They shouldn't be held accountable for what their ancestors did. So many children and animals. She gasped, thinking of Greta and Flower. Wallace's thicket. None of them had harmed any of her family. She flinched, thinking of her mother. Calista couldn't bear the thought of harm coming to her.

She shivered. This was what Mrs. Wilhelm didn't want to tell her. By coming here, she'd opened the way for Storm Haven's destruction.

"Courage." The word glided through her like warm spring air, and as soon as it spread into her mind, her shaking stopped, and a calmness settled in her chest. It wasn't Amara who fortified her. That was for certain.

She stood tall, rounding on Amara and the Moonwater witches whose fire flamed with such intensity that she couldn't let them come one bit closer.

"Stop." When she held out her hands, they trembled, but only so she would notice.

"Stand aside, Calista," Amara commanded. "We do not wish you harm, but we want our revenge. Some have waited for centuries. You won't deny any of us now."

"I understand you've been wronged. Terribly. Your lives stolen by ignorant, fearful people."

"Exactly. And now they and all of their spawn will know the pain that the Moonwaters have suffered.

"But your *magyk* isn't about revenge."

Amara drew herself up into an indignant pillar. "You are very wrong, Calista! Our *magyk* has everything to do with it. We were tortured and murdered because we healed the sick when every other healer had failed. Because we prospered even in the harshest of times. Because we were different. We're entitled—"

"No!" Calista's voice thrust through the air like a spear and brought Amara's eyes level with hers. Calista didn't dare falter now. If she broke this intense moment by letting her gaze shift so much as a second, she'd lose. If she failed, then the village and everyone in it ceased to exist—so did the farmers and their fields, their livestock. Her mother would be gone. Her home. She couldn't allow that to happen. "Your *magyk* isn't about destroying life. In your book, you wrote it's about protecting and cherishing it. You said that true *magyk* resides in those two acts. *Harm no one!* That was your first line. You can't destroy everyone and everything in Storm Haven."

Amara remained unmoving, but at her back the color of the flames softened and the heat on Calista's face lessened.

"Protecting and cherishing," Amara's voice was barely audible, and then she stopped speaking.

Calista was sure Amara had heard what she said. Now she hoped her great-grandmother was reconsidering her dreadful decision.

Amara stepped back into the clustered witches who drew around her. Their murmured voices rose and fell, but Calista could only make out a few words.

"Never!"

"But remember…"

"She's right about…"

Wallace looked up at her. "Still, that black ooze is a serious threat. I won't describe what it did to one hapless squirrel."

She didn't need for Wallace to describe what happened. She'd seen the earthworms' futile attempts at escape.

"I fear for my family should it spread beyond the cemetery. We need to know why this ugliness is being released into the world and how to stop it." He pointed an ear at the witches. "They'll know."

Calista knelt next to Wallace and whispered.

"You're right, but I can't risk interrupting them. They no longer seem as sure about destroying all of Storm Haven."

He looked back at the huddle of witches. "I'm trying to remember what my grandfather told me about deliberations. It was something about the longer they took, the more likely it was that those deliberating wouldn't reach agreement."

"If they can't agree, then perhaps they won't take any action. We must let them have as much time as possible, mustn't we?" If only she could use the time suspension spell again. But she couldn't. Before she thought about just how fiery all of these witches could become in an instant, Calista stood and said loudly, "Take your time to decide, but Wallace and I are returning to Storm Haven. If you destroy it, you will also destroy us. I don't advise that because that means there will be no more Moonwater witches."

"Wait!" Amara commanded. "We have decided to give you one day to leave Storm Haven and to alert those you feel deserve mercy. One day, Calista, and then we descend."

"So much for indecision," she said to Wallace.

The witches had returned to talking. Some spoke louder than others. Amara was the loudest.

"They have the time we agreed on. Now I want to discuss other issues my great-granddaughter has raised."

Calista quickly reached down, and with Wallace's consent, she scooped him up. Without turning around, she marched down Vengeance Mountain. She had a day, but since Amara seemed eager to continue their talks, Calista also had a bit of hope. The witches might still choose the right and honorable way of witches. If not, she—along with everyone in their path—would not exist shortly. She'd give others warning, but she had no intention of fleeing her home.

Chapter Thirty-Six

With each step down the mountain, Calista's doubts grew. What was she thinking to challenge Amara? It didn't matter that she was her ancestor. It mattered that no witch had ever been more powerful. While Amara could destroy everything around her with a nod of her head, all Calista might accomplish was a fumbled magic trick. Even though she'd improved, and even though Amara said she possessed true *magyk*, she didn't have full confidence about working spells correctly every time. She grimaced thinking about the tailor's sewing machine and Wallace's sudden flight into her room. She didn't want either of those kinds of *accidents* to happen again, especially now at this critical time.

With a sense of doom pushing at her back, she loped downhill until she came to the fork in the road where she'd frozen the villagers in time. Just outside their grotesque circle, Simon paced.

He'd broken free of the stocks, but she'd been sure he'd do that. What surprised her was how comforted she felt at the sight of him. She had to be truly upset to feel such a need for his presence, but she had no time for those feelings right now.

"Best set me down and deal with Mr. Pinehurst," Wallace said.

"Right." Calista let Wallace hop to the ground. "Simon," she called to him.

Simon whirled, fists clenched, but he relaxed as soon as he saw her. "You! Where have you been?"

"I've been to see the witches." She pointed toward the mountain.

"There are more like you?"

"Many more. I went to ask them to stop the black

ooze in the cemetery, among other things."

"The what?"

There's no time to explain now." She glanced over her shoulder at Vengeance Mountain, almost expecting to see advancing flames in spite of the short reprieve the witches had promised. But the mountain remained, as always, cold and forbidding.

"At least tell me about that remarkable piece of statuary!" Simon pointed at the villagers.

Some held their fixed arms high, ready to hurl stones. Bailey still thrust his pointed tree limb at where she'd stood before casting the spell. Others, including Mrs. Pinehurst, bared their teeth. They all stared at the spot where Calista had been before suspending them and their hatred in place. Such a state to be caught in. Surely they'd be ashamed if they could see themselves.

She sighed. All of that hatred was directed at her, and she'd done nothing to harm any of them. Where did this hate come from? And what could prevent it? What a miserable cycle it set up. Hate. Revenge. More hate. Down here, she'd faced the outraged villagers who wanted witches dead. Up at the summit, she'd faced the witches who wanted the villagers dead. She'd never felt the need for her mother so strongly. Miriam's absence was terribly wrong.

Simon stood waiting for her to explain the frozen villagers.

"I cast a spell to save myself from stoning. They came at me with every intention of killing another Moonwater witch. I had no choice."

When he looked puzzled, she said, "I see there's much you don't know about the Moonwaters and Storm Haven."

"Then you'd best tell me."

"Of course. I'll explain on the way to my

cottage." Calista started away, but halted. "I can't leave them here without defense. I don't care what miserable people they are." She hesitated, knowing that if she released them from the spell, she couldn't corral them again, not for two more days. Another dilemma.

The words came to her again. *Harm no one.*

No. There was no dilemma. There was only one choice. She faced East and held out her arms. The villagers sprang to life, thrashing, hurling stones and babbling in ugly, guttural sounds, which soon fell away and became a drone of confusion. It was obvious they were uncertain about why they'd gathered, who they were prepared to stone, and who they were screaming at.

The sound of several people's footsteps came from behind the boulder, and Mr. Lowery trudged steadily up to Calista. Behind him came the blacksmith and Mr. Bennet, followed by the tailor. The elders came next and Parson Garrison last, huffing and mopping his forehead despite the cold.

Simon crossed his arms, ready to take them on if they'd come to recapture him, but none looked in his direction. Their faces held fear, and all of them darted nervous glances at the mountain.

"We've conferred and decided that the signs are very clear," Mr. Lowery said. "The giant is about to descend."

"No, Mr. Lowery. There is no giant." Calista faced the villagers. "The Moonwater witches of the past are returning."

The villagers drew close, whispering and pointing at the mountain.

"What did she say?"

"Witches!"

"The Moonwater witches?"

The mythical giant was no longer the fearsome

threat. Now the real danger lay before them, and fear replaced all of the hatred on their faces.

"I'm looking for a way to save the village," Calista said.

"Save the village?" Mr. Lowery asked, his voice quaking. "Surely, even they won't do harm to all of Storm Haven."

"I'm afraid that's their intention. They plan to destroy everything with fire just as they were destroyed by your ancestors. You have one day to leave, then they're coming."

A collective gasp escaped from those gathered. Bailey threw down his tree limb and ran. Others followed him toward the village. She guessed they were off to gather whatever they could before fleeing to safety.

The blacksmith shifted his gaze up to the peak, and then he looked back over his shoulder. He seemed to be thinking of how he'd escape. Pastor Garrison clasped his hands in prayer, and the tailor fumbled with the tape hanging around his neck, his fingers shaking.

"I can't promise I'll succeed in stopping them," Calista said.

"You can only try, and we are grateful for that," Mr. Lowery said.

Today the magistrate had a noble look about him. He was taking on the challenge of a leader and even though he might not succeed, Calista was pleased at his quiet determination and the touch of bravery in his eyes. He wouldn't be one to pack up and flee.

"Mr. Lowery, you must return to the village and tell everyone about the Moonwater witches—that they were never evil women to be feared. Tell them that what their ancestors did was terribly wrong. I'll try to steer their revenge to where it belongs—the old section of the cemetery. I'm going there now."

From his face, she knew she'd been right. He'd heard about the unjust and violent deeds of old Storm Haven.

"I was a young boy when my father told me what happened. I thought it was a fantasy, something like the fairy tales in our storybooks." He swiped his hands over his eyes as if he wished he could wipe away the images of what his father had told him. "I'll tell the villagers what I know."

Simon's aunt was slowly backing away when Simon shouted, "Matilda!"

She made a grave error when she responded to her real name and faced her nephew. All eyes turned on her, and Matilda searched for a way to slip off, but Simon didn't let her escape. "Admit to these friends of yours how you poisoned my mother and tried to poison me. I never dropped that deadly concoction into your food, now did I?"

Matilda shriveled like a salted snail, and sputtered a denial, but it was barely audible even in the hush.

Some of the villagers who were still there stepped away from her, but others seemed ready to defend her.

"She isn't the real Mrs. Pinehurst, and we'll prove it to you." Calista pointed at the villagers. "She should be in custody until we can hold a trial, Mr. Lowery."

Even as shaken as he clearly was, the magistrate didn't let panic keep him from his duty. He took Matilda firmly by the arm. The blacksmith took the other.

"Come," he said, "Until we have all of the facts, she can wait in the village jail."

"No," Matilda screamed. "I don't want to be locked away. I want to escape this wretched place!"

Mr. Lowery and the blacksmith strode off with Matilda, tugging and protesting, in tow. The remaining villagers trooped after him.

Once they'd started down the road, Calista caught the words, giant, myth, witches, and revenge. Confused and fearful voices picked up that last word.

"Revenge for what?"

"What have we done?"

Mr. Lowery silenced them. "Listen, all of you. These are the old stories you must hear." He began telling them about the Moonwater witches, and the suddenly mute villagers followed him and listened.

Chapter Thirty-Seven

Mr. Lowery's voice faded in the distance, and Calista felt a great measure of sadness. The villagers hadn't known about the murders before today. All they'd ever known was some vague superstition about a giant. The only crime they were guilty of was ignorance of their history. She had to convince her ancestors that their revenge had to be directed only at those who'd lit the fires and tightened the noose.

"Well done," Wallace said.

"For the moment, but there is still much we have ahead of us." Calista struck off toward home with Wallace leaping along on one side and Simon matching her strides on the other.

"So now you have to tell me about this black ooze and those true stories of early Storm Haven," he said.

As they walked, she described the horror of the old section of the cemetery and then explained the history of the Moonwaters.

Simon shook his head. "I'm afraid my family was part of all that, but I never knew. My mother and father only told me I should avoid the cottage by the cemetery because the people were very" —he fell silent, searching for a word — "different."

"At least they tried for a kind way of putting it. Or did you substitute 'different' for another word?"

"I don't remember, Calista. I was young."

He was very clever at dodging the truth, but she'd let the matter drop.

"Once we reach your cottage, do you have a plan for saving Storm Haven and everyone in it? I suppose that includes us."

Without breaking her stride, she looked up at him.

"I have no plan whatsoever."

"That is truly not what I wanted to hear."

When they came to the cottage, Calista hoped to find her mother already returned from Scrawly Springs, but when she looked inside, the kitchen stove was cold and the rooms silent and empty.

"I'm off to see if my family's safe and if that black ooze has made inroads into our home," Wallace said.

"Of course." Calista knelt and touched him. "If it has spread this direction, please come back here at once," she said. "Bring your family. We're on a little higher ground, and being here may keep them safe until I have time to sort this out."

As Wallace disappeared around the side of the cottage, worry crushed her heart. Her mother gone. Wallace was off to face a terrible danger.

Once inside the kitchen, she shivered, rubbing her hands over her arms, but the chill came from inside. It had nothing to do with how cold the house was.

"I'll get us some warmth." Simon gathered kindling and set a fire inside the stove while Calista brought Amara's book to the table. "I only hope my great-grandmother has left me help for this situation." She thumbed quickly through the familiar pages until she came to ones she hadn't yet read.

So many stories were about ailing animals and failed harvests. Spells hidden within these wouldn't help. A few pages later, she read:

"The first to fall ill was old Murphy from down by the bog. His eyes yellowed to the color of a black cat's and his skin grayed, so that before he departed Storm Haven forever, he looked more like a regenerated corpse than the powerful man we'd all known as Bog Man Murphy. Next to fall into the clutches of this unknown ailment, was…"

Calista swept her fingers across the lines and brought forth the hidden spell. Quarantining A Dread Disease. She sat back in the chair. Would the black ooze qualify as a dread disease? If it did, maybe quarantining it would be the same as sealing it off from the rest of the cemetery and keeping it inside the gate to their farm. It couldn't hurt to try because she had nothing else.

"What's that?" Simon asked, looking over her shoulder while stoking the kindling into a blaze.

"I hope it's the spell that will stop the advance of that horrid menace in the cemetery."

"Then I say you'd best get on with finding out." He busied himself snapping more sticks in two and feeding them into the fire.

For a moment, Calista watched him, focused on his task. What sort of man was this? Strong. Yes. Yet vulnerable. She'd seen him within reach of death's grasp. But mostly he was surprising. He not only accepted her for who she was, he encouraged her to use the powers she possessed. He even understood Wallace, and when he'd told her why he avoided her as a young man, he'd sounded ashamed. Shame was something she hadn't expected from him. Still, she'd seen what his past was like, and she didn't want any of that in her life.

Absolutely never.

She returned her attention to the book, and read the first line of the spell. *You must use a fist-full of salt.* They had salt and certainly a fist-full. She looked up. "Simon, please hand me the large white sack in the top cupboard." *Spread it evenly on a level surface.* She opened the top of the sack after he'd handed it to her, reached inside, and with the grains cupped in her hand, sprinkled them onto the table. *Draw an unbroken line from end to end while saying, "Salted line across this face, keep the threat in safest place."* With one finger, she made the line and repeated the words, and she then stepped back. Unlike the other spells she'd worked, nothing unexpected happened. The only way she'd know if she'd cast a successful spell was to go and see.

She made for the back door. "I'm off to find out if I've corralled whatever is coming up from those graves."

"I'm coming with you." Simon set the heavy lid of the stove into place with a clank.

She stopped with her hand on the latch. She always associated the clank of that lid with her mother busy at the stove. The twinge of worry about her mother was there again, only stronger. Something had been troubling Calista about her mother's absence from the moment she'd ridden off. Since her encounter with Amara and the other Moonwater witches, she'd grown more and more certain that she and her mother must be together. She wished she understood what was brewing inside her. She'd never felt the absence of her mother as severely. She'd worried if she was late, and panicked when she hadn't returned from the village the night she'd twisted her ankle, but this was more than panic. This was an urgency stemming from something she couldn't identify.

Simon placed his hands against the door on either side of her head and looked down at her. Worry etched his face. "I know you are more than capable of taking care of yourself, Calista, but from what you've described, you're up against something that even you might not manage on your own."

He was frighteningly close, but thank goodness he wasn't touching her. She couldn't think when he did that. "You may be right, but I'm the only one here at the moment who can at least try to stop this disaster." She ducked under his arms and unlatched the door, letting the chilled air sweep into the kitchen. He followed her, and on her way down the step, she said, "But I do need your help." She made straight toward the cemetery with Simon at her side.

"Anything."

"My mother's still off in Scrawly Springs and I need her to return home right away."

"I'll fetch my horse and be off as soon as I can." He caught her arm and brought her to a halt. Tipping her chin up, he came so close his breath warmed her lips. "Be careful. You have become very important to me."

She stepped away, and then shocked by what had just happened—mostly by the feeling of his warmth—she backed toward the cemetery. Stumbling on a root, she did a quick turnabout, then she made her way around the side of the cottage.

Instead of being upset, she should be grateful. He was helping her when she needed it most. What had Wallace told Simon? *You've come to Storm Haven at the proper time to do justice and help Calista.* But that's all he'll do, she vowed. Once this is done, he must return to his life and I must return to mine.

The thicket came into view, and for a moment she hesitated. Colton stood in the middle of Wallace's home, the muzzle of his gun pointed at her hare's nesting place. To the side, Micah sat on the squire's horse, the mare's eyes wide with fear and her head straining to be free from Micah's control.

Behind them, the black ooze lapped at the cemetery gate. Already the iron bars bowed from the pressure, but something—she hoped it had been her quarantine spell—was keeping it from spilling through the open spaces and across Wallace's thicket.

She clenched her fists and marched toward Colton, determined to get rid of his threat to her friend once and for all.

Chapter Thirty-Eight

Colton shifted his attention from Wallace's home to Calista, who charged straight at him.

"Put that gun away, Colton, and get out of here while you can." Calista pointed toward the cemetery. "The horse has more sense than either of you. She knows how dangerous that wretched matter is. If it breaks through the gate, it will destroy everything in its path."

Colton glanced toward the gate. "It don't look like more than a little upset tar to me. Witch tar most likely. And it don't seem like it's coming through now, does it?"

"Not yet, but I can't promise it won't." Calista put herself between Colton and Wallace's nest. "Leave."

"Not until I get what I been hankering for. I spotted that gray rabbit diving in there," — he pointed at the bush that hid Wallace from view— "and I aim to have it in my bowl tonight."

The mare neighed and pranced, kicking up chunks of dirt. Micah yanked on the reins, and she reared, pawing the air. "Stupid dang thing!"

She wished the squire could see what was happening to his prized horse. He'd take care of Micah in very short order. She was sure of that.

A cold shaft of wind swept down on them. The horse reared again, this time throwing Micah to the ground. "That's it!" Micah shouted. "Colton, forget that danged rabbit and shoot this thing. It's nothing but trouble to me."

A tight slit of a smile spread across Colton's face. He cocked his rifle, put it to his shoulder and aimed at the squire's horse.

"No!"

Colton shoved her aside. She stumbled back and

sat hard on the ground. How could she call herself a witch if she couldn't find a way to disarm this monster? She looked on, angry at being helpless and remorseful for not having the talent to do what a Moonwater witch should be able to do—cast a spell of her own without resorting to a book. Now she understood so much about her mother, how she must have felt this same helplessness and remorse many, many times.

She thought of the squire and how beautifully he once sat astride this horse's back. Both so elegant. That cold shaft of air stung her face again, and she felt the same chill as when she encountered the cemetery ghosts. She searched around her, but no spirits appeared. Still, one of them had to be here. It was icing her to the core. Even Colton shook with cold and couldn't keep the rifle steady.

She might not have a spell at the ready, but she had herself. Taking advantage of the small distraction, Calista ran at Colton, shouldering him aside at the moment the gun discharged. The gun shot into the air and across the cemetery wall. The horse galloped off and Calista sat back on her heels, suddenly drained.

Micah advanced on her. "You stupid witch! I'll track that horse and shoot it myself."

Calista had a lot to say to Micah about being stupid, but watching him trudge off with that wretched Colton she kept her mouth sealed. She wanted them gone, so she could concentrate on the task in front of her. The horse had a good head start and somehow Calista knew that mare wasn't about to let Micah or Colton track her down.

The black ooze still pressed up against the gate, and the bars were more bowed than when she'd first arrived. She couldn't possibly enter here, so she went to the front of the cemetery and swung open the main gate that faced the road. She glanced up at the iron lettering that arched overhead, Storm Haven Cemetery Welcome Forever.

On her way inside, she ran straight into the irate ghost of Squire Nielsen.

"Isabelle!"

"Who?"

"My horse! I saw how that brute treated her. I saw her condition."

"You were in the thicket just now?"

"Of course I was! You told me what was happening. You needed to tell me to throttle that monster, but you didn't. I was helpless."

That stopped her. She hadn't sent a message to him. She did think of him. She did picture him astride the mare. Perhaps just the thought was enough to call him.

"I want that cruelty stopped immediately!"

"You're shouting at me, Squire Nielsen, and I really don't need that at the moment. I have a great deal to manage, and all of it is urgent." She drew a deep breath. "However, I understand how you feel. I care deeply for your horse. For Isabelle. And I will try to rescue her from Micah. But right now, I'm extremely concerned about the old section of the cemetery. Have you seen—"

"Of course I have. Every one of us has. That mass of wretched creatures has made inroads into our part of the cemetery, but fortunately, something has halted its progress."

Me, Calista thought. *I think my line in the salt did it. Draw a line and stand firm.* She set her jaw. *And then cross all of your fingers.*

"Calista. I'm so relieved to see you." Mrs. Wilhelm appeared at her side. "Forgive me."

"For?"

"For concealing the great danger you'd unleash. But you see I didn't want to discourage you, and I hoped when the witches met you, you'd remind them of the true magical heritage they passed on to you." Mrs. Wilhelm shook her head. "I understand that didn't happen and they're descending the mountain bent on wiping Storm Haven from this earth." She knotted her fingers together. "Very, very sad."

The squire came so close to Calista that she felt ice crystals form on her eyebrows. "Before the witches arrive, I want to know who murdered me. It's the least you can do."

"Why is it always me, Squire Nielsen? Don't you think I've done enough for people who treated me and my family like outcasts?"

"I did not."

"Perhaps, but you did nothing to make the Moonwater D'Whites accepted, did you? And your very noble ancestors seemed to have turned suddenly blind while your villagers murdered my ancestors. Your grandfather was alive when they hung my great-grandmother. Why didn't he stop that?" In spite of the cold, she leaned into him and he backed up.

"My apologies," the squire said.

"Oh, very nice, indeed. Apologies aren't enough anymore, Squire. I'd like some of that justice for *my* family."

"Please!" Mrs. Wilhelm shouted so loudly that the squire and Calista fell quickly silent. "Thank you. Now let's set to work to bring justice to everyone in Storm Haven, shall we? No partiality. Only fairness. And as fast as possible. Storm Haven should be free of as much guilt as possible before it ceases to exist."

Mrs. Wilhelm always worked on being fair, so Calista decided to do the same. She hoped that there was still time to stop the witches from carrying out their plan, but if not, then as many wrongs as possible should be made right.

"I'll do what I can to see justice come to as many in this cemetery as I can."

From behind her, Wallace said, "That is all that anyone could expect. Well done."

"Wallace! I'm so glad to see you, but really, you must stop creeping up on me. You set me on edge with your sudden appearances."

The hare didn't answer, but she was sure he smiled. She was beginning to think he appeared like this for the very purpose of keeping her alert.

Wallace bent an ear toward an approaching ghost.

The Jones Boy flew toward her, wringing his hands. He halted and held them out, pleading. "I heard about it, Calista. The witches coming. Before they comes down the mountain to take Storm Haven away, I got to ease my mind by telling what really happened that day."

"About the squire's murder?" she asked.

"Yes. I, uh … I," he stammered.

The squire advanced, but Mrs. Wilhelm stepped in. "Wait. Let him speak."

"Like I said, I were there. In the wood," Luther said in a sudden explosion of words. "But before I say what I know, I want to tell you why I was there."

"Get on with it!" the squire shouted.

"It were Colton who tricked me into meeting up with them that day. He said he had a job for me, and when I got there, he told me what he wanted. I said no. I didn't want nothing to do with a nasty job like that one. He says if I help him just one time, he'll let me be. He'll let me learn my baking trade, and he won't never trouble me again. If I don't, he'll fix it so I lose my place at the bakery and can't get work anywheres else in Stone

Haven." He looked around as if he expected someone to jump out at him.

"So you helped him." Calista didn't want him to stop telling the story now. She glanced over her shoulder to check the advance of the black ooze. It was creeping forward, but its progress was barely perceptible.

He nodded, still darting his eyes to different places in the cemetery. "When I met up with Colton, Micah were there, too. And that's the first I hear about them set on stealing the squire's horse." Luther looked up at the squire. "Sorry to say, but Micah hated you for courting Miss Selena."

"Selena Wakefield?" Calista asked.

The squire crossed his arms, fuming but quiet.

Luther swiped his nose with the back of his arm and sniffed. "All I was supposed to do was spook the squire's horse."

"All you were supposed to do?" The squire lunged. He swung his arm, and his fist went through what once was Luther Jones's chest and out the other side. "Damn!"

That blow didn't satisfy the squire, and it didn't much bother Luther.

"But he didn't say he was set to kill you. 'I mean to take his horse, so as he won't have Selena and that fine mare, too.' That's what he says to me. I should have knowed killing was part of it because everybody in the village would spot that horse straight off. But, you see, I was scared and not thinking like I should."

"Micah killed the squire?" Now, Calista was impatient for the answer.

"No." Luther darted his eyes even faster around the gathered ghosts and dropped his voice to a whisper. "I spooked the horse. I did. And I tried to get out of there, but Colton, he grabbed me, you see on account of…"

Farmer Kennewick's ghost settled next to Calista.

"On account of…" Luther stammered again and then stopped.

The squire burst into particles like an exploding firecracker, but he quickly collected himself. "Out with it!"

Luther seemed to be pleading for help, then he began again. "They weren't done with me yet. After the squire … well, they had more on their minds about me doing things for them." He blinked as if he fought back tears. "Colton lied. You know about leaving me be at Mr. Bennet's bakery. He never meant to. And once I done that to the squire, the two of them, him and Micah, were out to make me do more that was bad. If I didn't do what they said, they were telling the magistrate they seen me kill the squire."

"What bad things did they plan?" Calista asked.

"They tell me to leave the back door to the bakery unlocked. They have plans for thieving from Mr. Bennet. Then they have plans to take money from all the tills in Storm Haven, and I'm supposed to help by doing whatever they tell me."

"You are an idiot! Get to the point!" the squire yelled. "Who killed me?"

Farmer Kennewick stepped forward and Luther shrank behind a tombstone.

"It was me."

All eyes turned on Farmer Kennewick's ghost. "I done the killing, but on accident. I knew Micah and Colton were up to no good, and I knew it was Colton that was leading my boy into bad trouble. I decided to put an end to him ruining my boy more than he already done. I took my rifle and followed them into the woods. I heard the plan. I seen what happened. My shot was meant for Colton, but when that horse spooked and reared, it put the squire dead center where I'd aimed."

The misery in his voice silenced everyone.

"I hightailed it out of there that day and was heading for the magistrate to confess my crime, but I never got to the village. My heart seized up on me, and I died with this on my conscience. This and how I'd treated my two children." He looked at Calista. "You've helped me ease some of the pain, but you'll never take away the pain I have about Micah. He might've been a better man if I'd been a better father."

"So how do I get justice when you're already dead?" The squire thought a moment before thrusting his face at Calista. "You!"

Calista stepped back, but when the ghost lunged another step closer, she held her ground. "Not again!"

"You must figure out a way to get me justice. Micah and Colton didn't kill me, but if they hadn't ambushed me, he" —the squire pointed at Farmer Kennewick— "wouldn't have accidentally shot me."

Calista's first thought was to tell the squire he could get his own justice for a change. Then she remembered how it felt to deliver the farewell note to Minnie's husband and hand Grace Kennewick her mother's locket and the scolas her father had secreted away for her. She remembered how it felt to ease Ida Lakeshire's mind about her diary. And when Simon's aunt was led away to face a fair court, that had been gratifying. It was all about setting things to rights, and that put her own mind at ease.

She lifted her gaze to the squire. "Yes. I'll do exactly that."

The look on his face shifted from angry to grateful. Once all of the anger vanished, he stepped away, and with a stricken look, said, "I loved Selena very much, and she me. We planned to wed."

The sorrow in his voice touched Calista. No wonder Selena had left the village after the squire's death. Poor Selena. Poor Squire Nielsen.

Calista reached out to touch him, and the sadness that seeped into her hand made her heart ache for the two of them even more. She sought out Luther Jones behind the tombstone. "And what about your story? If we're meting out justice, I want you to have your measure as well."

Luther's voice came soft and sad. "I'm here now on account of Micah."

"Micah killed you?" Calista faced him.

"He didn't aim to." Luther shook his head, a dejected slump rounding his shoulders. "I didn't think Micah would do me harm. We was friends once, but he turned real dark after Selena left. When I told him he shouldn't ought to go along with Colton's plans to take money from all the stores in the village, he shoved me hard. I know it were an accident how I hit my head on that rock, but it weren't an accident about the shoving."

Calista had heard enough. "I have just one day, but I'll see that everyone in the village knows what Micah and Colton have done. If there's time, I'll demand that the elders try them in an open court." She took a breath, before saying, "And, Squire, if I can save the village, I'll save Isabelle and bring her back to health."

Again, she waited, considering what she was about to do before she said what would bind her to these words.

"I promise."

Chapter Thirty-Nine

The squire finally had his answer. His death had been an unfortunate accident caused by two would-be thieves, the bullied Luther Jones, and a distraught father. And poor Farmer Kennewick had relieved more of his guilt.

Calista struck out toward the main gate of the cemetery with Wallace in the lead. On their way, many silent but very worried-looking ghosts intercepted them.

"Can you keep that evil from pouring over our graves?" Mrs. Lakeshire's wispy bird-like voice was almost lost under Squire Nielsen's bluster.

"You must stop that horror from advancing," he said, stepping between them and the exit. "It will take away any trace of who we once were."

"I'm doing my best, Squire. But I have the witches to attend to as well."

She and Wallace started for the gate again when Mrs. Eleanor Pinehurst thrust a vague hand into her path, bringing Calista to a halt.

"If that spills over our markers, even the one I hate will be destroyed. I'd rather have a poorly chiseled gravestone than none at all."

"I understand, and I'm on my way to make sure your sister is punished for what she did. I'm sure Simon will do his best to have your name beautifully carved into a new stone." Even while Calista made her promises, she feared that there wouldn't be time to keep them.

She looked up at Vengeance Mountain, hoping to see the usual cloudy shroud covering its peak. Instead, the mountain top was in flames.

They'd promised her a day! How dare they break that promise. Instead of a day she didn't seem to have but minutes. Her ancestors had to at least give the people time to flee and her time to finish this business of bringing justice to her village.

"Wallace! We must hurry."

She wrenched open the gate, and they ran. Already the cold winter day felt like the beginning of summer. The temperature rose with each long-legged leap she made. Out of breath, she drew up short, panting. "Wallace. Go home. Take your family and leave."

Wallace rose to his tallest measure. "Now is not the time to abandon duty. I've left instructions with everyone in the thicket. They all know what to do whether the danger comes from the black ooze or the fiery mountain."

Calista reached down and touched his small but sturdy back. "Then it is up to us."

"Indeed, but something or someone's coming our way." He perked up one ear and looked down the road toward the way they'd just come. "Listen."

It was faint at first, but then the unmistakable sound of hoof beats became clear. Wallace was right. Someone was riding toward them. It could be Micah on Isabelle. Or Colton out to do more harm.

She stood her ground. Whoever was coming at them would not catch her with her back turned. In the distance, she made out the vague shadows of a large and powerful horse, riding ahead of a smaller animal. Big ears. Stocky legs.

In only a few moments, Simon's tall figure mounted on his impressive stallion became clear. Coming quickly behind him was Flower and the most welcome sight—her mother on Flower's broad back.

Calista ran toward them, relief spreading throughout her.

Miriam drew Flower to a halt and leapt down. She

gathered Calista to her and held her. “Simon made my return sound very urgent. Are you all right?”

“Yes, but I needed you here.”

“And here I am.” Her mother hugged her closer before stepping away and taking a paper from her satchel. “I have proof from the apothecary in Scrawly Springs that Colton bought the poison. He said it was for rats, but it won’t be hard to prove he handed it to Matilda.” She glanced up, her eyes reflecting the advancing flames. “Is that what I think it is?”

“I’m afraid so,” Calista said.

“Simon explained what the Moonwater witches have in mind.” Miriam took a wide stance and faced the mountain. “How dare they.”

There was a fierceness about her mother, the same fierceness Calista had seen lately when something threatened their safety.

Simon, who’d held back until they’d had a moment together, now came to them. “I was hoping by this time that you’d have a plan, Calista. How’s that coming along?”

“Slowly.” She shook her head. “No. Not at all, I’m afraid.”

“Good plans do take time,” Wallace said.

Simon glanced down at Wallace and nodded. “Very true. So since it seems we might not have a lot of time” —he stared up at the mountain— “I want to help. Tell me what you need me to do.”

For a rogue and a thief, he was disturbingly gallant. And Calista wished she knew the answer to his question.

Then suddenly she did. “Take the proof of your aunt’s guilt to the magistrate. If justice must be done quickly before those Moonwaters mete out their own, then that will be one more wrong made right.”

“That’s excellent. Step one in a plan,” Wallace said. Calista couldn’t have a better familiar than this hare.

While this didn’t solve the problem they faced with the witches, it might mean that Eleanor Pinehurst would find peace for a brief time. It also meant that she’d carried out another promise, and doing that had become very important to her.

Once again, Simon looked up at the mountain, lines of worry creasing his face. “That’s a very large fire.”

It had grown, but it had stopped moving down the mountain toward them. The witches must still be in heavy debate over their course of action. That had to be why they advanced, then hesitated so frequently.

“Calista, please. Come with me. You, your mother, Wallace. We must try to escape.”

She shook her head. “I can’t. It’s wrong to run away and leave the innocent without trying everything to change the witches’ minds.”

He looked down at her. “You can’t go up against that and survive.”

The fire seemed to singe the clouds.

Miriam handed the sworn testimony of the apothecary to him and drew Calista to her. “Simon, you carry the evidence to the magistrate. I will stay with Calista. Together we can survive anything.”

Her mother’s words comforted Calista and bolstered her confidence. “Please go, Simon. Let my mother and me do what we can—what we must.”

He brushed her cheek with his finger. “You always amaze me,” he said, quickly mounting his horse. “I’ll deliver the proof right now.” With one last look back at Calista, he galloped toward the village.

Miriam turned Flower toward home. “Go girl,” she said, sending the mule to the barn. Then Calista and

Miriam, still clasping hands, faced the mountain and climbed as quickly as they could toward the flames. They rushed to confront the witches and hopefully save their village.

Wallace raced to keep up with them.

"*Courage.*" That familiar feeling of someone being at her core to encourage and support her was there again. "*Courage.*" The second time the feeling was so strong inside her that Calista was sure her mother sensed it.

Breathless from the climb, Calista gasped. "Did you feel that?"

Her mother gripped her hand, and her own fingers went from tingling to pulsing at the tips.

"I felt something," her mother said, smiling. "Love."

Of course. What else could be so powerful as to still her heart when she was panicked or keep her moving ahead when fear gripped her and threatened to stop her. Silently, she thanked whatever or whoever came when she needed that courage the most.

"Look," her mother said.

The fire had come much closer now. The witches, each a flaming torch, came steadily on, Amara in the lead. Her determined stride was so like Calista's that Calista imagined it might be herself coming down that mountain toward her. She and Amara were much alike, yet Calista knew she'd never deliberately destroy anyone or anything. That was where their similarity ended.

Soon the heat grew so intense that Calista and Miriam had to cover their faces with their arms.

Wallace took shelter behind them.

When the witches stood within a few feet, Calista shouted, "Stop! You said we had a day. Are you not keeping your word now? Isn't the word of a Moonwater witch good anymore?"

The intensity of the heat lessened and a moment later Amara stepped away from the cluster of flames. "Miriam." She held out her arms, but Miriam didn't respond.

"You fear me?" Amara asked.

"No. I fear for you and for all Moonwater witches," Miriam answered.

"I'm beyond being harmed by anything or anyone, Miriam, but say what is in your mind." Amara cocked her head, listening.

"You, of all the Moonwaters, should know what you're planning is wrong. Our family was never vengeful. We forgave and set ourselves free from the heavy burden that revenge imposes. If you allow this indiscriminate destruction, you will break the ancient vow that has bound us as advocates to protect life all these centuries. That will damn you and every witch standing behind you. That is why I fear for you."

"Let me—"

Calista interrupted Amara. "You are wrong in wanting to burn Storm Haven. And you're about to destroy the last of the Moonwater descendants."

Amara opened her mouth, but again Calista stopped her. "You're the only one who can guide the rest onto the right path. You're the most powerful of all the Moonwater witches."

"Very nice of you to say so, my dear, but—"

"Didn't they hear anything I said when Wallace and I came to you?"

"If you'd only listen—"

"Punish those who were guilty of your murders and whose grim remains now threaten to engulf the innocent," Miriam pleaded.

"To remove every trace of their existence will be

the very worst punishment anyone could mete out to the blameless." Calista's voice was filled with urgency. "No record of their lives—good or bad? No stones that mark their remains?"

Amara shook her head. "I wish you both would stop interfering—"

"We won't stop interfering. Not until you and the other Moonwaters remember your true *magyk,*" Calista said.

She reached for her mother's hand, and when she did, the familiar tingling Calista had felt so often surged between them. That feeling grew, until a white heat flashed up Calista's arms and into her chest. Her mother's face mirrored what she felt. Holding up their clasped hands, they looked at each other.

"You are filled with such *magyk*, my sweet," her mother said.

The stir of *magyk*. That's what that tingling in her hands had been all along. That was what had grown in intensity since she'd delivered that note to Farmer Lakeshire. It hadn't been Amara's warnings at all. And now, her mother's *magyk* had broken free after all these years from the restraints she'd used to keep her family safe. Together, they'd tapped into something very powerful. Now Calista understood why she'd needed her mother at her side today more than any other time in her life.

"Do we allow these witches to destroy Storm Haven? What do you say, Calista?"

"I say we stop them."

"Agreed."

The question was how. Calista had no spell to call on. All she had was a fierce determination to keep the witches from making a horrible choice. But she had her mother, whose hand was still clenched in hers, pulsing with an energy that continued to grow.

"Please stop all of this nonsense," Amara said.

As Calista gripped Miriam's hand more firmly, darkly bloated clouds swooped overhead, blotting out the light, and in the next moment, those clouds released a torrent of rain.

This was the kind of rain that brought mud sliding into Storm Haven. It was the kind that filled the creek to overflowing and flooded the fields. Calista's clothes grew heavy with water. Her hair became plastered against her head and her cheeks. Drops slid down her forehead and dripped from the end of her nose. Her mother looked as if she'd stood under a waterfall. And poor Wallace. Nothing was nearly as miserable looking as a soaked hare.

When the deluge stopped, only Amara stood before them.

Calista was certain her great-grandmother was about to unleash a punishing spell on them. How shocked she was when Amara tipped back her head and laughed.

Wallace poked his nose out from behind their feet.

"Well. Well. Well," Amara said. "It seems I underestimated the both of you. That was something of a spectacle." Amara brushed wet curls from her forehead.

"The others. Where are they?" Calista hadn't wanted to destroy them.

"I would imagine they're off to dry themselves. They're not used to being drenched, you know." Amara didn't sound angry. "Come." She held her arms open. "I need to hold you to me again."

"Only if you promise—"

"Calista, stop. I'll do what I believe is right. You will not bargain with me. Do you understand?" She folded her arms over her chest, closing off the welcoming embrace.

“Then what have you decided is right?” Miriam asked.

Amara took her time before answering. “The Vengeance has been long in coming, you understand.”

“But—”

Amara held up a finger. “Hear me until I’ve finished. You made a strong case for *adjusting* our plan. We considered what you said and were about to—”

Calista started to speak again.

“I said wait.” Amara flicked one finger and Calista found she couldn’t speak.

“Thank you for your silence,” Amara said, smiling and looking pleased. “Now, I can hear what the Moonwater witches are trying to tell me.” She cocked her head, hearing what Calista could not.

“You’d best go and leave me to placate them once they’ve dried off. I hope that you haven’t stirred up more anger than was already there.”

She turned and was out of sight in the blink of an eye, leaving Calista and Miriam without an answer to their question. What had the witches decided to do?

Chapter Forty

Calista, Wallace, and her mother started back toward Storm Haven as another dusting of snow covered the ground. Calista shivered and pulled her wet shawl closer, but it gave her no warmth. They came to the fork in the road that led to the square. Three wagons loaded with furniture rattled from around the boulder and toward Scrawly Springs. Several men on horseback followed them. Some villagers were heeding her warning and leaving.

A babble of loud voices talking over each other came from the village center. Calista and Miriam halted and looked at each other.

"This sounds as if there are still enough people left to form a mob, and it has been unleashed again," Miriam said.

Calista agreed. "And it's time that mob is dispersed forever, don't you think?"

"Indeed. Let's hope we still have time to do that."

When the familiar square came into view and they could see what was happening, they stopped again. Simon, towering over everyone and clearly angry, stood at the hub of villagers. There were only a few onlookers—the elders, the blacksmith, some younger people, craning to see the magistrate. The rowdy villagers that remained seemed more interested in the spectacle of a trial than in their own safety.

While everyone else shouted or waved fists in the air, Simon's lips were sealed, but his eyes shot sparks of fury. His aunt stood at Mr. Lowery's side.

Mr. Lowery held up his hands and shouted for quiet. When the noise dropped to a level that everyone could hear, he called on Simon. "Present the evidence you claim to have, Mr. Pinehurst."

Simon stepped up front. "I've asked the Healer to speak to you first." He waved the bent figure of the town Healer forward.

"Mr. Pinehurst asked me to tell about his father's illness and death." The Healer had always been ancient in Calista's eyes, but now he looked less like the stooped elder she remembered and more like a root of a medicinal plant. He cleared his throat—a rheumy sound of the very old. "When I was called to the good farmer's side, I believed his heart was simply giving out and suggested rest and my special compound of ginger and cinnamon. He followed my advice and seemed to recover, but the symptoms returned later, and then he passed."

"Did you consider that he'd been poisoned?" Simon asked.

The Healer shook his head. "No."

"But my father's symptoms could have been those of poisoning, isn't that true?"

"Yes. I didn't suspect poison because there was no reason to."

"Poor judgment," Miriam said softly, shaking her head. "Why not consider all possibilities of an ailment? And shoddy healing as well, if you ask me. Ginger and cinnamon go well with jam, but a compound of them alone would do nothing for an ailing heart."

"You should be the town Healer," Calista told her. "They'd all benefit."

Miriam smiled. "I doubt they'd agree to that. It's only when they've exhausted all other sources that they come to the cottage at the end of the road."

Simon thanked the Healer and held out a paper to Mr. Lowery. "The apothecary in Scrawly Springs has given this as proof that Colton Kennewick bought arsenic from him on several occasions. All of the dates he set down are within a few days of the onset of a serious illness or a death. Mr. Pinehurst and Mr. D'White are two. The other is my mother, Eleanor Pinehurst."

"She's standing right in front of us!" someone shouted from the crowd.

The crowd had bolstered Mathilda's confidence, and after her little slip earlier, she was back to behaving as if she was indeed Simon's mother. "It was my sister who died. I am his mother! How could he turn on me in this way?" Matilda held out her hands to the crowd. "All of you know me. I'm a good person falsely accused by her own blood. He has even attempted to poison me. Remember those bottles of poison he ferreted away in his pockets? He's lying!"

"She's darned noisy for a dead woman," another said, and the crowd broke into nervous laughter.

"She's lying. That woman's my aunt, my mother's twin, Matilda. She poisoned my mother, then my father, and by accident, Mr. D'White." Simon's ferocity silenced the crowd. "She tried to kill me, but I didn't succumb, thanks to Calista and Miriam. They saved my life."

At the mention of the two women's names, people shifted feet, and a nervous ripple went through the crowd. Simon pointed at the paper Mr. Lowery held in his hand. "See that last purchase? That was one day before I almost died. And I saw Colton sneaking from my house the back way on that same day."

Mr. Lowery read the letter from the apothecary, then looked out over the square. "If my memory serves, the dates of these sales do coincide with those tragic deaths, but this letter names Colton Kennewick, not Eleanor or Mathilda Pinehurst, as the person who purchased the poison."

"My aunt paid Colton to bring it to her and to

dispose of the evidence."

Mr. Lowery stroked his chin. "I'm afraid there's simply not enough to prove your mother" —he hesitated— "or your aunt did anything wrong."

Even though the magistrate was coming to the wrong conclusion, he still attempted to be fair.

"At last someone is using common sense," Matilda said.

It was clear that Simon fought to keep his temper in check. "Then bring Colton Kennewick here. That letter implicates him. Let him tell his story."

"Nobody's seen him of late." Mr. Lowery signaled the blacksmith. "Have you seen the young man?"

The blacksmith shook his head.

"Then until we can locate the fellow, I have no choice but to release this woman. I will keep this statement. Bring Colton here and let him tell the elders his story."

A smile spread across Matilda's lips. For a moment, Calista thought Simon might do something foolish and lunge at his aunt, but he turned his back on her. The crowd parted as he pushed his way through to his horse.

He rode at a gallop across the square and reined in next to Calista. "Did you see that?"

"I did. We will prove her guilty."

"I'm off to find Colton. What of that?" He nodded at the mountain, which was smoldering, but not in flames anymore.

"Oh, they're coming, I'm not sure what they plan to do. We may still be in grave danger. Right now, they're drying off." She smiled.

"As you should be. Here." He handed down his heavy coat. "I'm trying to imagine what you did."

"I'll tell you later. Go find Colton and bring him to the magistrate."

"I'm on my way," Simon said, before galloping off.

"He's such a handsom—"

"Stop," Calista told her mother a bit too sharply, as she placed half of Simon's coat around her mother's shoulders.

Miriam shrugged. "Whatever you say, Calista."

"We should go home. Even with Simon's coat, we'll both freeze unless we keep moving." She glanced up at the mountain. "The witches seem to be taking their time coming down to wreak havoc, so we'd best see if that spell of mine is still holding the black ooze from spreading. And I want to be at the farm when they do arrive to remind them that we are family. I fear they might forget in their fiery frenzy."

"Good idea," Wallace said.

Together, they left the square and hurried down the road toward the cottage.

They'd come to the path leading to their door when rifle shots brought them up short. One. Two. The sound ricocheted from behind the cottage, leaving a hollow echo of violence in the air.

"Colton." Calista bolted toward the sound. "Wallace," she shouted over her shoulder, "go home." At the barn, she drew up short. Flower lay on her side, a pool of blood forming under her shoulder. Colton stood over her, his rifle now aimed at her head.

Across from him, Micah stood grinning at Calista. "Mules ought not go stubborn when told to get out of the way."

"Darned fool thing moved!" Colton cocked his gun at the same time. "You need a lesson in minding what you're told."

"Stop!" Calista hurled herself at his legs and toppled him.

They rolled in the snow. Colton on top for a moment still gripping the rifle. Then Calista on top pressing the rifle across Colton's throat. The rifle went off again, this time splintering a barn door plank and sending chickens scuttling off in every direction.

Colton thrust hard with his hands against her shoulders and sent her to the side and onto her back. She leapt to her feet confronting him, his good eye fixed on her, and his lips drawn back in the tight grin of a hunter sure of a kill.

"Why are you here?" Calista demanded.

"I heard there was some of you looking for me." Colton rested the rifle across on arm. "You got that Pinehurst fella to telling things about me, haven't you, witch?"

"He's been telling what he thinks is true. You go to the magistrate and give him your version, Colton Kennewick, and let him decide which of you is being truthful."

"Let's get out of here, Colton," Micah yelled and pointed at Vengeance Mountain. "I don't like the looks of that."

It did seem that the fire was moving downward again. The witches must have finished drying themselves, and either Amara had persuaded them to focus their hatred on the truly guilty or they were coming to cut a wide swath through the village and across the farms of Storm Haven.

Calista glanced down at poor Flower, but her mother was already crouched next to her and applying pressure to the wound in her shoulder. Calista would leave Flower to her mother. Right now, she had Colton to disarm and Micah to scare away.

"You'd best run now. What you see up there is The Vengeance on its way." She looked up at the approaching fire. "I'd say you have only a few minutes."

"She's not lying about that, Colton. Let's get." Micah started away, but stopped when Isabelle pounded around the side of barn, her nostrils flared and her ears back. She halted just behind Colton, who whirled to face her.

"Here's that danged horse of yours, Cousin. Seems she can't stay away from you."

"Forget the stupid thing. Come on!"

"I'm with you, just as soon as I take care of this witch with the mouth full of lies about me. I never had truck with no poison." Colton raised the butt of his rifle and was ready to bring it down on Calista's head. "Got some last words?"

Isabelle reared, her forelegs slicing through the air.

Micah yelled, "Look out!"

The horse charged Colton at the same time the rifle discharged. The bullet went into the sky, and Colton fell backward, dropping the gun. Isabelle came down on his chest with her hooves. He curled into a tight ball and buried his head between his arms. Isabelle struck again. This time Colton's shoulder bones snapped, a sickening sound, and he fell onto his back, screaming, then silent. When he no longer moved, Isabelle backed away, snorting and dipping her head up and down, her black coat sleek with sweat. Her eyes were wide, but she didn't bolt. Instead, she came to Calista's side.

Calista laid a hand on Isabelle's neck. "Thank you."

Micah scrambled to his feet. Calista picked up Colton's rifle. She held it pointed straight at him, and he stayed on his knees. "You've lost your claim to Isabelle, and you're on your way to the magistrate to tell how you and Colton ambushed the squire."

He studied her a moment before a slow, unpleasant smile crept across his lips. "You got no proof of that."

He was right. The two witnesses were dead, and she wasn't about to testify how the ghosts of Farmer Kennewick and Luther Jones had told her what happened.

"I know it was you and Colton."

"Yeah? You was there? You seen it?"

"Get up."

He got to his feet, staggering at first, and then he grabbed his hat from the ground and jammed it on his head.

"Never come here again if you wish to live, Micah. I swear I won't hesitate to shoot you."

"I knew you didn't have nothing but your own twisted ideas about me. When I come again, and I will, you won't see me until it's too late, witch." He wasn't steady on his feet and he stumbled, making his way around the back side of the cottage and toward the cemetery.

Calista almost called out to him that he was going the wrong way—too close to the old cemetery and the black ooze— if he planned to return to his farm safely, but she remained silent. Micah would not get her help in any fashion.

She wasn't ready for Isabelle's charge after Micah. He jerked around to look back. His eyes went wide. The mare came straight at him. He ran, zigzagging, but she tracked each change of direction. Her hooves pounded deep holes in the snow.

Calista chased after them. It was as if Isabelle were herding him, and when he came to the cemetery gate, still bulging with the black ooze, she stopped and stood pawing the ground.

He couldn't return the way he'd come. Isabelle had that escape blocked. He either had to push through the gate and wade into the rotten remains of the Storm Haven ancestors or make his way across the thicket that was Wallace's territory. He started through, but he'd taken only a few steps when hundreds of hares surged out of hiding. They tripped him. They clawed at him. They, too, seemed to be herding him toward the cemetery gate.

Micah, his face red with anger and confusion, searched for a way out. The hares leapt at his legs. Isabelle snorted and reared, her hooves barely missing him. Desperate, he faced the cemetery and charged straight for it.

"Micah, no!" Calista called.

But he leapt over the gate and plunged waist deep into the black ooze. At first, he waded through it, but quickly he came to a halt, unable to go forward. He tried to return the way he'd come, but with each turn, he became more deeply mired. It rose like a slow tide up to his chest. He raised his arms overhead, a silent scream on his lips.

While her spell was keeping it from spreading across the thicket and toward her cottage, it still moved within that barrier like a hideous thick sea. Now with Micah in its midst, it rose in a wave and folded over him. His screams and the horror of seeing Micah pulled down into the wretched blackness would stay with her forever.

Chapter Forty-One

Calista stared at the place Micah had stood only moments before. A sinister silence surrounded her, and the smell of decay turned her stomach. The hares had vanished as quickly as they'd appeared. She felt the rising heat, and when she looked up at Vengeance Mountain, she had only minutes to get out of the way. She prayed the Moonwater witches were passing Storm Haven without stopping. She prayed they were headed to the exact spot where she was standing and not the village, and she prayed she had time to escape.

Miriam ran toward Calista, shouting. "Come. Get away from there. Now."

But there was no time left. The witches had arrived.

Miriam gripped Calista's hand and yanked her back as the columns of fire splintered into the enflamed insects from the old stories. They swarmed past the cottage, swooped into the air, and hovered over the cemetery.

For a moment, the sky fluttered with white hot wings of destruction, and then the incendiaries dove over the cemetery gate and descended on the old section. The black ooze exploded into flames that towered into the sky. Those fiery tongues were going to be visible all the way to Scrawly Springs. Certainly, any Storm Haven villagers who'd stayed behind were cowering in their homes right now. Calista feared they wouldn't be spared once the witches were finished here. She feared she and her mother might not escape their ancestors' revenge.

Courage. The word came like a cool breath this time. Whatever sort of spirit it was, it seemed to know when she needed warmth and when something cool would bring her comfort. It knew her very well.

The pounding of hooves brought her around quickly. Simon was bearing down on them, his great stallion sending muddied clumps of snow flying off to the side.

He was off his horse and on the ground the moment he reached where Calista and Miriam stood.

"You're safe!" He had her in his arms before she could escape. Then he released her when she tried to pulled away. "I saw the flames. I knew they came from here." He stared at the cemetery and the smoldering remains of the old section.

The insects hovered overhead, but they were high enough now that all they managed to do was melt more snow on the ground and dry Calista's and Miriam's still-damp clothes.

The figure that came through the side gate took her time. It was as if she were enjoying a stroll through a beloved and familiar place. When Amara stood in front of the three of them, she examined Simon as carefully as she had everything on her way to them. "A Pinehurst by the looks of him."

"He is." Calista glanced at Simon.

"What?" Simon asked, glancing in the direction Calista was looking.

She held her forefinger to her lips, hoping Simon would wait until she could explain what he couldn't see or hear.

"Most of them were honorable. None of them were on the hanging committee as I recall," Amara said.

Calista stepped to Simon's side. "He only just learned about that history when I explained."

Simon was staring at her, but he remained silent.

"Just as well. Leave the old stories where they belong from now on. They've served their purpose. The myth of the giant is gone. The villagers won't be hiding behind that anymore." Amara faced Calista. "Now tell me how you managed to hold back that vile residue of our murderers for so long."

Calista explained how she'd found the quarantine spell about Bog Man Murphy.

"Very clever."

Miriam wrapped one arm around her daughter's shoulder. "Calista is more than clever."

Simon started to speak, then he must have understood that Miriam was talking to that invisible, silent entity, and he stopped.

"Yes, she is," Amara said. "My quarantine spell, heh? I never expected it to be used in that manner, but how grand that it worked."

Calista recounted how that section of the cemetery had grown increasingly dank and sour until that foul substance surged from the ground.

Amara smiled. "Of course, we rattled a few bones with our tremors, and that last one was a clear signal that we would soon descend."

"Why would they" —Calista searched for the right word, but couldn't find one— "*bubble* up to the surface like that? Wouldn't they want to stay out of sight? You know, avoid you?"

"It's not them. It's the earth herself who heard us and wanted them gone, wanted herself cleansed. We sent notice, and she paid attention."

"Earth wanted them destroyed by fire?"

"Well, the witches deserved that. Justice, you know." Amara looked out over the old section of the cemetery. "We've finished."

"Does that mean you're not burning down all of Storm Haven?" Miriam asked.

"It does. We've had the justice we deserve, and

we're leaving any issues of injustice or unfinished business to you. Mrs. Wilhelm tells me you've done an excellent job of setting things to rights for those who ask."

"I've tried," Calista said.

"Well then, this is goodbye, my dears. It's time for the Moonwater witches to return to the mountain and find the peace we've longed for." She started away and then stopped. "There is one old story that you might dredge up. This one could make Storm Haven much more enticing for visitors and residents as well."

"What is that?" Miriam asked.

"In the old days, Vengeance Mountain was known as Fair Weather Peak." She smiled. "It could be that again. I'd consider proposing the change to the village council, and we'll be sure it lives up to that old name."

Amara vanished in the drone of insects. The air cooled, and more light winter snow fluttered down from the sky. It came gently, a clean white blanket quietly covering the blackened area where steam still rose into the air. The old part of the cemetery had not one headstone remaining. No traces of the rock wall that once separated it from the rest of the graves remained. It wouldn't take long for the snow to remove the last traces of the scorched earth.

Calista sniffed the air. It smelled pure and clean. The sour scent of old guilt was gone. She smiled. "Purified."

"And are you going to explain what was happening just now?" Simon pointed to where they'd been standing.

"That was my great-grandmother. She thought highly of your family."

"That's a relief."

"Come, you two," Miriam said. "We still have

things to do."

When they returned to the barn, Colton lay as Isabelle had left him, but now with a light dusting of snow, he resembled a toppled statue.

"More justice?" Simon asked.

"Yes, but not by my hand," Calista said. "It was Isabelle. He was about to hurt me, and she came to my rescue."

Simon knelt and felt for a pulse. "He's still got a heartbeat, but it's faint. Best get him into the shed. I want him alive to tell what my aunt did."

"Thank you, Simon." Miriam said. "I'll see to Colton Kennewick after I tend to Flower."

Simon carried Colton into the shed, laid him on a wooden bench, and covered him with a blanket.

With some help, Flower made it onto her feet and Miriam finished cleaning the wound, and then gently applied a healing ointment.

"Is she going to be all right?" Calista asked.

"It will take time. Luckily, the bullet didn't shatter any bones, but it tore through some muscle and tissue that will make her leg painful for some time. Poor dear." Miriam wiped her hands and slowly led the limping Flower to her stall.

Miriam examined Colton's shoulder before slowly pulling his arm away from his body until his shoulder bones clicked into place. He moaned, but he didn't move when she bound his arm to his chest with a clean gauze and tucked some crushed herbs under his gums. "This will ease the pain for now, but even as badly hurt as he is, I don't trust he'll stay put."

Simon took down a coil of rope and lashed Colton to the bench. "He'll not go anywhere now."

"Simon, you will stay for supper," Miriam announced.

Calista frowned. She didn't like how her mother encouraged him. True, he was interesting. He was someone who didn't judge her or shrink from who she was. But that only made her more nervous about the man. If she were going to be honest, that made it very difficult to keep him at the comfortable distance she needed for him to stay at. She must never forget who he was under that tall, ruggedly handsome exterior. She must never forget what awful things he was capable of doing.

"We must talk about your aunt," Miriam said with a pointed look at Calista. "If justice is in our hands, then let us see it is done. Am I right, my sweet?"

Grudgingly, Calista nodded.

Supper was a hot soup and bread, and as they took seats at the table, Calista refused to look at Simon. He'd taken her father's chair as if it were his proper place. Well, it wasn't. It was her father's, and no other should be sitting there.

The only sound in the kitchen was the clink of spoons against soup bowls. Simon had emptied his and was already ladling more of the thick broth from the tureen, while Calista had barely touched her food.

Miriam broke the silence. "I can make sure that Colton's pain is bearable," Miriam said. "And now that his shoulder's in place, it will heal properly."

"I'm not as keen on sparing that evil person pain as you are." Calista sliced the end from the hot loaf of bread with a hard scrape of the knife across the board. "He deserves to be punished. Poor Flower. He was partly to blame for the squire's death, and he was set on ruining poor Luther Jones's life."

Miriam placed her hand over Calista's. "I'm doing this so Simon can take him to the magistrate and so that he can stand trial. We must make him tell the real story and be sure Matilda Pinehurst is punished along with him."

Her mother was right. Calista had no argument against that. All that had happened since she'd bumped into Simon's aunt at the bakery had taken a toll. It was making her downright cranky. That's what had her snapping at her mother and what had made her appetite vanish. She stirred her uneaten soup and set the slice of bread aside. She had every reason to be upset—the near catastrophe with her ancestors, and, of course, Simon Pinehurst, who had the appetite of an ox. He was already serving himself a third bowl of soup and had finished off four large chunks of bread. If he didn't stop eating, she imagined him cleaning out the last of their meagerly stocked pantry.

"Calista?" Her mother's voice brought her attention back to the table.

"Sorry. I'm thinking about … Flower."

"Come. Help me with the numbing tea, and then we'll have an early night of it."

Together, they brewed and then administered the tea to Colton. When he fell into a painless sleep, they draped his limp body over the haunches of Simon's horse.

"I'll see that he's delivered into the hands of the law," Simon said. "I'll be at the inn for the night." He grinned. "I doubt that my aunt has left the door unlocked for me."

Since Calista still remained silent, Miriam thanked him and then added, "In the morning, we'll arrive at the square to demand another hearing. This time Colton will testify."

"He may need prodding to make sure he does so honestly. I'm going to tell him that my aunt has confessed. We now have her word that he gave the poison to my father."

Calista had to admit that it was a good plan, and she had an idea for how to make it even better. "Then we will tell your aunt that Colton has already said she paid him to bring the poison to her and take the empty bottles away. We need to frighten them both."

"Excellent." Simon rode away with Colton's legs dangling off to one side, his head on the other.

Miriam hugged Calista. "You and Simon make a perfect team. I'm sure those two are as good as convicted."

"We are friends, nothing more." Calista yanked free from her mother's arm and stomped into the house.

"Calista, stop. "Miriam charged up the steps behind her daughter. "This has been a trying time, but don't make it an excuse for rudeness."

"I'm sorry." Calista collapsed into one of the kitchen chairs, the one Simon had taken, the one that was rightfully her father's. "I will be more myself after some sleep."

"Apology accepted," Miriam said, gathering the plates and setting them into the sink. "These will wait until the morning when I have the energy to scrub them clean." She stood behind Calista and pressed a cheek against hers. "Well done today, Witch Moonwater."

"I think we should make that Witches Moonwater," Calista said, and then, yawning, she made her way to her room. She was grateful to fall across her bed and close her eyes. Tomorrow, one more injustice would be righted. Tomorrow, she'd be able to tell Eleanor Pinehurst that her sister was going to pay for her crime, and soon, her true name would be engraved properly on her tombstone. The sigh that escaped her lips was all about satisfaction. And how nice that was for a change. Instead of feeling hopeless, she was feeling hopeful at last.

"Well done, indeed." The soft flush of encouragement she'd felt so often these past weeks came again, but this time it had more shape, like a soft, but deep-voiced whisper.

She bolted upright, all thoughts of sleep gone. She searched the room, but it was empty, yet she felt a presence. "Who ... what are you?"

Laughter filled her head. It was a rich baritone sound that she'd recognize no matter how long it had been since she'd last heard it.

"Father?"

There was no answer, but the feeling of strong arms wrapped around her and drew her into a familiar safety.

"Now let me tell you of goddesses and faraway lands where noble deeds are done and stalwart heroes live."

"You've been the one fortifying me when I needed it most. You wrote that passage in Amara's book about having courage when I faced danger."

"Of course. You could have managed on your own, but a small nudge of encouragement served to make your tasks a little easier. That's what fathers are supposed to do, isn't it? Lend support when needed?"

"Why can't I see you? I see all the other gho…" She couldn't finish the word. She didn't want to think of her father in any way, except as the man with strong arms and a gentle voice that told her stories, stories that changed her from outcast to someone special in this world where being different was often a crime.

"You don't need to see me. I have no regrets or unfinished business in this world. I lived the way I thought right and fitting. I had you. I had your mother. I had the most perfect life. Isn't it enough to always feel me at your side? To always know I love you and am so proud

of the goddess you are?"

"But I miss you so—"

"Courage, my lovely goddess. I'll be here when you need me again."

And with that, the room became empty and silent, except for the rapid tapping of her heart.

Chapter Forty-Two

That next morning, Calista woke, blinking at the ceiling and willing her father to come back. She ached for his presence and his laughter. But in the cold light of the winter's day, she was alone. She pushed aside her quilt and dressed. There was much to do, and lying in bed wasn't going to accomplish any of it.

She wrote a note for Matilda Pinehurst. In it, she explained that Colton had told the magistrate how he'd delivered poison to her and taken the empty bottles away. "You'd best present your side of the story as soon as possible." Calista signed it, "A friend."

She and Miriam made their way toward the village square, but when they came to the Pinehurst house, Miriam continued past. "I'm anxious to know if the magistrate will hear Simon and accept the evidence. I'll meet you in the square," she said. "Take care, my sweet, and come soon."

Calista veered off toward the Pinehurst house. She slipped the note under the door, and, before hiding across the road, tossed a few pebbles at a window. She crouched behind a bush and waited. The woman would either bolt or she'd brazenly accuse Colton of the murders. Either way Calista planned on making sure that woman stood before the magistrate. She'd killed her own sister and Mr. Pinehurst. *But she also killed my beloved father, and for that she is going to pay one way or the other.*

While Calista stayed out of sight, the wagons that had fled Storm Haven the day before rattled back along the dirt road. The same men on horseback followed. Word must have spread that the danger was over.

It seemed like hours before the door to the

Pinehurst house opened. At first, Calista thought Matilda wouldn't see the note at all, but it caught her eye. She snatched it up, glancing around as if she expected to find whoever had left it still lurking nearby. Ripping the small envelope open, she read the note before crumpling it and stuffing it into her satchel.

Now what will she do? Calista wondered. She prepared to sprint after the woman if she decided to hitch up her buggy and ride off, but Matilda shut the door firmly behind her and struck off toward the village. Confidence radiated from her face.

Suddenly, Calista had doubts about today. That woman had seemed so sure the magistrate would believe her. And Calista knew the hearing could come down to Matilda's word against a Moonwater's. Even if Colton testified to save his own miserable self, he had no standing in the village, so Calista followed Matilda, feeling less confident that she'd see justice done this day.

Calista had expected to see the square filled with curious onlookers. Instead, only Miriam and Simon stood at the magistrate's door when Matilda stomped up and shook her fist at them.

"Lies! All of it. How dare you turn on your own mother, Simon Pinehurst." She burst into tears that were so real, Calista stayed her distance, shocked and confused. Matilda truly believed she was in the right. She truly believed she was Eleanor. There was no other explanation for such an authentic outpouring of distress. Were there people like that in the world—those who were steeped in guilt, but denied it even to themselves?

Matilda raised such a fuss that the square began filling with curious villagers. The magistrate's door flew open. He and Mrs. Lowery, her eyes wide with alarm, stepped onto the porch. Matilda seemed to be near collapse. Mrs. Lowery supported her while Mr. Lowery fetched a chair from inside. Matilda slumped into it, sobbing.

That woman was one amazing actress.

The elders arrived when Parson Garrison rang the church bell, and then Mr. Lowery signaled the blacksmith. “Bring Colton Kennewick.”

When Colton walked out of the one-celled jail, he leaned heavily on the blacksmith. His arm was still bound to his chest, and he stared at the ground, his hair falling forward over his eyes. Calista felt a surge of sympathy from those gathered around her. This was not the way she’d expected today to unfold. Both of the wickedest people in Storm Haven should have been found guilty by now and on their way to punishment. Instead, she feared they’d be let free.

Once again, Simon set out his case. “Clearly, Colton Kennewick is guilty of helping to poison my mother,” Simon said.

Mr. Lowery held up the apothecary’s statement. “I’ve checked the dates to confirm that the poison Colton bought was about the same time as the mysterious sickness struck down the four villagers.”

Colton shook off his hang-dog look and turned on Matilda. “It weren’t me who sneaked poison to them. You told me that poison was for rats!”

Matilda set up a wail that must have been heard at the very peak of Vengeance Mountain.

Mrs. Lowery patted her shoulder and gave her water.

Sputtering, Matilda pointed a shaky finger at Colton while glaring out over the crowd. “Lies. I tell you. Look at him. He’s always lied. He’s always been a disgrace to the Kennewicks. Now you will take his word against mine?”

Calista’s fingertips flared with heat. How she

wanted Simon's real mother here to see what Matilda was up to. If only she could take on her sister and show her up for the liar she…

Wait. Squire Nielsen told her that when Isabella was in danger from Micah and Colton, she only needed to ask for his intervention. "You needed to tell me to throttle those monsters, but you didn't. I was helpless." That's what he'd said. And Mrs. Wilhelm … what did she tell me? "W*e* must be asked if you want us to intercede. And you must do it in the right manner."

I'm not sure what "the right manner" means. If she called Eleanor and asked for her help, would she come? The only way to know was to try. "Okay, Eleanor," she said softly, "come and *throttle* this sister of yours."

The leg of Matilda's chair splintered, and she landed with a thud on the magistrate's doorstep. She'd barely gotten to her feet when her cape blew up into the air and over her head. She fell back against the door and slid once again onto her ample bottom.

Sudden gusts of wind sent snow spiraling like tiny tornadoes that surrounded Matilda. The rest of the square remained untouched by this startling flurry, and the anxious villagers backed away, glancing this way and that. A buzz of nervous talk came from the crowd.

"What is this?"

"Witchery. That's what!"

"Those Moonwaters again. My guess."

Some fled the square, clutching their children's hands.

Mr. Lowery grabbed Matilda by the arm and hauled her to her feet, but as if someone had shoved the woman, she stumbled and this time fell from the stoop and into the snow. She scrambled to stand and held onto the porch railing. If she let go, Calista was sure she'd land face down. Her eyes were wide and her cheeks pale as the snow that dusted her skirt and shawl.

"I'm so glad you called on me, Calista. This is the most fun I've had in a very long time."

Calista looked in the direction of the voice, and there stood a familiar ghostly figure. "Mrs. Pinehurst. You came."

"Well, you called me for help. I couldn't resist."

"I'm glad you heard me. I was worried that—"

"I heard you very clearly, Calista. Grand job. Moonwater caliber."

"Thank you." Calista couldn't help but feel pride after that compliment. Perhaps she had come fully into her power at last.

"My pleasure. Now watch what comes next."

With that Eleanor sent Matilda rolling across the square like a runaway barrel.

"Oh no! Maybe you should stop." Calista shouted, and more villagers scattered to their homes and shops. How curious this must seem to everyone else, who couldn't see or hear Eleanor Pinehurst.

"Not until she confesses," Eleanor said, and that next minute, Matilda was upright, her toes barely reaching the ground. "Tell them what you did, sister, or I'll take some justice of my own."

Matilda tried to shake free, but her sister's ghostly grip at the back of her neck wasn't about to let go.

With a simple request for help, she'd transformed a passive, observant ghost into one able to haul the living up by the back of the neck. This newly found power made Calista giddy and more than a little nervous at the same time. She remembered her father's words from one of his stories. "With power comes responsibility."

The only people left in the square were the elders who huddled behind the blacksmith, their hands in prayer. Colton crouched where the blacksmith had left him, fixed and staring. Mrs. Lowery quickly ducked into her house and shut the door with force. Simon stood next to Miriam, looking mystified, while Miriam fought to keep from smiling.

Mr. Lowery scurried to the stricken Matilda. "What is wrong with you?"

"Tell him, Matilda. Tell him what you did." Eleanor shoved her sister at the magistrate, and the woman fell sobbing into his arms.

Since Matilda was a good deal larger than Mr. Lowery, it was fortunate that Simon stepped forward and kept them both from toppling to the ground.

"So, Aunt, are you ready to tell what happened?" Simon asked.

"Yes," she gasped. "Just get her away from me."

"Her?" Mr. Lowery looked at Calista, who stood behind him, and then at Miriam, who was off to his right. Neither was close to the hysterical woman.

Matilda stammered out her confession and included Colton's part in the poisoning. Surprisingly, she had only told him she planned to poison rats.

For heaven's sake. Colton was really an innocent dupe. Maybe for the poisonings, but not for anything else.

Miriam was on her the moment she'd finished. "And my husband? How could you do this to him?"

"I didn't mean to harm Mr. D'White. It was by accident," Matilda said.

Mr. Lowery drew Miriam aside. "It's time for the elders to decide how these two will be punished."

The elders huddled briefly, but it only took a short while before they sentenced Matilda to twenty years, and if she survived those twenty years, she was to be forever banished from Storm Haven.

"She'll serve her time in Scrawly Springs," Mr.

Lowery said. "It won't do to have such a long-term inmate here. We'd have no place to house another wrongdoer."

When it became time to sentence Colton, Mr. Lowery pronounced, "Colton Kennewick is not guilty of knowingly assisting Matilda in poisoning her sister or her husband. Therefore—"

"Wait!" Calista shouted. She stepped closer to Colton and made him look up into her determined face. "You may not have known what Matilda planned to use the poison for, but you were responsible for Squire Nielsen's death."

Colton glared at her. "I don't know what you're talking about."

"Come and get him, Squire," she said just loud enough that only Colton could hear her.

The cold descended on Colton like a splash of icy water. He shook. His lips quivered. Like a trapped animal, he searched for a way to escape. "I … were there, but I didn't shoot him. I swear! I don't even know who done it. The shot came from the trees."

"But you were indirectly responsible for his death. If you and Micah hadn't ambushed him, he'd still be alive."

Colton choked. He pried at the invisible fingers around his throat. "Make it stop!"

"Tell what happened, and I will," Calista said.

Colton croaked out the story, and it was very much the way Farmer Kennewick had described what happened.

In a whisper, Calista said, "Now everyone knows, Squire Nielsen. You have your justice."

He released Colton and floated away to stand next to Eleanor Pinehurst.

It took a few moments for the crowd to

reassemble and settle down. When the shock of Colton's strange behavior and confession had subsided, the elders huddled. It didn't take long for them to decide his punishment either. They gave Colton five months in the village's one-celled jail with each Sunday in the stocks, so all of the villagers on their way to church would see him. After those five months, he, too, was banished from Storm Haven forever.

"If you return," Mr. Lowery said. "It will be the hangman's rope." He signaled the blacksmith. "See that this fellow is locked up immediately and that Mrs. Pine … I mean, Matilda is on her way to Scrawly Springs before the hour. I'll be back with the papers for their town jailer." Mr. Lowery went into his house as the blacksmith led Colton and Matilda away.

Although it seemed a light punishment for both Matilda and Colton, Calista didn't relish more death. There had been enough. "I hope you're content with the elders' decision, Mrs. Pinehurst. Squire Nielsen," she whispered behind her hand.

"I'll be fine with it as long as my proper name is carved into my stone."

"I know that Simon will see to it."

The squire bowed and vanished.

Calista felt a chilly, light touch like that of a hand on her arm, then Mrs. Pinehurst said, "Thank you, dear. I'm off to tell the others about all that's happened today!"

All that's happened. The black ooze was gone. The Moonwater witches had taken their revenge and spared the innocent. Micah, who'd caused both the squire and poor Luther Jones to die before their time, had been well and truly punished, and Isabelle was safe in her care. Colton and Matilda were on their way to cells. But the most remarkable event was that she'd called ghostly spirits to intercede, and she'd done it without any spells that required special words or special props like cinnamon bark or a snip of her hair. She had to figure out exactly what that meant for her future as a witch.

She felt another hand touch her arm, but this time it was warm and firm. “Is something wrong?” her mother asked.

Calista shook her head. “Nothing at all.”

After seeing that Colton and Matilda were locked securely in the jail, Simon came to where Calista and her mother waited. “I’m staying in the village to talk to the stonecutter. Will you come to see my mother’s new stone when it’s in place?”

“Yes, of course,” Calista said. She had to be there when her last ghostly favor was finally completed. Her last favor? Maybe not, but she hoped that there were no other requests waiting for her right away. She needed some time off.

Chapter Forty-Three

The day the stonecutter positioned the new headstone on his mother's grave, Simon fetched Calista from the cottage, and together they walked to the cemetery. Wallace joined them when they came to his thicket.

The stone was grand. So much larger than the original one. The ghosts clustered around Eleanor Pinehurst, who couldn't stop running her fingers over the letters that spelled out her true name.

"This is exactly right, and so beautiful," she said to Calista. She looked with longing at her son, who couldn't see her joy. "Will you tell him how much this means to me?"

"Yes. I will." Calista glanced over her shoulder. "But I do think he knows already."

Simon and Wallace stood off to the side, Simon looking perplexed whenever Calista talked to the empty space around her. She found it interesting that he strained to hear the other side of her conversation.

Ida Lakeshire flitted next to Calista. "Splendid work."

"My pleasure," Calista said.

"Do you know Farmer Lakeshire has come to see me twice since you gave him that note? That pleases me more than I can say."

"Wonderful, Ida."

Minnie Wakefield quickly settled next to Ida. "When my daughter comes, I hope you'll bring her to say hello. I don't think she'll visit on her own, you see. We didn't get along."

How sad, Calista thought. A mother and daughter had been at odds in life and now Minnie had no way to make their relationship whole.

"Is that what you wrote in your diary? How you disagreed?"

Minnie nodded. "But thanks to you, she'll not read my misguided thoughts. And she won't discover how very poor we really were."

"Poor?"

"We had to sell our land bit by bit to see that our girl could have decent clothes and we could have food."

All that village talk about Farmer Wakefield hating to till the soil had been untrue. It was exactly like gossip to spread speculation so it appeared to be fact. No wonder the stove was ancient and the house bare. The Wakefields were struggling to live by not replacing the old and selling what they could to keep their home.

"Can I deliver some message to her? You could dictate it, and I could see that she finds it on the mantle." Calista grinned. "I'm much better at those kinds of stealthy missions these days."

Minnie clutched her hand in a gentle, icy grip. "Oh, I'd be ever so grateful."

"Done then," Calista said.

The squire pushed between Ida and Minnie. With a gallant bow he said, "My apologies, Calista Moonwater D'White. You've set my restless spirit at ease. Micah and Colton have paid for their part in my murder, and I've already seen Isabelle in your barn. She'll be a beauty again very soon, I'm sure."

"You've forgiven Farmer Kennewick?" she asked.

"Of course. And that miser … I mean poor wretch, Luther Jones, as well."

Calista smiled. "Very gracious of you, Squire."

He faded into a mist, and Luther Jones took his place in front of her. "I heard what happened to Micah.

Sorry he met such a bad end. I really mean that, you see. And I heard Colton got his comeuppance. It was yourself what done that, and I thank you for setting things to rights for me, too."

"There's just one thing," Calista said. "My boots."

He shrank away from her. "Your what?"

"The boots on Minnie's back porch. They were mine, Luther Jones."

"I didn't know they was yours. I thought Minnie'd left those behind, and they were still good and all, so—"

"Never mind. But do you know where you put them? I only have one pair now and I don't like wearing them in the barn to do the mucking out."

He scratched his head, looking more confused than usual. Then he found the answer he was searching for because he grinned and looked up at Calista. "They be at the back door of the bakery. I put them there that day we was at the Wakefield house."

She'd collect them on her next visit to the village. "Thank you, Luth—"

She had no time to finish before Farmer Kennewick, his face pulled into sorrow, pushed Luther aside.

Was he going to yell at her for what happened to his boys? "I'm sorry for—"

"No," he said. "None of it were your fault. It were all mine. It were me who should have been a better father to Micah. He needed attention, and I gave him none. And I should have sent Colton packing when I seen the evil in him. He were a bad seed, but I let him stay in my house too near to Micah anyways. Thank you for all you done. I'm more at ease now that I told about the accident. That was a heavy burden to carry to the grave."

Farmer Kennewick vanished and Mrs. Wilhelm,

who was settled on top of her weeping angel, clapped her hands together in silent applause. "Calista, you are one very successful Moonwater witch, my dear, but I knew you would be. And look at what has happened to Miriam! How wonderful. She's found her *magyk* at last. I'm almost giddy, and that hasn't happened in a very long time."

"My mother is a powerful Moonwater. And a brave one," Calista said.

"Indeed. And she can expect some visits from us here quite soon." Mrs. Wilhelm pulled out a sheaf of paper from her dress pocket. "Your success has given many more of us hope. With the two of you—"

"Wait." Calista held up her hand. "We must have some time to sort out what has happened. I still want to work on my *magyk* ... just to be very sure, and my mother is new to her power."

Mrs. Wilhelm tipped her head from side to side, considering. Then she said, "Your word has always been good. Time it is for you both."

"Thank you." Calista felt the weight of promises lift from her, yet she knew she'd come back to this place and listen to other entreaties because now she understood how important it was for those who had unfinished business in this world. And she'd discovered that it gave her pleasure to help them. With her mother lending a hand, the load would be much lighter.

She waved goodbye to the ghosts and, with Simon, started away.

"One of these days, will you tell me the other side of those conversations?" he asked.

"Of course."

Wallace hopped through the side gate and up to his thicket. "Well, done, Calista."

"I wouldn't have succeeded without you."

"Let's just say we work quite well as a team, shall we? And now I have to catch up with my family. I've neglected them for some time. When you need me, you know where I'll be."

"Goodbye, Wallace," Simon said. "See you again, too, I hope." He bent low and offered his hand.

"Of course," Wallace said, placing his paw in Simon's hand and eyeing Calista. "I'm quite certain you have good reason for staying here a very long time." Then he scuttled under a dense bush, leaving Calista with her cheeks burning.

Calista gritted her teeth. That Wallace. He was no help in getting rid of Simon Pinehurst. But now was the time to make sure Simon returned to his farm and let her be. "Goodbye, Simon. I'm sure Wallace is mistaken, because I believe you're bound for other parts."

"And why do you think that?"

She didn't want to open the conversation about where she uncovered her information. If she did, he'd find out about her method of discovery and all that she knew about him. She'd keep that secret to herself, thank you very much.

"Intuition." She smiled, hoping the smugness wasn't evident.

"I do have to finish a job for someone, but I don't plan to leave Storm Haven forever. I have the farm to take care of now, don't I?"

"I suppose." She backed away toward the cottage. "I hope you finish whatever job you have, and may your farm prosper."

He was next to her in two steps, and firmly gripping her arm, he turned her to face him. "Wait. We can't part like this."

Those images of him that she'd seen each time they'd touched, of his thievery and womanizing, came clearly to her again. She pried his fingers loose. "You're mistaken about that." She strode away and when his footsteps still came from behind, she broke into a run.

He caught her before she reached the cottage. "What are you afraid of, Calista? It can't be me. I think you're afraid of trusting anyone enough to love them. Am I right?"

"No. I simply do not want to be with you."

He fell back as if she'd slapped him. "I see. So you have someone else you care for."

She didn't answer. It was better to let him think there was another man than to have to explain her reasons for not wanting him.

"Then I wish you happiness." Simon walked to where he'd tied off his horse. He yanked the reins free and mounted.

Once he galloped off, she squared her shoulders and brushed her hands together. "Good." Now she could get on with her life. She had Greta to tend to. And Isabelle. Flower's dressing needed changing and a new poultice applied. Then she'd bake some of her cinnamon spice muffins and see if Mr. Bennet had changed his mind after all that had happened. Even if he refused to buy her muffins, she'd retrieve her boots while she was there. And she hadn't had any time to explore more of Amara's book, so she most certainly planned to do that.

It gave her a sense of relief to have so many tasks ahead in the day, and she hummed while she knelt next to her goat.

Half way through milking Greta, she sat back on her heels, with the milk filling only part of the bucket.

"Is something amiss?" Greta asked, giving her the baleful stare that only a goat can.

"No. I'm thinking about—"

"A very big mistake." The voice came from

behind her and Calista turned to see Flower eyeing her and swishing her tail.

"Flower! You talked to me."

"I finally have something to say. What do you think of my observation?"

"I have no idea what you mean."

"Simon is what I mean. You'll not find a better man anytime soon, if ever. Certainly not in Stone Haven. And I've been to Scrawly Springs. Nothing there for you, my girl. What is wrong with you?"

Calista didn't have an answer, so she went back to milking Greta. Her bottom lip slipped into a pout and a tear ran down her cheek. This was ridiculous! Everything was set to rights in Storm Haven. She even had plans to go before Mr. Lowery and propose the name of Vengeance Mountain be changed back to Fair Weather Peak. Storm Haven was going to be a wonderful place to live once again. She'd study more of Amara's *magyk* and maybe even start her own book. She wiped her eyes and pressed them with her fingers. She had to stop this nonsense.

"Admit it," Flower said. "I'm stubborn, but you are the most stubborn human female on this earth. I've never seen the likes before."

Flower had some very strong opinions, obviously. "That is just hurtful." Calista yanked the bucket up by its handle, sloshing some warm milk onto the ground. She stomped off to the spring house.

"Hurtful or truthful?" Flower brayed after her.

Calista gritted her teeth. She was sorry her mule had suddenly decided to give her an opinion. She took her time in the spring house, moving butter to a different shelf, and then back. She counted the eggs and recounted them.

She'd ignore that mule if she started up again.

And she'd remind her she depended on the one named Calista to change her dressing. "That's me, Flower. You depend on me," she said to nobody as she set the basket of eggs down. At the door she swiped her hair away from her face. "What a tangle you are!" When she pulled her shawl closer against the cold, she found spots on the bodice and the edge of a pocket frayed. "You will have a good hot bath after all of the chores are done. And some mending's in order." She stomped back to the barn, irritation needling her at every step.

Fortunately, Flower was munching straw and had returned to her silent self, and Calista avoided those eyes that tracked her while she put a new bandage on the mule's shoulder.

She curried Isabelle and filled her water trough. She'd just about finished when Isabelle nosed her shoulder. "Flower's right, you know, dear. Just think of poor Squire Nielsen. How he'd give anything to have his Selena again. Don't be foolish and throw your chance at love away."

Calista sat heavily onto the fresh straw and cradled her head. "Not you, too!"

Chapter Forty-Four

That night, when Calista opened Amara's book, she took her time turning the pages until she came to the last entry. Calista liked revisiting the early entries and remembering how she'd struggled to master the spells. She wished Amara had written more, and she was disappointed that there were only a few more page with writing. She waited for the runes to assemble into words; then she leaned over her writing table and read.

My final thoughts: I had nothing left from my ancestors to guide me. This is why I chose to create a book of magyk. It helped me learn my craft, and it was a way to pass on what I could to those who would come after me.

About love: I've come to treat love as a gift to accept with gratitude and give back freely once that it was mine. I never thought I'd find it, but it came with a wonderful man from Scrawly Springs, and it has changed how I will live my life. At last, I have someone to share my dreams with, and I'm no longer the lonely girl of the village.

"No!" Calista pushed up from her chair and paced. Was there a conspiracy afoot? One to drive her into Simon's arms? They simply didn't know his true nature. Well, she did, and she would not fall prey to his charm. She would certainly not let a thief into her life.

Returning to her writing table, she brushed her fingers along the lines, but no hidden writing revealed itself. She'd hoped for more spells that might help her change the village into a place that welcomed her and her mother—a village that wouldn't shun or mistreat those who were different anymore.

At least the next passage wasn't about love.

About Magyk: The practice of magic takes time and patience. It takes a generous heart and a mind open to possibilities. While anyone can gather magic into their hearts, only some will be claimed by magyk. It comes in many disguises, but it is always a hunter, tracking and testing its target. I first sensed it as a caressing breeze, then a sturdier wind that wrapped me in its arms like a lover. Once it made sure I was worthy, I found myself cocooned inside a funnel—my magyk arrived like a tornado and it swept me up.

Calista looked at her hands. Her *magyk* had stalked her. It had tested her. The increasing intensity of that tingling had been a precursor to what happened on the mountain when she and her mother faced the Moonwater witches. Her *magyk* had arrived like a lightning storm.

Once magyk has taken you, these simple spells I've set down are unnecessary. Think your command and it's accomplished.

"Of course." Amara had hidden the spells inside stories of her daily life to protect them from prying eyes, but she'd also crafted her *magyk* from these stories. Calista didn't have to create a book. She had Amara's to guide and teach her everything from stopping time to helping the remorseful dead, and she'd improved slowly. She remembered how she'd unwittingly coaxed the squire to witness the way Micah mistreated Isabelle, but at the time, she didn't have the power to ask for him to intercede. Later, she'd only had to beckon Mrs. Pinehurst and the squire with a wishful thought, and they'd not only come to the square, but when she asked, they'd rattled Matilda and Colton into confessions.

This might mean she'd have to be very careful about what she asked for. A simple request—for say—the tailor's sewing machine might bring it hurtling into her room. She frowned, thinking of the challenges she might be up against with this new power.

She turned to the final page of Amara's book.

My warning: This is a magnificent power, but it comes with incredible danger and terrible responsibility. Courage is all that you

That was the end of the book. What did Amara mean to write and why didn't she finish? Calista went to bed with the words, "magnificent power, incredible danger and terrible responsibility" racing through her head.

Her dreams were as troubled as her waking thoughts. She tossed so much that she twisted herself up inside her quilt and had to get out of bed to shake herself free.

"Enough." Giving up on sleep, she went into the kitchen and stirred the embers of the stove fire into flames. She filled the kettle with water and set it over the iron plate. Putting the dried leaves from last spring's Chamomile into the teapot, she waited for the water to boil, and then sat to let the tea brew.

Of course, she was often alone, but she'd managed her whole life with just her mother and father. Her animals—until today, that is—had been good company. Wallace. For goodness sakes, she had him. And if she had to be by herself, she counted those solitary moments as precious. They allowed her time to think or dream without interruption.

She poured her tea and blew into the cup to cool the drink a bit, then sipped.

Simon Pinehurst could not invade her life. She would not allow it. The hot Chamomile trickled down her throat and eased the tenseness inside her.

Before she could stop it, the feel of Simon's arms around her crept into her thoughts, and she looked across the table to where he'd been. His scent came to her and she closed her eyes, letting the aroma of leather and lime blend with the Chamomile.

If he wasn't a scoundrel ... but he is. End of story.

When she'd finished the tea, she went to the sink and rinsed her cup. The Chamomile had helped. Perhaps she could sleep now and not be tormented.

"Love! So highly overrated."

"Courage."

She whipped to face the kitchen. "Father?" But no, it couldn't be. The word hadn't glided along the edges of her mind like the other times. This was a voice. A woman's voice. "Amara?"

"Yes, Calista. It is your great-grandmother. That unfinished passage you read in my book? I intended to write that "courage is all you need to manage magyk and accept love." But I didn't have time to finish because those who were filled with hate came to take me away. I died that day, but I tried to leave the women who would come after me a very important message."

She felt Amara's arms slip around her shoulders. *"Oh, my dear, be careful not to overlook a stalwart hero."*

Amara was gone as quickly as she'd come, and now it wasn't solitude she felt, it was sheer and complete loneliness.

There was such a difference between the two feelings. A canyon of difference. How had she failed to notice that before now? She hated to think she was the stubborn human female that Flower said she was. What bothered her most was that Amara believed Simon belonged to the world of stalwart heroes and not that of rogues.

"Someone please tell me what I'm to do because I have no idea." She sank into a chair and rested her forehead on her arms.

"Calista?"

The scent of leather and lime permeated the air. She sprang to her feet and faced Simon Pinehurst, who stood on the other side of the table.

"How are you here?"

"You might tell me. I was packing my bag to leave in the morning and suddenly I am in your kitchen."

"Yes. I see that." She felt as cornered as a mouse by a cat and backed away. "You … you should leave. At once."

"That's fine with me, but it might be a friendly gesture to at least offer me a ride back to my house. It is, after all, late and dark, not to mention cold. And I came away—more to the point—you whisked me away without so much as a coat."

"Sorry. I … I…" She bit down on her lip to stop sounding like a stammering fool. "Flower. Of course. She's yours. All yours." She shook her head. What was she thinking? Flower was still hurt and couldn't carry anyone, especially someone the size of Simon. "No. Isabelle. She … she is fine and … and a good horse. Well, you know that. I'm not telling you anything you don't already—"

"Are you not well?" Simon stepped closer to her. "Your eyes are—"

"Tired. That is all. They are tired." She yanked open the door.

"And red with crying. Can I help in some way?"

"Yes! By leaving and never coming here again. Thieves are not welcome. Not ever!"

"Calista, for heaven's sake, stop. I'm not a thief, and I'd like to know how you came to believe that of me." Simon reached out and touched her arm.

The scenes of his thievery flooded through her. A

darkened room. A desk. A knife blade that flicked open a locked drawer. A key. Then a safe and nimble fingers turning the key in the lock. With a click, the drawer popped open. Money. A jewelry box. Inside that box, pearls and a ring that sparkled under the candlelight.

She blinked, trying to force the images to stop, but she only succeeded in changing the scene. This time it was a romantic encounter with sweet kisses. Promises of love—not from Simon, but from the woman he caressed. His smile as he bid his farewell. Then sadness and apologies—all his. "You misunderstood, I'm afraid. I'm so sorry," he told this beauty.

The woman's tears streaked her face, then her palm stung Simon's cheek. And she was gone, leaving him alone, his eyes those of an abandoned pup.

"Talk to me, Calista. Explain why whenever I try to tell you how much you mean to me, you shut me out.

She pulled away from his touch.

"If you don't have any feelings for me, fine. But then why did you call me to your kitchen?

She couldn't have called him, but what if she had? *Someone, please tell me what I'm to do now, because I have no idea.* Those were the words she'd uttered just before he appeared. Oh dear. Her *magyk* did come with complications.

She thought back to the day at the cemetery when she'd confided her secret to Simon and he'd met Wallace. At no time did he flinch. He took her for who she was, a Moonwater witch with a unique familiar and the propensity for gathering ghosts to her.

It was time to take another chance on this man. She sat at the table.

"I know who are by your touch."

"I don't understand."

"Remember, I am a Moonwater."

"That is impossible to forget."

"I see things about people's lives when I touch them. I saw how you kissed and jilted those women—those *many* women. And I saw you take money and jewels from a locked drawer and again from a safe. Please don't deny it because you can't."

He sat across from her. "True. I've kissed some, well, a lot of women. For some reason, they like it. That I will not deny. But I have never stolen anything. What you saw was me recovering stolen property. That's what I do. I work for a detective company and my job is to reunite people with what thieves have taken."

"You steal from thieves?"

"Yes. I suppose you can put it that way. The insurance companies appreciate me, and the people who have their property returned do, too. I'd really feel so much better if you would appreciate what I do as well." He ran his tongue over his lips. "I'm parched. May I have some water?"

Something inside her flared, not anywhere near her heart, but in that secret space she'd only just discovered when she looked into his eyes.

"Water. Yes." Now parched herself, she rose and poured some from a pitcher into two glasses. When she handed one to him, their hands touched and what passed between them made her gasp in surprise.

"Don't shut me out. Please trust me when I say I love you, Calista Moonwater D'White, and I believe you love me. We can take this leap together if you're willing." He set the glass on the table and drew her to him. He winced, as if preparing for rejection.

She'd never thought anyone but her parents would say that to her. She never thought she'd be in an embrace where she felt as safe as she had when her father held her. Yet, here she was. The tingling in her fingers, that *magyk* that now surged through her in a steady current, combined with another force, one just as powerful. Love.

But there was one last question, one last doubt. She stepped away but stayed inside the circle of his arms, looking up into his face. "How do I know I'm not just another conquest? I don't want the kind of goodbye you've said to others."

Simon shook his head. "Calista, you can never be conquered. You're the conqueror in this matter, and you will have my heart captive forever. I want you for my wife."

Wife. A word Calista had never thought would apply to her, the ungainly girl of Stone Haven, one of the Moonwater witches who could not enter the church even to be wed.

Her eyes widened. "The church!" She said that before she could stop the words.

"What about the church?"

"I'm forbidden … I mean the Moonwaters are forbidden."

Simon smiled. "Oh, I think not, particularly if you've just accepted my proposal of marriage."

Had she accepted his proposal? She hadn't said yes out loud, but she'd thought it. And that thought seemed the right one.

"And so I have," she said, looking up at his boyish grin. She let him draw her close to him again and rested her head against his chest. His heartbeat made a steady sound, and this time when images from his past filled her head, they were of her standing with him, facing down the hatred of the village, sharing tea at this table, talking as he chiseled his aunt's name from his mother's stone. They'd already built a history together, and now she imagined the future that they would continue to build.

She returned his embrace, remembering Amara's words about the gift of love.

"What a beautiful gift you've just given me, Simon Pinehurst."

The End

Notes

I deliberately set this story in a vague yet seemingly early time, somewhere on the North American continent. I've kept it regionally neutral, but I had New Hampshire in my mind while I wrote it. The mountains, the seasonal changes with snowy winters and hot summers seemed perfect.

The spring house is something today's reader might not recognize. It was something that my grandmother told me about when I was little. She said that their family's spring house was a small single room made of river rock and constructed over a spring. It stayed cool year-round, so they could store milk, their churned butter, and eggs. Remember there was no other refrigeration before the mid-1800s when the ice box became available. The electric refrigerator wasn't in wide use until the 1920s.

Magic v. *magyk*. The first is used to describe what a magician does with different kinds of tricks. The second has a deeper, more mystical meaning, a sacred and other-worldly practice.

Evernight Teen ®

www.evernightteen.com

www.ingramcontent.com/pod-product-compliance
Lightning Source LLC
LaVergne TN
LVHW091027080826
845145LV00002B/382

* 9 7 8 0 3 6 9 5 1 4 4 6 2 *